The Carnelian Phoenix

Jacquie Rogers

© Jacquie Rogers 2022.

Jacquie Rogers has asserted her rights under the Copyright, Design and Patents Act, 1988, to be identified as the author of this work.

First published in 2022 by Sharpe Books.

For Peter

Best regards,
Jacquie

Table of Contents

Prologue: January AD 212 1
Chapter One 4
Chapter Two 11
Chapter Three 20
Chapter Four 30
Chapter Five 39
Chapter Six 47
Chapter Seven 58
Chapter Eight 68
Chapter Nine 76
Chapter Ten 85
Chapter Eleven 96
Chapter Twelve 108
Chapter Thirteen 119
Chapter Fourteen 130
Chapter Fifteen 140
Chapter Sixteen 148
Chapter Seventeen 159
Chapter Eighteen 170

Chapter Nineteen 179
Chapter Twenty 190
Chapter Twenty-one 199
Chapter Twenty-two 210
Chapter Twenty-three 222
Chapter Twenty-four 230
Chapter Twenty-five 241
Chapter Twenty-six 252
Chapter Twenty-seven 261
Chapter Twenty-eight 272
Chapter Twenty-nine 282
Epilogue 294
Notes and Acknowledgements 295
Place Names 298
Glossary of Terms 301

Sed quis custodiet ipsos custodes?
"Who will guard the guardians?"
Juvenal, *Satirae 6, 1347.*

Prologue: January AD 212

Rome

Senator Bassianus Valerius waited for his wife to leave the house before he took his own life.

He watched from his book room as her litter was carried downhill from their rambling old house on the Quirinal. She would be gone all afternoon, shopping and gossiping with her wealthy friends.

His daughter was in Etruria for the end of year festival, visiting his brother Faustus on the family estates. His son was far away, serving in Britannia. Everything was in place. He summoned his steward Silenus and asked him to ready the bath. The man looked upset as he left the book room.

The senator opened the roll of papyrus on his desk to where he had paused the day before, when his oldest friend had burst into the house. Senator Proculus Caecilius was panting and red-faced after hurrying on foot up the hill from the senate house. Bassianus nodded as Proculus gasped out that a notice of proscription had been issued by Emperor Caracalla. All those suspected of being supporters of the Emperor's recently assassinated brother, and co-ruler, Geta, were to be arrested. Their lands and belongings would be confiscated; their lives were forfeit. Proculus feared his friend's name would be on the list, well-known as he was for advising both imperial brothers in happier days.

Bassianus picked up his pen, adding a line to his will.

Further, I bequeath half my entire estate to my beloved mentee, our illustrious Emperor Marcus Aurelius Antoninus Caesar.

He hoped this legacy to Caracalla would persuade the suspicious Emperor to let the Valerius family retain some property. It was a desperate hope. He sanded the wet lampblack ink, rolled the document up and sealed it, pressing his engraved ring into the hot wax. He looked round the room. All was as it should be. One last thing: he tugged the ring off his little finger, and slid it into a small packet already containing a letter. Without his authorising seal the packet could not be sent by the official mail. But his steward Silenus would know to avoid the imperial messenger system, and would send this letter privately to Faustus. Bassianus had also readied a separate sheet of directions, with a note of farewell. He folded the papyrus, wrote the woman's name on the reverse, and propped it up against the packet in plain view. Silenus would pass the message on. She and the child would be safe in Etruria, on the family estate. He could trust his brother Faustus to provide for them.

At the soft knock, he rose stiffly and joined Silenus for the short walk through the deserted house to the bath suite. All the household slaves, except Silenus and his wife Drusilla, had been given the afternoon off. At the door Bassianus handed Silenus manumission documents freeing this most loyal slave couple, kissed him on the cheek, and let himself into the steamy bath suite. Silenus lingered by the door till he heard his master lowering himself into the warm water. After a moment or two, there was a faint moan and a splash. Silenus thought he heard a sigh, perhaps of sorrow, perhaps of completion.

The old steward wiped his eyes and went back to the book room to find his master's instructions. Then he went to the kitchen. A fair-haired young woman, a stranger, was sitting with Drusilla. A tiny girl was in the woman's lap. The child looked up shyly, hazel eyes gazing at him. The pair were dressed in rough travelling clothes. The young woman was weeping silently; Drusilla, kind-hearted, was holding her hand. The little girl tried to comfort her sobbing mother, reaching for the tiny silver fish strung round the young woman's neck. Silenus nodded at them, and gave the mother a heavy leather purse and the folded sheet of papyrus from his master's desk. Then he left the room quietly. He did not see the woman depart, her head drooping wearily over the child in her arms as they passed quietly through the back gate to begin their long journey north. Neither did he note the hooded figure who slipped out of a doorway to follow them.

Quiet fell on the house of the Valerii.

Chapter One

May AD 224
Bo Gwelt villa in the Summer Country, Roman Britannia.

Beneficiarius Consularis Quintus Valerius stirred awake, the sweat of a bad dream on his brow. Cool air flowed from the bedchamber window which was open to the fragrance of the British night. Moonlight flooded the room; the shadow of Minerva's owl passed over the sheen. He stretched out his hand for the pool of warmth in the bedding where the woman had been sleeping. Her scent reached him, rosewater mixed with the intoxicating smell of her skin. The last wisps of his recurring nightmare fled.

Lady Julia Aureliana turned from the window, her light robe stirring in the breeze. Quintus wrapped himself in the woollen bedcover and crossed the room to join her, pulling her close. The night-drowned marshes spread out before them, trees and bog-encircled islands silhouetted against the moonlit Mendip Hills. To the north-east the conical tor of Ynys Witrin rose smooth from the surrounding marshes.

'That's the Fairy Hill, isn't it?'

'Really, Quintus? A senior Roman officer and initiate of Mithras knowing our British legends?'

'Aurelia told me. It seems she has some mixed beliefs.'

THE CARNELIAN PHOENIX

Julia smiled, her gaze back on the hill silvered by the hanging moon.

'Yes, there are still some among us who hold the old stories to be true. Nothing in Britannia is quite as it seems, including our daughter.' She left the wooden shutters folded away from the window, and took Quintus by the hand.

'Forget about fairy kings. Come back to bed, it's chilly.'

***

Londinium, a week later

'I'm pleased our womenfolk seem to be making friends.'

Governor Aradius Rufinus gestured to the two women, one tall and fair, the other petite with nut brown hair coiled elaborately around her neat head, strolling arm-in-arm through the gardens of the Governor's Palace. Servilia Vitalis said something low-voiced to her companion, and Julia laughed, head thrown back. Her amethyst-coloured evening robe stirred as she walked.

The governor smiled benignly at his little wife. As so often the case in the Roman upper classes, Aradius and Servilia were distant cousins and had known each other from early childhood. It had been thought in their refined circles that the birth injury which left Rufinus crippled would rule out a career following the *cursus honorum,* the conventional path to success in public office for young Roman patricians. He and his perceptive wife had proved their families wrong, and had overcome considerable discouragement to rise to the peak of ambition, when Rufinus was rewarded for loyalty and appointed governor of the British province.

'I haven't known Servilia Vitalis long, sir, but I doubt anyone could help but like such a gracious and amusing lady. Least of all Julia, who appreciates wit and perception more than most.' Quintus saw that Rufinus was still smiling, and added, 'I have hopes that once my mother and sister meet Julia, they will find her charming and cultured, and welcome her into my own family.'

Rufinus beckoned to his Governor's Man to accompany him into his office, where they sat down in front of the window. Rufinus poured good Spanish wine into two engraved glasses. He changed the subject.

'I am grateful to you, Quintus, for agreeing to travel to Rome as my representative. I owe my position here, and probably my life, to your courage and sense of duty.'

Quintus waited. His superior was not a man to be hurried. A well-dressed slave knocked and entered, handing the governor a linen packet. Rufinus pushed the packet across the table.

'Here are your formal orders for your mission to Rome, with a brief you should find useful. Also, a letter of introduction to the chief imperial minister at the emperor's court, Senior Praetorian Prefect Ulpian. Before you go, I wanted to go a little deeper into your mission. The prisoner escort guard taking the traitor, Gaius Trebonius, and his confederate, Cassius Labienus, for senate trial in Rome, has today embarked for Gaul. There is no need for you to be with them; Centurion Felix Antonius is experienced, and has hand-picked his men. But the gravity of Trebonius' attempt at usurpation, his status as my predecessor, and his connections at high levels in Rome warrant sending a senior British officer to witness the trial.'

Quintus nodded.

The governor continued. 'Once you're in Rome, I have an additional goal for you — which I prefer to make as a request. With all I owe you, there is no question between us of commands.'

Quintus kept his peace. Rufinus drew breath.

I have reason to fear for Rome and for our young emperor. I had word just yesterday that the joint Praetorian prefects, Flavianus and Chrestus, are dead.'

This news jolted Quintus out of his calm.

'Sir! How — why? Is Councillor Ulpian safe?'

'It was my cousin Ulpian himself who wrote to me, in cipher. I have no details yet, but I gather the prefects were executed on the orders of Augusta Julia Mamaea. Ulpian believes they were plotting his death.'

Quintus was shocked beyond measure. The highly-respected jurist Ulpian had served on imperial councils since the days of the great Emperor Septimius Severus, the commander under whom Quintus had fought in his youth. At the glittering court of Mamaea and her adolescent son, Emperor Alexander Severus, Ulpian was renowned as the most brilliant of their advisers. From the moment Alexander came to the throne on the assassination of his hated cousin, Elegabalus, the famous legal scholar had been their chief adviser. But given her son's tender years and pliant disposition, it was the empress who ruled in effect.

'You must understand, Quintus, my cousin has been determined to root out corruption and abuse of power in the government. Augusta Mamaea, a strong, fiercely intelligent woman like her Severan predecessors, wants Rome to return to its traditional values. Ulpian supports her in this. He believes that the law should be a tool to create a more just society. He wants to help young Emperor Alexander lead an honest, cultured and broad-minded court.'

Quintus frowned. He had himself foresworn any political ambition when he returned to Rome, from the war in Britannia, to find that his senator father had been forced into suicide under Emperor Caracalla. From that moment he had turned his back on the standard career path into high office expected of his class. Instead, he had set aside his grief while pursuing his duty to safeguard the borders of the empire. But the drive to uncover those who caused his father's death was not buried deep, and never left him for long.

Governor Rufinus, soft-spoken as always, had said something else. Quintus begged his pardon.

'No need to apologise, *Beneficiarius*. I was recalling that you yourself were an officer in the Praetorian Guard at one time. Did you know either of the dead prefects?'

'No, sir. It was a long time ago.'

Quintus saw no need to add that from what he heard, neither Chrestus nor Flavianus had shared his own standards of integrity. His brother-in-law and oldest friend, Justin Petrius, had continued to serve in the Praetorians for years after Quintus had transferred to the special imperial service at the Castra Peregrina. Justin had only recently retired from soldiering to farm his lands in Etruria. Quintus had divined over the years that Justin remained in the Praetorian Guard despite, not because of, the mores of that elite cohort. His sister, Lucilla, had occasionally hinted to Quintus how difficult it was for her husband to square the circle of duty to the men of his cohort with the reality of the corruption within the Guard. To Quintus himself, his old friend had breathed not a word of his struggles, but Quintus knew what Justin's loyalty must have cost.

'This news alarms me, sir. I fear the senior prefect's position may be precarious.'

THE CARNELIAN PHOENIX

'I'm glad you understand, Quintus. I do fear for my cousin. He has publicly vowed to clean up the Stygian mess of the Praetorian politicking in Rome. But we have seen attempts to restrain the Praetorian Guard before. I do not believe they will quietly accept the stripping away of their power.'

Neither did Quintus. Even the mighty Septimius Severus had failed to achieve that. If that revered soldier-emperor could not permanently wrest power from the Praetorians, what chance had an elderly legal philosopher, and a boy Emperor?

' So, sir, my other mission…?'

Aradius leaned over to pick up the refilled wine jug. He poured carefully. Only when they both had recharged glasses did he answer.

'Once you have carried out your public orders — ensuring the traitor Gaius Trebonius is safely escorted to Rome, to stand trial in the Senate for his attempted coup, and then witnessing his execution — your real mission begins. I need you to be my secret eyes and ears in Rome, Quintus.

'The truth is, maybe not tomorrow, nor next year but at some time, the Severan dynasty may come to an end. It was weakened by the ruthlessness of Caracalla. His successors, the short-lived Macrinus and weak deluded Elegabalus made matters worse. Both died without heirs. It is only the strength of will of our Syrian princesses that has kept the Severans on the throne. That can't last forever. And then we may have to live through another Year of Five Emperors, with all the bloodshed and chaos that will ensue. I want your help to safeguard Britannia, to protect this island province from any fire and fury to come. While you are in Rome, ostensibly enjoying your home leave, I need you to watch and listen for me. Bring back any warning signs so we can prepare.'

Quintus had not expected this. It was treasonable to make any reference to the death of an Emperor, let alone the end of a dynasty. Governor Rufinus must truly trust him. Under the warm glow of this honour, though, Quintus knew that his mission could easily become dangerous. There would be few he could share the Governor's fears with. Tiro was stoutly loyal but had no idea about Rome and its politics. Was it even right to take Julia with him, knowing as he did how fragile the regime may be?

He drained his glass in a single swallow, and stood, saluting the governor solemnly. 'I swear by Mithras the Lord of Light, by Jupiter Optimus Maximus, Roma Dea and all the gods of Rome to discharge my duty. I will do my best to gather whatever information I can, sir.' He let out a long breath, held unconsciously under the gravity of his oath. 'And I will do whatever lies in my power to protect your cousin Ulpian, and the emperor.'

Rufinus stood clumsily, positioning his club foot carefully before stretching out his hand to grasp Quintus's arm.

'My friend, I knew that already. Just find out what you can, and come back safely to Britannia. And Quintus—'

'Sir?'

'Spend some time with your family. You're going a long way to see them. Make sure Lady Julia is made welcome.' The governor smiled fleetingly, and turned to greet Servilia and Julia as they came indoors for dinner.

Chapter Two

Augustodunum, Gaul

'Is it always this hot in Gaul, my lady?'

Julia glanced sideways at Tiro. His face was perspiring, and wasn't enhanced by a black eye several days old. His tunic was sweat-darkened. He looked decidedly uncomfortable as he jogged up and down in the saddle. It was an early summer day, bright enough to make the straight, tree-shaded avenue ahead of them glint white. Puffs of fine dust rose from round their horses' hoofs.

So far their journey south-east from Gesiacorum on the north Gaulish coast had been pleasant. The roads were wide and well-maintained, the inns were large and comfortable by British standards, and all their hired mounts had been acceptable. The accompanying carriage carrying their luggage kept up with them on the good roads; all three of them preferred to ride. By Julia's reckoning, they should arrive at Augustodunum well before sunset.

'You may find Italia even warmer, Tiro. And Rome itself can be a furnace in summer.' She beckoned behind to the young courier escort. He cantered up, and at her request pulled a rolled-up straw hat from her saddle-bag.

'Here. Wear this. You don't want to arrive in the Eternal City looking like a beetroot, do you?' With hat donned

Tiro's face appeared less scarlet, but he still looked miserable.

'What is it, Tiro? You seemed so excited about coming to Rome, but ever since we left Bo Gwelt your face has been as long as a horse's.'

The young *optio* stared ahead between his own horse's ears.

'It's nothing really, my lady. Only, in Londinium — it wasn't the same. I thought it would be fun to catch up with the lads, have a drink and a laugh in the taverns. But the lads didn't seem interested, and I told them if all they could do was drink and blabber on about town gossip, well, I wasn't bothered. And then one of them threw a punch. I soon had him on the floor.' His mouth hardened. Julia had seen that look before, when trouble was about. Mostly trouble launched with Tiro's fists. 'Well, for one thing, old Felix wasn't there.   Course he wasn't, he's on the road ahead of us with the prisoner escort, guarding that treasonous rat Trebonius.' Tiro sat upright again. 'Solid sort is Felix Antonius. He helped us get the job done in Corinium, all right. I'll crack a jar of wine with Felix in Rome, when we catch him up.'

'You'll have some good stories to swap when you see your friend again.' Julia allowed this happy thought to percolate. But Tiro's face quickly dropped again. So, not just the heat, or the punch-up in Londinium.

'But — I …well, it's Britta too.'

She waited, giving him time. Julia knew Tiro had quickly fallen for her housekeeper and childhood companion, but she wasn't sure how Britta felt in return. Clearly the Londoner intrigued and flattered the Summer Country woman, but Julia wondered if what he had to offer would be enough.

THE CARNELIAN PHOENIX

Even so, she was startled when he said, 'I asked her to marry me. Straight up, proper marriage with a home and everything. I've got good money coming in since my promotion.' His mouth twisted.

Julia sighed. 'Let me guess. She's not ready to settle down.'

'I don't understand, Lady Julia! What more could a girl want — a home and family, a respectable man with a future ahead of him? I just want to look after her.'

Julia did know. She thought the competent, forthright Britta unlikely to settle into quiet motherhood, after running a large household and helping with the Aurelianus estate in recent years.

'Just give her time, Tiro. She's used to looking after herself. Who knows? By the time we return to Bo Gwelt she may be missing you so much, she'll listen with a kinder ear.'

He looked more cheerful. 'You're right, my lady. And anyway, we'll soon catch up with Felix and those beers.'

***

Julia had travelled in the western provinces as a girl, accompanying her grandmother to luxurious watering places in Gaul and beyond, but even she was impressed with Augustodunum. The city was set on a hill surrounded by great rivers. The approach road took them past terraced estates, some with palatial residences. She gazed in awe at the huge temple to Janus before they passed through magnificent granite walls, entering the city by the north gate. Here, they paused briefly in the self-contained guard plaza while Quintus was saluted and his pass checked. They were promptly waved through. Their *mansio* for the night was some way along the main street, flanked by the forum on one side and several luxurious houses on the other.

'Better than the inn at Calleva, Tiro?' Julia murmured, as their horses were taken in charge by grooms.

'It'll do, my lady,' he called back, disappearing quickly towards the beckoning steam plumes of the bathhouse.

'You're late, Tiro,' said Quintus severely, when Tiro came into the dining room an hour later, hair still damp from the baths. A young girl was setting plates of shellfish on the low table in front of them.

'Sorry, sir.'

Julia smiled as Tiro gingerly lowered himself into reclining position on the couch next to her. 'Look, Tiro. British oysters, barged in from the coast and then all the way here up the Liger and Adrus rivers.' She watched in amusement as his initially eager face clouded over.

'I'm not touching them, and you shouldn't either, my lady! Fresh oysters brought to Londinium from Rutupiae on the same day are a treat sure enough, but these have spent too long in the heat. Not safe.'

'Nonsense. They've been kept alive and fresh in barrels of brine the whole way,' said Quintus, the laugh lines around his eyes showing. 'Come on, try them.'

Tiro cautiously poked a spoon at the oyster the serving girl offered him, closing his eyes as he swallowed. He nearly choked, saved by a back thump from the Governor's Man. 'Urgh! What is that slime?' He spat the oyster out indelicately, while Julia laughed.

'I told you he might not like the cumin, Quintus.'

Quintus grinned. 'Best get used to spicy sauces, Tiro. They're well-loved in Rome, I can assure you.'

Tiro curled his mouth in disgust, but it was noticeable that he ate heartily of the roast duck with hazelnuts, and the asparagus that followed. By the time the shy girl had come back to remove the dirty platters and lay out a dessert course of excellent local cheese and sweet pastries, he appeared fully reconciled to Augustodunum cuisine.

'Another, sir?' He poured resinated wine into their glasses, adding water and a little honey. Julia, who had relished the shellfish and enjoyed the duck, declined the wine and dessert. She excused herself while the men shared the second course.

On her way back from the latrine, she was accosted by the serving maid.

'Domina? May I speak to you for a moment?'

The girl glanced round, hesitating before drawing Julia into a little storage room, piquant with spices. Amphorae of fish sauce and olive oil were stacked against the walls.

Julia recognised her accent, and was surprised to realise the girl was a native from her own region.

'You are of the Dobunni?'

'Yes, Domina. I grew up in a village near Corinium. I came to learn the restaurant trade with my uncle here. It's a good job, and his chef is training me well. But that's not what I wanted to tell you. Only —' the girl paused, looking troubled, 'your husband, the Governor's Man, is he looking for someone here? I don't want to get into any trouble.'

Julia took the girl's hands in her own. 'No, my dear, we are travelling privately on family business. Don't be afraid, you can tell me. What is your name?'

'Locinna, Domina.'

'Well, Locinna, I am Lady Julia Aureliana, of Bo Gwelt. You may call me Julia. How can I help you?'

If anything, Locinna looked more apprehensive. She pulled her hands away, folding them in front of her long tunic, face worried.

'If you *are* Lady Julia, then you must know the witch.' Her mouth trembled.

'The witch?' Julia's eyebrows shot up.

'Yes, my lady. The red-haired witch, Fulminata, with an owl brand on her cheek. She was here …'

'Fulminata was here?' Julia spoke loudly, and the girl went pale with fright.

'Please be quiet, someone will hear!'

Julia controlled herself. Her lowered voice sounded grim in her own ears.

'Locinna, tell me what you know. When was she here? Do you know where she was going?'

'Two, or was it three days ago, maybe? They were heading south, there was someone they had to meet, and they were anxious to get there quickly —'

'They? Someone was with her?'

Fulminata had been outlawed from Britannia by the Sisterhood in Aquae Sulis, punished by the Wise Women for the murder of one of their own. Julia had borne witness as the Sisters had branded the furious actress with the mark of Minerva, and cast her into exile. How had she survived to get here? The laws of the Sisterhoods were absolutely respected throughout Britannia, and beyond. No-one seeing the owl of Sulis Minerva on the woman's cheek would give her food, shelter, or help of any kind.

Julia grasped the girl by her narrow shoulders. 'Describe her companion! Was it a tall fair man, masterful, wearing a green cloak? Quick, girl!'

Locinna stared at her. She opened and shut her mouth before getting out, 'No indeed, Domina. No-one like that. He was a poor, pathetic thing really. Young, very thin, dark curly hair. He seemed a sad sort, not up to much and …well, strange in the head, if you take my meaning. She shouted at him a couple of times, stopping if I came into the room. Although she was speaking the British tongue, and I took good care to pretend I couldn't understand.

THE CARNELIAN PHOENIX

That's how I heard her name, when the poor boy said, 'Fulminata, you have to help me. Just get me home, and then I'll reward you. You can have all the money.' A right nasty piece she is, that scarred one. She kept him shut away in the room after that. The next day, they just upped and left.'

'Was there a messenger? Or did she meet someone else here? Which way did they go?'

'She met no-one that I saw, my lady. They were here that one night, and then just vanished the next day, before dawn. Like magic, it were. I dunno where they went. I told you she were a witch.'

Julia doubted that, but clearly Locinna knew nothing more, or was too scared to say. She thanked the girl, promising again there'd be no trouble coming her way, and headed back to the dining room thoughtfully.

Quintus and Tiro were locked in a debate about Gallic wine.

'It's highly regarded these days,' Quintus said, leaning back on his couch and admiring the ruby colour of the vintage in his wine glass. Tiro was shaking his head.

'I've seen these Gauls in the Londinium taverns. They toss their wine back without any water. The wine may be good, but the way they drink is shocking.' He looked so disdainful of his Gallic cousins that Quintus burst out laughing. ' Tiro, you're such a hypocrite! You are the worst one for drinking yourself under a table I've met in a long time!'

'Oh, well, that's British beer, sir. I would never guzzle wine like they do over here.'

'That's because you can't afford the best wines, like the Massilian. It's judged to be as good as Falernian in Rome.'

Tiro subsided into a mumble; it was apparent that he had never deigned to try Massilian wine, or wasn't willing to pay the steep price.

Julia smiled, the slight frown easing off her face as she watched Quintus. He was leaning back on his couch, wearing a comfortable civilian tunic, thoroughly relaxed. His grey eyes were narrowed in humour and a grin lit up his suntanned face. Julia hesitated, reluctant to spoil his sunny mood. He reached over for her hand, pulling her down next to him.

'Julia, it seems my optio here has sworn off the drink. Tiro has become a new man since we left Britannia. No Gallic wine for him. Or maybe it's his money pouch that is sworn off the booze.' He paused at her slight hesitation in joining the joke.

'What is it, my darling?'

Julia opened her mouth to deny, just as Locinna entered the room. The British girl's downcast eyes and hasty movements as she gathered the plates and leftover food were more than enough to alert the ever-watchful Governor's Man. He said nothing while the girl busied herself, but as soon as she'd left he turned to Julia.

'What's going on, Julia?'

She explained. Tiro choked on his overlarge mouthful when she mentioned Fulminata, and Quintus stood up quickly, his face drained of humour. He paced the room silently for a while. Julia felt her stomach drop. Quintus was more disturbed than surprised by what she'd told him, it was plain.

'So, we have missed Fulminata and her companion, who I take to be Lucius Claudius. You remember that Lucius got away at Corinium?' Julia and Tiro nodded. 'The governor's briefing notes told me he had been traced to the Cantii coast, and it looks likely he shipped out to

Gaul from there. We didn't know where to, or whether he was travelling with someone. The governor thinks he is still involved with a criminal network extending beyond Britannia, possibly with political links in Rome itself.'

'You don't think he could cause more trouble, do you?'

Quintus said nothing, merely frowning. Tiro winked, as if to say, *'It's just the boss being his old close-mouthed self.'* But Julia noted that the happy look on Quintus's face had fled.

It would be a long time before she saw that look again.

Chapter Three

Augustodunum, Gaul

None of them were in the mood to extend the evening after that. Tiro saluted and departed to his room, muttering something about an early night. In their own chamber Quintus slid under the striped bedcover next to the dozing Julia. The bed here was better than most, but did not bear comparison with their feather-filled couch at home in Bo Gwelt. He held Julia close while her cool skin warmed. She stirred, tugging her long fine hair aside, and turned to him for a sleepy kiss. He lay still as her breathing slowed and she settled back into sleep.

Familiar troubling thoughts crept up on him.

Life was so precarious, like the treacherous flash of a sword in battle dealing life or sudden death. He thought about his young brother Flavius, solidly here one moment, then gone beyond evanescence the next; Quintus's own touch-and-go fight against fevered pain and disability in Eboracum after the Caledonian battles; the unknown moment of conception that created his daughter, Aurelia; the mischance of losing Julia, the woman he loved, and the luck of finding her again many years later.

And now, Fulminata and Lucius passing through Augustodunum, barely days ago. Into his restless mind came a vision of Fulminata, in league with the troubled young Lucius and flanked by the rebel Gaius Trebonius and his right-hand men, the Labienus brothers. He remembered events in Britannia the previous spring, during the attempted insurrection. Antoninus Labienus had died after losing a fight with Quintus back in Lindinis. Then Trebonius and Cassius Labienus had both been captured at Corinium, and were now disgraced prisoners on their way to trial in Rome. But Lucius …that strange young man who had set fire to Bo Gwelt and killed Julia's brother, Magistrate Marcus Aurelianus. How had he got here, apparently in league with the outcast and branded Fulminata?

It was understandable that the witch had left Britannia after being sent into exile by the Aquae Sulis Sisterhood. Any reported sightings of her in Britannia would mean her death. And Lucius — his father, Bulbo Claudius, had died in the villa fire too, trying to rescue him. His aunt Claudia was likewise in disgrace and unable to help him. Quintus remembered that Lucius had fancied himself in love with Fulminata. She might think he could still be useful. Locinna had said they were travelling south, that there was someone they had to meet. Quintus made up his mind. From tomorrow they would need to travel faster. They would catch up Centurion Felix Antonius and accompany the prison escort in person. Just in case. The leisurely honeymoon tour with Julia was over; in his bones he feared the chase was on.

Everything in this world was ephemeral, he thought. Including his father's senatorial reputation, leached away into the bathwater with his lifeblood. The scars on his right leg twitched. He felt apprehensive, as if the happiness he had rediscovered with Julia in Britannia was passing away with each step closer to Rome. He held her tight until she moved in her sleep, warm and real.

***

Four days later, the road south, towards the great commercial city of Lugdunum, took them parallel to a low range of hills on the west. The land sloped between lowering crags towards the confluence of the mighty rivers Sagonna and Rhodanus, as they approached the final bend of the highway. The day's heat was raising pale dirt from the horses' hoofs, leaving their following luggage wagon hidden in the haze of their wake. Quintus peered ahead, stiffening as he pulled his horse to a sudden halt and flung a hand up. His skin prickled, and he wrinkled his nose at a familiar and unwelcome smell.

The stink of death.

He and Tiro dismounted hastily, signalling to Julia to wait behind.

A bloodbath lay before them. Dead soldiers were scattered across the road and into the ditches like untidy scarecrows. At first, Quintus detected no movement or sound, apart from the calls of an interested family of carrion crows. As he stepped closer, keeping his footsteps quiet, a figure leaning over one of the bodies straightened up. It was a man, ragged and dishevelled, but well-armed with knife and sword. He turned, straddling his victim.

'We got here first. These are our pickings. Back off, or die!' He sounded as if he meant business, and judging by his ragged assortment of clothes, he was the kind of itinerant ruffian who had nothing to lose.

Quintus and Tiro drew their swords and ran towards the man, who had been joined by another, shorter ragamuffin. It was obvious the pair were at best battlefield looters, picking over the dead bodies; at worst, they were finishing off the final lingering victims of an ambush.

'Oh, Jupiter Best and Greatest! It's Felix!' Tiro tried to push past, but Quintus had seen what was happening. He pulled on Tiro's sleeve, saying fiercely, 'That one's for me. You take the other.'

Tiro needed no further invitation. The shorter of the two men was holding a heavy bag, which he seemed reluctant to abandon even in self-defence. That was his last mistake. Tiro lifted his sword in both hands and slashed it downwards, hacking the man's hand clean off. He screamed, and fell forwards onto his face, dropping the precious bag of swag onto the road where it discharged a motley collection of daggers, coins, decorations and phalera, all obviously stripped from the surrounding corpses.

'You filthy thieving crow!' spat Tiro. He knelt heavily on the man's back, grabbing a hank of his long greasy hair to pull his head back, then reaching round to slit his carotid and windpipe. A quick kill.

Meanwhile Quintus had approached the other man. He was still standing astride a body, which Quintus had recognised with a sick sensation as Centurion Felix Antonius.

'He's mine, and his gold is mine!' the man growled. He waved his sword in warning. Quintus saw a heavy purse still attached to the officer's belt. Governor Rufinus would have issued funds to defray the costs of the prisoner escort party on their way from Britannia to Rome. Quintus lifted the point of his *gladius* as if about to cut the purse off the wide leather belt. His opponent was so obsessed with the money — excusably, as it would probably keep him in food and shelter for months, if not years — that Quintus had an easy job of it. As the man lowered his own sword to strike away Quintus's blade, Quintus brought up his dagger in his other hand and sliced deep into the man's solar plexus, severing the artery there. The second man was soon dead.

Quintus rolled the body away from the Briton, and looked round, swallowing hard. A torn standard lay in the dirt: the vexillation sign of the Londinium cohort, the prison escort hand-picked by Governor Aradius Rufinus to take the greatest criminals in Britannia to Rome. In the centre of the carnage lay the dead figure of Gaius Trebonius. Former governor of Britannia Superior, and before that, legate of the famed Second Augusta legion. The former liaison officer and friend of the younger Praetorian Guardsman, Quintus Valerius, during the long-ago Caledonian campaigns of Emperor Septimius Severus. More recently the leader of the insurrection Quintus and his allies had nipped in the bud at Corinium, barely months ago. Now Trebonius lay curled on his side, knees gathered in, hands tied together, a look of surprise on his broad dead face, and a settled pool of blood under his torso.

Quintus turned back to Felix Antonius. His red-crested helmet had been knocked off his head and his harsh-featured countenance was turned skywards, staring open-eyed as if searching for rescue from Mount Olympus. His red uniform was smudged with dark oozing patches; his cuirass, covered with bronze phalera awards, slashed across and slick with blood. His right arm was nearly severed, but now Quintus saw that blood still pulsed slowly from the wound.

Tiro yelled, 'Felix!', and flung himself onto the ground by the old soldier, causing the gathering birds along the road to rise in alarm. Felix still clutched in his left hand his red centurion's vine stick, and Quintus realised the man was alive when it quivered.

'Let me through!'

It was Julia, who had scrambled off her horse and run over as soon as the two looters were disposed of. Quintus

THE CARNELIAN PHOENIX

moved back to allow Julia access, but she had to push Tiro roughly away. She glanced at the hacked arm, ordering quickly, 'Tear off the bottom of my robe, a wide piece right round. Quick as you can!' Quintus hurried to obey, and watched as she wrapped the linen tightly above the hideous slash and knotted it hard, uncaring of the faint moans from Felix. The blood flow slowed, but she looked sombre as she felt for the soldier's pulse. She shook her head. 'We've come too late, he has bled too much.'

Tiro crouched on the ground, chest heaving as he reached for Felix.

'Sir…Felix Antonius … speak to me.' The grizzled head turned with effort, and Felix looked at Tiro with glazed eyes. Tiro prayed, 'Please Jupiter, I beg you — save this man! I will dedicate the best altar in Gaul to you, make any sacrifice you like, just save my friend.'

Felix's good hand twitched again.

'Hush, Tiro, he's trying to say something!'

Quintus knelt down in the bloody dirt, his ear close to the soldier's mouth. He could hear Felix gasping, the gravelly voice a mere whisper. There was a long pause while Quintus listened intently. Julia continued to tear more of the sea-coloured border off her riding dress, balling the fabric and thrusting it up under Felix's hacked cuirass in an effort to staunch his abdominal bleeding. Tiro rocked on his knees, distraught.

Eventually, Quintus stirred and sat up. He closed the centurion's eyes gently. His worried fancies of the night at Augustodunum came crowding back to him. He looked at Julia, who stood up stiffly to check the rest of the party. All dead.

'I'm so sorry, Tiro.' The *optio* seemed to realise his superior was speaking, and raised bleary eyes to Quintus.

'You see, sir, he was — he was my only family. When my parents died it was Felix who pulled me off the streets, starving and hopeless. He got me into the Londinium cohort, underage as I was. He taught me soldiering, everything I know, saved my life several times, made me want to achieve. To do him honour. The day I was presented with my bravery phalera, he told me how proud he was. I never called him Father, but that's what he was to me.'

Quintus touched his shoulder, before getting to his feet, considering the wreck around them. It was utter devastation. A score of men hacked savagely to death. The only sign of life was from Julia, crouched in the verge on the side of the road, being uncharacteristically sick.

Quintus often found that the scene of a crime told its own story. He frowned. A score of bodies, but one was missing. Cassius Labienus, Roman patrician and co-conspirator of the attempted British coup with his elder brother and Gaius Trebonius. Antoninus Labienus had died trying to persuade Julia's tribe into rebellion at Lindinis. His younger brother, Cassius, had later stepped forward to champion the self-proclaimed Emperor Gaius Trebonius at the battle of Corinium. Quintus had recognised him then: a tall, fair man so like his brother, of arrogant posture and sweeping gestures. Quintus had fought him to a stand-still on the road outside the city of the Dobunni, and arrested him at the new governor's orders.

'We need to move on now, Tiro. Get this slaughterhouse scene sorted.' He reached for the younger man's arm, but Tiro pulled away sharply.

'*Futue te ipsum!*'

THE CARNELIAN PHOENIX

Quintus eyed his *optio*. Telling your superior officer where to put himself was both insubordinate and crude, but he would let the insult go — this once.

'Felix has passed on, Tiro, but these dead soldiers, your comrades and compatriots, need respect and care. You do them disservice.' More gently he added, 'We'll make sure he has a worthy memorial. He was an honest man, and a proud soldier.'

Tiro remained slumped by his friend's body till Julia, looking pale and heavy-eyed, persuaded him to his feet. Quintus went to inspect Trebonius again. There were no wounds other than the back stabs. He rolled the body over, looked more closely and signalled to Julia.

'Any thoughts?' She looked more her professional self.

'Neat stabs. Between the ribs, straight into the heart from behind. I would say a thin, sharp knife.'

'Not a *pugio*, then?'

She considered. 'You're the soldier, but…I think these stabs were made by a finer blade. Perhaps a filleting knife?'

'From a fishmonger?'

'Or a well-equipped kitchen.'

'Hmm. Julia, I have the feeling there's something here we're not seeing.'

'Apart from Cassius Labienus?' So she had noticed, too.

'Well, yes. But more than that.'

Tiro rejoined them. He was swaying but clearly trying to pull himself together. Quintus clapped him on the shoulder.

'It doesn't look like those two scavenging crows were the attackers here. You have sharp eyes, Tiro. Find me what's missing. Perhaps in the ditches?'

Tiro nodded and moved away to search the road and verges, full of early summer wildflowers. The cowslips looked tired and dusty, but large clumps of hellebore and startling blue lungwort filled the gaps, attracting butterflies of all colours.

'Sir! Here! Careful where you walk, there are a couple of footprints near the edge of this ditch.'

Julia craned down to look. 'What's so interesting?'

But Quintus had seen: two clear footprints where the dirt was damp, a third smudged behind. 'A civilian.'

'How so?'

'Look around, Julia. Everyone here is wearing standard soldiers' boots, caligae. Hobnailed. Except the person who stood over here for a moment.'

Tiro was hunched over in the ditch, carefully searching the ground between the profuse flowers. He lifted something up, then scrambled back up the verge, where he stooped once more to check the foliage. He held out a pair of fine whipcord loops, originally cinched together but then slashed to release whomever they had shackled.

'Like the cuffs I carry. Cut off with a weapon that had just a little blood on it.' He nodded at the ditch plants. 'Sticky leaves, smeared dark red.'

The two soldiers looked at each other.

'Lucius?'

'Or Fulminata. Or both,' Quintus said. He looked up from studying the hand shackles. 'That fits with Governor Rufinus's intelligence that Lucius had crossed to Gaul, being in league with plotters in Rome.'

'But the ambushers, sir, they must have been British. Apart from us, who knew the party would be coming this way?'

'The Londinium garrison knew. And the governor would have written to the imperial authorities, to alert the

THE CARNELIAN PHOENIX

Senate that two traitors were being sent for trial from Britannia.' Quintus tucked away the whipcord. His shoulders sagged momentarily; he would have to tell them. 'I already know where the ambushers are from. It wasn't Britannia.'

The other two looked startled. He was forced into a brief laugh. 'No prophecy or divination on my part, I'm afraid. Felix managed to tell me the soldiers took Cassius Labienus with them. And he identified them. He told me their shields bore the symbol of the scorpion.'

He saw they looked puzzled still. Of course, like Felix, they were British. And too young to remember the insignias of the cohorts brought overseas by Emperor Septimius Severus. 'They were sent from Rome. My former colleagues, the Praetorian Guard.'

He turned away, feeling infinitely weary and not wanting them to see his chagrin and shame. He had let down Aradius Rufinus, who had placed so much trust in him. The usurper Trebonius would never receive the judgement in the court of the Roman Senate that he deserved.

Now, Quintus knew the web of the British rebellion really did stretch across the empire, and was more deadly even than he had dreaded.

Chapter Four

Lugdunum, Gaul

The north gate to the city of Lugdunum was not much further, but the day's heat had already soaked away into cooler dusk as they rode slowly past the sacred precinct of Condate, above the rivers. The west-facing marble side of the great altar glinted where the lowering sun hit sparks off gilded letters, the names of all the Gallic states. Ahead was the greatest mercantile city in the three Gauls, but Quintus, musing, had never been less observant of a city built to impress. His companions rode in silence: Julia looked shaken still, and Tiro was clearly thunderstruck by his loss. Quintus guessed that he himself was the only one of the trio who fully appreciated that their trip had been turned upside down by the deadly ambush.

Lugdunum was glittering in the light of flaring cressets by the time they had reported the attack to the authorities, and a burial detail had been sent to retrieve the bodies. Quintus stayed on at the army barracks long enough to write a hasty report for immediate dispatch to Londinium. Tiro escorted Julia to the large city *mansio*. This official hostelry took pride of place on the island lying in the embrace of Lugdunum's twin rivers. As he passed along the wide streets to join the others, Quintus barely noted the magnificent temples dedicated to the imperial cult, befitting the birthplace of Emperor Claudius. He was

THE CARNELIAN PHOENIX

thinking about the attack: who had been killed by the attackers, who had apparently not, and *why*.

The inn was busy with travelling officials and local dignitaries coming and going. The harassed reception clerk gave Quintus a package delivered some days ago. He turned it over, surprised. In the dining room he found Julia, changed into a clean tunic and yellow pleated overdress, sitting alone. She was still pale, but composed. Tiro had gone to the adjacent bathhouse, doubtless to wash away his sorrows, along with his travel dirt. Good — he could talk to Julia without bringing back the blood and disaster to Tiro.

Julia looked inquiringly at the package, and signalled to the attendant slave to pour wine while Quintus opened the cloth wrapping. It contained an ivory tablet letter addressed to *Beneficiarius Consularis Quintus Valerius, travelling in Gaul, to be collected. From Lucilla Valeria, Rome.*

'Strange. It's from my sister.'

Quintus broke the threaded seal to discover that the upper parts of each hinged side of the tablet contained notes inscribed in the wax; the lower parts had been hollowed clean to make room for a small item packed between the ivory covers. He unwrapped a gold intaglio ring. It would perhaps fit a woman's hand or the little finger of a man.

'Ahh…'

He passed the ring to Julia. It was fine gold, narrow-shanked and fitted with a red gemstone. She held it up to the light. The image of a bird had been carved delicately into the carnelian gem. With the lamp backlighting the stone in flickers, the image seemed to be bursting into life from translucent carmine flames.

'What a beautiful ring!'

Quintus was examining the letter, shaking his head.

'This is almost impossible to read. Why didn't Lucilla use her secretary? Can you make out what she says?'

'But Quintus, why has she sent the ring? Is it yours?'

'Read it,' he said, holding the tablet out to her. He took the ring back from Julia and looked closely at it.

She saw his problem. The stylus strokes ran together awkwardly, and the lines of writing drooped slightly as if the correspondent was unused to writing on wax. There was some truth to this impression, as Julia realised when she made out his sister's name in the same hand, and crammed in as a tight afterthought at the bottom of the tablet. She read aloud the cramped words.

'Greetings, dearest brother,

We have just accompanied Mother to Rome from Uncle Faustus's estate in Etruria. Sad news — Uncle Faustus has passed away. I send you our father's signet ring. Father sent it ... ' I think the next bit says ' *...with a secret letter...to Uncle Faustus just before his own death. Uncle kept...* 'there's a smudge here ' *... hidden, and told me about them when he was ill. I found the letter among Uncle's private papers after the funeral. Father was adamant that Faustus should pass the ring and the enclosed letter to you, once you came of age and were settled in Rome. And then, of course, you never did settle back in Rome. I'm not sure about the...* ' I can't make out the next bit, Quintus. ' *You must forgive Mother, she is so...* 'next two lines also unreadable ' *... wish you joy of ...* ' Nope, smudged again here. I think it may say " *in Britannia*" . The last bit says — ' *Mother is here with us, and ... so Justin thinks it best to accompany her. I wish I could come, but... and long to see you when you arrive in Italia and ...*

THE CARNELIAN PHOENIX

'Then I think Lucilla adds at the bottom — ' ... *I can't stop her, so will wait*
I embrace you.
Lucilla'

'That's odd.' Julia's face was screwed up, puzzled.

'What is?'

'Why would your sister send a valuable ring by the post, when we're on our way to see her anyway? It's waited with your uncle all these years since your father died. She's obviously received your letter telling her the route we are taking to Rome, as she knows we're currently in Gaul. And what does she mean, not being able to stop your mother?'

'Why indeed?'

Julia shot him an irritated look. He gave her a smile of apology.

'Little of this is clear to me. But I wonder more about the "secret" Father sent to Uncle Faustus, and the "them" Faustus kept hidden.'

He searched the linen packet again, this time extracting a rolled and sealed scroll of papyrus, flattened by time and travel. He lifted away the old seal, still intact, and carefully smoothed out the page to read. The ink was faded; he tilted it to the light. His brows knotted.

Julia watched, her face showing anxiety as time passed and he did not speak. He closed his eyes for a moment or two, then re-read the letter. At last he let it drop from his hand.

'Quintus? Is it bad news?'

'Bad news? I don't know; perhaps. But too late — this comes far too late.' He sat in heavy silence, elbows propped on his knees, gazing hard at nothing. Julia knelt down in front of him.

'Quintus? My love? What's wrong?'

He felt he was struggling to speak, needing to drag in heavy breaths. Julia picked up the dropped letter. 'May I?'

He nodded, not lifting his head, as she scanned the precise neat writing. It was dated early 212, addressed to *Tribune Quintus Valerius of the Praetorian Guard, at Eboracum in Britannia*, and signed and sealed by Senator Bassianus Valerius. The letter was brief, but Julia needed to read it twice to absorb the contents.

The senator wrote that he was on a list of those proscribed under the new regime. He knew his life would soon end. He wanted his son to know he had behaved as befitted a Roman patrician, and regretted little in his life, apart from not being able to see his beloved sons Quintus and Flavius and his lovely daughter Lucilla again. He asked Quintus not to discuss the contents of this letter with anyone but his brother Faustus, especially not with Quintus's mother.

'For Hortensia would not understand, and in her pride and hurt might take damaging action. I have not always been the best of husbands, Quintus, though the gods know I have tried. However, she is my wife and your mother, so I say no more.

In recent years my affections have strayed. I must tell you that I found happiness with a lady, a younger woman of respectable equestrian class called Fabiola. I cannot tell you how we met, to protect her and others, but if you understand the symbol on the ring you will perhaps guess our secret. We have a daughter, a tiny creature of beauty and sweetness. Your mother has no idea, and I would not shame her with divorce or any other arrangement, so my relationship with Fabiola has remained hidden. I am sending Fabiola and the little one to shelter with Faustus at the farm.

THE CARNELIAN PHOENIX

I beg you, when you return to Rome, to extend what protection you can to my darling Fabiola and my child. I hope you will take on this burden and find it in your heart to forgive me. I have tried to protect the family estate and our proud old name, but Emperor Caracalla has turned against me despite the years of affection between us. I fear I can do little to prevent his punishment of me, however uncalled for. Do not look to see me alive when you return, my son.

I am immensely proud of you, Quintus, and know that wherever your career takes you, honour, loyalty and love will guide your steps.

Your affectionate father,
Bassianus.'

Julia put the letter down on a side table, and still kneeling, wrapped her arms around Quintus. He began to shake, still covering his face. She held him as the shudders gradually eased.

'There's so much he never knew, Julia.'

'About what, my dear one?'

'About — Flavius, dying in Caledonia. About my time in Eboracum; you and Aurelia; about me turning my back on his beloved Praetorians and becoming an imperial investigator, trudging the dusty roads of the east all those years. He says he is proud of me, but what have I ever done to deserve his pride? He left me a sacred trust, to protect and shelter his chosen woman and their child — my sister — never knowing I couldn't do that for him. Fourteen years too late, Julia!'

When they went to bed he lay awake, feeling the comfort of Julia's embrace long into the night.

***

At dawn, as the fowls in the yard below clucked to be let out, and the household slaves started clattering in the kitchen, Quintus fell into an uneasy dream.

In the dream, a young woman carrying a little child was hurrying away from the old house on the Quirinal, through darkening streets. There was the sound of children playing, but he could not see them. Quintus tried to catch the woman up, but his scarred right leg suddenly broke open into terrible twisting wounds. As he stumbled and fell onto the cobbles, the woman quickened her pace ahead. But the faster she hurried, the faster nebulous danger pursued her.

He woke to find Julia, white-faced, vomiting into a chamber pot.

'The British oysters attacking you?'

Julia turned a pale face, speechless. Quintus summoned the chamber maid and ordered ginger tea. The maid lifted her ill-plucked brows at the expense, but hurried off obligingly when Quintus gave her money. Julia insisted she was feeling better, and they both joined Tiro downstairs for breakfast. He looked unusually sombre but greeted them both readily.

Quintus handed hard-boiled eggs, bread rolls and local apricots cooked in honey and mint, across the table to Julia. He was surprised and relieved to see her eating; she nodded her appreciation. He turned to his *optio.*

'There was something else Felix said to me, just a snatch between mumbles.' Tiro looked up.

'Felix thought Cassius greeted one of the Rome party as "brother"'.

Julia broke in. 'How many Labienus brothers are there? We know about Antoninus, who died at Lindinis. And Cassius, no doubt now on his way to the nearest port on a fast horse. Was there another?'

THE CARNELIAN PHOENIX

Quintus rubbed his scarred leg thoughtfully. 'I don't know, Julia. The Labienus family is a patrician one, of high repute and status — was, anyway. But my family had no connections with them. They had far more money, for a start, and I suppose the brothers entered public life with higher-profile patrons and support.'

As he spoke, a flash of last night's dream came back to him. The young woman disappearing down a narrow alley in Rome, followed by…whom? Why did that feel familiar? He didn't know the girl; even if he had, she was fleeing with her head covered and her face turned away. The house she'd come out of was not visible in his dream, but still…He felt there was something there he knew. Perhaps he had dreamt of his old home on the Quirinal? Yes, that was it! She was walking away from the servants' entrance, down the back alley behind his house. That's how he knew the street. He and Flavius had spent hours as children playing in that very spot, with other lads —

'Sir?' Tiro dragged him out of his reverie. 'May I take some time before we leave to arrange a funeral for poor Felix Antonius and the Londinium lads? I must pay my respects, and make sure everything is done right.'

'Of course, Tiro. Would you like me to come?'

'No, sir.' It was said respectfully but firmly. 'This is something I need to do myself, for Felix.' Tiro's face was set; Quintus sensed the Londoner was relieved there was something he could offer his dead mentor.

'Off you go, then. We'll pack and bring the horses to meet you. Come to the river docks when you've finished. We're going by ferry from here. Whatever it was that really happened to our prison party, you can be sure the survivors will be taking the fastest possible route to the coast of Gallia Narbonensis.' He looked grim. 'From there, they'll ship out to Rome. And we must hope we can catch them.

Chapter Five

Massilia, Gaul

It took a full week of travelling by river and road, through a countryside of vineyards and olive groves, to reach the southern port of Massilia. The summer was ripening into the bright heat of late June as they journeyed south. The locals wore knee-length tunics instead of the trousers of northern Gaul, and Tiro heard less and less of the Gaulish tongue.

The quaint harbour city of Massilia could not help but charm. They passed through the east city gates onto a built-up peninsula stretching to aquamarine waters on three sides. It was an old and pretty city, with dainty Hellenistic buildings reminiscent of its long Greek colonial history. Tiro remembered that the hero of the British conquest, the great general Agricola, had been a native of Massilia. Quintus could have told him that the Massilian geographer Pytheas had long ago sailed from the vast deep-water harbour here, on the first ever Roman exploratory expedition around the unknown savage islands which became Britannia. Tiro's education, mainly of the street kind, did not stretch that far.

Julia was still struggling with the aftermath of food poisoning, and although she tried to pass it off as just a delicate stomach, Tiro could tell she was weary of the journey. She looked pallid and thinner of face. She refused to travel in their luggage wagon, though, saying being cooped up under canvas was enough to make anyone feel sick. By the time they arrived in Massilia, only her fortitude and superb horse-riding skills were keeping her in the saddle.

'Lean on me,' Quintus said softly to her, as the harbour-front *mansio* stable boys sprang to attention. He nodded to Tiro, handing over his official pass, 'Sort us out with the innkeeper, would you? I'll take Julia straight upstairs. She needs to rest a while in the cool.'

'Tiro,' Julia added with effort, 'could you go to the shops and buy me more ginger, please? It seems to help, but I've nearly run out.'

As Tiro headed off, Quintus said to him under his breath, 'Tell the inn-keeper we'll be here a while. She's too ill to travel tomorrow. We'll stay here a few days.'

The garrulous innkeeper nodded his head in sympathy when Tiro explained. 'Poor lady, I thought she looked done in! You British can't take the heat, can you? Different for us Massiliotes, of course — been here so long, even the mountains and sea can't remember us arriving. Well, you're in luck, sir. Our city is famous for its eminent doctors, ever since the times of Crinas; I can recommend a very good practitioner for your lady.' He may well have rattled on indefinitely in this vein, but Tiro was struggling in an effort to follow his rapid, heavily-accented Latin, and merely nodded, asking again more slowly for directions to the nearest market.

'Of course. Again, lucky.' The innkeeper beamed at Tiro's good fortune. 'Here in Massilia we have two marketplaces: the big daily one held in the city forum, and our local one. Today is harbour market day, and you'll find all sorts of stalls on the quayside as well as the weekly slave market. My cousin sells the most succulent shellfish at his stall, I can get you a discount…'

Tiro left quickly, jamming the broad-brimmed straw hat Julia had given him onto his head.

***

The harbourside was a bustling delight. People swarmed everywhere, dickering in street Latin and occasionally rapid Greek for every kind of produce. Tiro walked past the vast dockside warehouses, floors covered with *dolia* and wooden barrels and stacked to the ceiling with amphorae of local sweet wine, olive oil, and fish sauce from Antipolis. Beyond the warehouses were the market stalls, heaped high with local farm foods: asparagus, beans, peas, radishes, garlic and carrots. Carefully arrayed hillocks of eggs; early season cherries, peaches, grapes. There were rounds of young soft cheeses; mountains of seafood, of course. Tiro recognised sea bream and mackerel, and oysters. He shuddered, thinking of Julia. Other fish were a mystery, being caught, he supposed, from this strange tideless sea. He also steered round the stalls selling platters of small songbirds. The sight of their pathetic little dead beaks gaping wide was somehow upsetting; a fat pigeon or stuffed goose would be so much more appetising.

Merchants from the fringes of the empire and beyond were selling gaudy swags of fabrics, and piles of highly-scented spices, pungent and sweet in equal measure. It was all far more exotic than Tiro had ever seen on sale in Londinium. He found a spice stall with ginger, and managed to buy some without being fleeced too much, although he suspected he had paid over the odds. He recognised black peppercorns, bay leaves, fennel and poppy seeds. Other spices, eye-catching in their bright pungency, he could not tell: towering heaps coloured bright orange, rich brown, lime green. The stallholder, a swarthy man wearing silk robes and gold rings in his ears, assured him they were the best quality spices, brought at great cost from the fabled coasts of India. Tiro kept his hand tight on his purse, beckoned on by a growing clamour.

At the far end of the harbour, on the leeward side, was another market. Economically even more valuable, but much less alluring to the nose. Tiro was used to seeing slaves in Britannia, often born to slave parents, or children sold to pay family debts. The odd blue-painted Caledonian or raw-boned Irish captive would come to market too, in the aftermath of conflict north of the great wall of Hadrian. Such slaves would change hands at the Londinium market, but these were usually as individuals, not in groups being sold at once.

This was an altogether different market. The noise he heard was an amalgam of auctioneers' shouts and buyers' offers, raised above the chattering, weeping and the occasional slash of the slaver's whip. The smell — ah, Tiro thought, this was a smell he would never forget. A rancid blend he had seldom encountered, except in the gaol in Londinium, and at the amphitheatre one time he and his mate had been allowed to tour the underground animal pens before a gladiator-beast fight. It was the stink of fear, filth, sweat and despair. He swallowed, and pushed into the crowd.

Tiro was sensible about life, and understood as well as the next man how the world worked. Rome needed the labour of slaves to prosper, and after all, it was better for the poorest people to belong to a master who would feed, clothe and house them, than to die starving and cold in the streets. He thought ruefully of his own young life, hustling errands, stealing and begging for scraps round

THE CARNELIAN PHOENIX

the forum in Londinium. That was until the blessed Felix had scooped him up into the willing embrace of the Roman army. Where he had worked even harder. Just as well there *were* slaves, otherwise the army would have to do bloody everything.

He wrinkled his nose, turning his head in a vain effort to escape the worst of the smell. No risk of any slaves here dying of cold. They were sitting shackled in the blazing sun behind the auctioneer's rostrum, having been off-loaded from ships moored to the jetties nearby. The galleys were being washed, buckets of seawater sloshed across the decks and down the hatches to wash away the stain of slavery, before they were loaded with cargo for the return trip. Tiro looked round, curious to hear where the slaves hailed from as they were brought up onto the auction stage. There were people of every colour and country: pale-skinned northern barbarians; dark-haired labourers from Hispania; household and business workers from Palaestina, Arabia, Syria; high-nosed curly-haired captives from the Parthian Empire; and natives from beyond the great African desert, blue-black and gleaming in the heat. It seemed this was a market often supplied by pirates, bands of ruffians who would swoop down on defenceless coastal villages, kidnapping the youngest and strongest. That trade was supposed to be illegal, Tiro had heard, but there seemed very little prevention here.

To one side, surrounded by guards and eager customers, was a group of young girls. Tiro edged nearer. One of the girls, a small creature in her mid-teens, was being pulled to her feet. She was dressed in a long tattered orange-yellow robe, and had scuffed gaudy slippers on her little feet. Her hair, mid-brown with golden highlights, had come free of its pins and swung down over her face, but

Tiro caught a glimpse of small pretty features under the wing of hair. There was a roughly-daubed sign of some sort hung round her neck.

The auctioneer, an enthusiastic red-faced man in a grubby robe, was finalising the sale of a German prisoner of war who had been stripped to his loincloth to show his assets.

'A big man, tough hands, he'll do a hard day's work for you. Come,' he urged the crowd, 'come feel his muscles. You'll be amazed at his biceps, I warrant you.' He called on the buyers to free their purses, receiving a quick rally of bids in return. The hammer fell on the table, the fair-skinned giant was led away to his new owner, and Tiro's young woman was pushed up the steps.

'Right,' said the auctioneer, and Tiro thought his voice lost some of its former verve, 'I have a real bargain here, ladies and gentlemen. Young pretty lass, bred well, healthy, from Etruria, speaks beautiful Latin. Can even read and write. She'd be a bonus to any household. No record of bolting, no cheek to her owners, no thieving. I am authorised to offer a truly rock-bottom price for the quick sale of this slave.'

'What's wrong with her, then?' spoke up a man in the midst of the crowd. 'Why is she going cheap?'

'Oh, just a quick sale wanted.'

Another man at the front asked in tones of suspicion, ' So what's that sign round her neck for?' The auctioneer opened his mouth to bluster when a woman peered at the sign and read aloud, '*Vibia, failed prostitute. Refused customers. Did not earn enough to pay her taxes. For sale, by order of her brothel-keeper in Rome.*'

The auctioneer, perhaps feeling a sale slipping out of his sweaty paws, appealed to the crowd. 'Yes, maybe the girl did fail to please in that role. But she would still be useful to the right household. She has a beautiful singing voice.' He hissed at the girl, 'Sing, damn your eyes! Sing something, and make it good!'

The girl, Vibia, coloured, and lifted her hair away from her face. The auctioneer leaned down, saying something inaudible but obviously threatening. There were snorts of derision from the crowd. Some turned away. Tiro moved closer, bunching his ready fists.

Vibia cleared her throat, closed her eyes, and began a wavering song in a soft voice. It was a sweet little ditty, sung in the Etruscan dialect. As she sang, the girl's voice grew stronger. She did indeed have a lovely voice, melodic, perfectly pitched, and strong enough to hold the notes well. Tiro listened, enchanted. When the song ended he felt bereft. He wanted her to sing forever. Surely she was the victim of a jealous god, turned from nightingale into human form by Apollo or Mercury?

Some in the crowd didn't agree. There was a shuffling of feet, more exits. Someone shouted, 'Lascius, you old fraud. This was supposed to be a sale of girls for the brothels. You're just wasting our time here.' The auctioneer looked round anxiously, as customers drifted away.

'How about a warranty, good people?' A jeering call of obscenities was all the reply he got. His face darkened, and he pushed the girl, making her stumble. Tiro shouldered his way to the stage, raising his voice.

'Oi! You! Auctioneer. A word with you.'

The red-faced Lascius scowled at him. 'Either bid on the silly bitch, or get back on the boat, Briton!'

Tiro lost patience.

'I *could* buy her at half your starting price. Or I could come up there and smack you in your fat, red face. Take your pick.' The girl was staring at him, whether in horror or resignation, he couldn't tell. He threw a purse up at the auctioneer's feet. As the girl stepped down from the rostrum to join Tiro, she pulled the sign off over her head and dropped it in the dust. Round her neck hung a delicate silver necklace, a fish on a chain.

***

Tiro ushered Vibia ahead of him into the *mansio* chamber where they found Quintus sitting alone, sipping wine. The *beneficiarius* looked up, puzzled at the sight of the frightened girl. Tiro hurried to explain.

'Well, sir, I, err…I bought the ginger for Lady Julia all right. And then I thought as how a maid for the lady would be just the thing. You know, a body slave to look after her — while she's so poorly. Just till she's better.'

Quintus looked relieved. 'Not a bad idea, Tiro. I was never happy at Julia coming all this way without a maid, but she was so stubborn. We'll give the girl a chance. We can always sell her if Julia objects, or doesn't like her. After all, you seem to have struck quite a bargain price.' He smiled at the slave, who stood with downcast eyes, hair drooping once more. 'Welcome, Vibia. I'll show you up to our chamber, and introduce you to your new mistress.'

Tiro felt his cheeks warm a little, and blessed his constant concealing stubble. Best not to tell the boss why Vibia had been a bargain. He might not approve.

Chapter Six

Massilia, Gaul

The following day dawned hot and still. Julia was feeling no better, and after making a libation to the household gods and taking a few turns up and down the dockside, Quintus was still undecided what to do. Julia was still being stubborn, and true to form, would allow no doctor to be summoned.

'I'm a trained healer myself, Quintus,' she said in exasperated tones when he tried to insist. 'I know at least as much about medicine as any practitioner here. Just go away, and get that girl to bring ginger and lemon tea and yesterday's bread. The drier the better.'

He left reluctantly. The truth was, as he confided to Tiro, he was getting worried about losing time here, time that Cassius Labienus and his companions would make good use of.

Vibia slipped quietly into the dining room as Quintus and Tiro were finishing a breakfast of fresh bread with honey and dates.

'The mistress is asleep, Dominus.' Quintus tore a second piece off the bread, and the carnelian on his little finger caught the morning light glinting off the sea.

'Thank you, Vibia.' This was the usual signal for a slave to leave the room. Vibia did not do so; she was looking fixedly at Quintus.

Tiro appeared to notice nothing, having his face wrapped round a huge chunk of bread. Quintus cleared his throat in dismissal, but the girl dipped her head, saying in a low voice, 'May I speak with you, Dominus*?*'

Quintus glanced at Tiro, who took himself off, saying, 'I'll make enquiries about passage to Portus, sir.'

'What is it?' Quintus said. He felt distracted. His well-planned trip was unravelling badly, what with the ambush, Julia's food poisoning, and now the delay here.

The young girl coloured, looking intensely awkward. 'Sit down,' Quintus said, realising he had sounded harsh. What had Tiro been thinking, to buy this delicate creature instead of a more experienced and robust maidservant?

'Sir, may I ask your name?'

'My name? I am *Beneficiarius Consularis* Quintus Valerius.' He could hear the tight note in his voice. He forced himself to look calm.

'Forgive me sir, but would you be the son of Senator Bassianus Valerius, of the Quirinal in Rome? The nephew of Faustus Valerius, of Etruria?'

'Yes, but how do you know? What *is* this?' Quintus found he was standing, hand poised to reach for the gladius that was actually lying under his bed upstairs.

The girl's face had gone pale, except for red spots glowing on both cheeks. It was as well she was seated; she was quivering and holding on to the table edge.

'Sir, you may find this hard to believe. But I am — believe I am — umm…'

'Just say it! What are you, by Mithras?'

'I am your sister.'

Silence stretched out between them. Vibia still shivered visibly, silky hair slipping back over her face, as Quintus cycled between disbelief and astonishment. His mind flashed back to his father's letter. Could this slave girl somehow have found it? But he knew it was hidden in his kitbag. Anyway, what could she hope to gain without proof? Before he could say anything, she spoke again, her words rushing out.

'It's the ring, sir. I recognised it. It was my mother's before she gave it to my father. He wore it always.'

'My ring?' He lifted his left hand; the bronze ring on his ring finger, wrought with the little owl symbol of Minerva, was the love token Julia had given him in Eboracum thirteen years earlier. He grated out a laugh, this time meaning to sound harsh.

'You lying little vixen! Is that the best you can do? This ring hasn't been off my finger since you were a tiny tot.'

She lifted her desolate face to his, reaching a quivering finger across to touch the other ring he wore, donned only a week ago: the slim gold ring on his right little finger. It was so light, he had forgotten it. This was the ring she meant: his father's gold ring with the exquisite bird carved into the carnelian. She looked so shy, so begging, his heart nearly broke despite his resolve.

'My mother Fabiola gave this ring to my — our — father Bassianus. I saw it often.'

Quintus sat heavily, stilled by wonder and doubt. The words from his father's letter came rushing back: *…if you understand the symbol on the ring you will perhaps guess our secret. We have a daughter now, a tiny creature of beauty and sweetness. I am sending Fabiola and the little one to shelter with Faustus at the farm.* He squared his shoulders, holding the girl's gaze. Perhaps this slave knew the real Fabiola, had recognised him, had somehow arrived in Massilia to catch him, but how could he check her story?

'You say you are the daughter of Bassianus, my father? Tell me then, where you grew up. And explain so I can understand just how you come to be here in Massilia, right now, so conveniently at hand to gain a patrician brother's protection at your greatest need. You, a slave bought today off the dockside auction block!'

Vibia lifted her head, sweeping her gold-threaded hair clear of her soft young face. There was pride in her attitude, even a touch of hauteur that surprised him. That tilt of the chin, the upright stance with shoulders squared — he saw the familiarity, despite himself. The fairness of Bassianus had bequeathed her colouring, the eyes more hazel than the grey of his own. Quintus knew himself to take after his mother Hortensia, with his dark looks. But this girl — it was true, *deodamnatus*! — looked much as his sister Lucilla had in her mid-teens. She looked like Bassianus.

She gazed at him, a look of willingness to trust to his honour, his sense of family obligation.

'I will tell you,' she said, 'although it may sadden you to be reminded of terrible times. I don't remember the last time I saw Father — I was very young. But my mother described to me many times our escape from the wrath of Emperor Caracalla, that dreadful time of terror that savagely struck down our father. He sent us away north out of the city, with money and a letter for your uncle — our uncle Faustus. Such a good man! Faustus became another father to me, and gave us an honourable and happy home in Etruria. He had me educated, such a generous man. He said that the mischance of my parents meeting when they were unable to marry should not hamper my own future.

'Life became less happy when Mother died. All the doctors, and there were many, could not save her. And then Faustus began to sicken himself. In mind more than body, for he was an old man. He seemed to lose his way

THE CARNELIAN PHOENIX

about the farm. He would wander off into fields and copses, and I would have to send the slaves out looking for him. Eventually, he couldn't remember the names of the staff, even those who had served him like friends for decades. By then, he only knew me when I sang for him. He remembered the old songs, right to the end. He died last year, and then ended my life.'

She paused and he saw that she was crying. He hardened his heart, though he was beginning to believe her. But he was resolute. He owed it to his dead father, to Flavius, Lucilla, and even to his mother, to be sure beyond doubt. He thought bitterly of the actress turned pretend Druid-witch, Fulminata, who had carved a swathe of murder and rebellion across the Summer Country in Britannia only a few months ago. An actress who wrought terrible damage. He must be certain that *this* girl spoke the truth.

'How did you come to be a slave, and to arrive here in Massilia with such nice timing?' He worked hard to keep his voice calm and cool; he thought he had succeeded.

Vibia seemed to hesitate, as if wondering what to say. *Aha! Here come the lies.* And yet, *Please tell me more, I long to trust you, my sister.* Two forces battled in him, and he no longer knew which would win.

'Uncle Faustus apparently died without a will. There... was no provision for me. No money. The estate was sold with all the slaves, and I was not needed. The new owner disapproved of me, and I was — ' She drew a ragged breath, wiping her hands across her eyes. She looked directly at him. 'Brother, I was sold to a brothel. In Rome. After a while, I was unable to please the brothel owner. He hoped to get a better price for me in Gaul, and I was passed on to the merchant who sold me to your man, Tiro.'

'What do you mean, the new owner "disapproved" of you. What did you do to upset him?'

'Her.' Vibia said it absently, but there was a flash of pride in her tone. She glanced at his ring, and he remembered his father's mention of a secret associated with the carved intaglio. 'I will not pretend, not any more. Chance has put me in your hands. I will not deny my Lord, even as Peter the Apostle did, thrice.'

Quintus twitched unconsciously. He was an initiated worshipper of Mithras, the Lord of Light, but he had spent much time policing the troubled eastern province of Palaestina. He understood, with an icy feeling down his spine, the significance of his new ring.

Keeping his voice cool, he said, 'The bird is a secret symbol of the Christian cult, isn't it? I have heard that a phoenix bursting aloft from a fiery red stone signifies the resurrection of the man-made-God, Jesus of Judaea. Is that right?'

She held her head proudly still, but one hand reached up and grasped the slender silver chain round her neck. 'Yes. And here is another symbol of our faith, bequeathed by Peter, who was our first bishop and our greatest martyr after our Lord Jesus.' She held up to his intent gaze a tiny shimmering fish. 'Father gave this to Mother when he was baptised a Christian, a token of his love and faith. It is the only thing of hers I have.'

Quintus was struggling to breathe, battered by these revelations. If he accepted that Vibia was telling the truth, then everything he thought he knew about his father was uprooted, ripped out, tossed away. *Or was it? Was he not still a man of honour, a man who loved and was loved in return?*

While he was thinking this, he heard a female voice upstairs. A moment later a *mansio* slave knocked, popping his head round the door to say Julia was calling for her maid.

'Yes, of course.' He nodded, saying to Vibia, 'I need to think about all this. Come back later when Julia is asleep, and we'll discuss what is to be done.'

As Vibia's soft tread moved up the stairs, Tiro barged into the room. 'Sir, sir!'

'Well, did you find ships leaving this week for Portus?'

'No, sir, I didn't get the chance.'

'By all the Gods, why not? What was it this time? No more impulse purchases of slaves, I hope?'

'No, sir. But look who I found disembarking at the docks!'

Tiro held the door open wide to usher in a middle-aged woman in fashionable dress, who swept into the room with every indication of disapproval. Behind her stood a tall man with a soldierly bearing, wearing a faint look of apology. This was Justin Petrius, Quintus's oldest friend and husband to his sister Lucilla.

'Mother!' exclaimed Quintus.

Hortensia Martial was a shortish woman, the petite figure of her youth coarsened a little by age and child-bearing. She carried herself upright nevertheless, and her elegantly coiffed hair, discreet makeup and silk robes announced a widow of rank who invested in her looks. She held both hands out to her son, looking less than thrilled to see him.

'Quintus. At last. We've come a long way to find you. These ships from Rome are atrocious. You wouldn't have believed the extortionate prices of provisions at the ports, and the difficulty I had getting a cabin. And cooking space on board! Justin had to pester the captain continually to get space at the hearth for my girl to cook our meals.' She withdrew her hands from her son, gesturing at a spotty young maid waiting submissively by the door. 'Take my bags upstairs — you have booked chambers for us, Quintus? — quickly, stupid girl!'

Justin stepped forward, calm as ever. 'Let me see to the rooms and luggage, Hortensia. Quintus has hardly had time to greet you properly.'

Quintus took the hint. He drew a seat out for Hortensia. 'Please, Mother, do sit. You must be tired after your voyage. Let me pour you some wine. But why have you put yourself to all the effort of coming to meet us in Massilia?'

Hortensia looked at him sharply. 'Surely Lucilla wrote to you?'

'Well, yes, but her letter wasn't entirely clear. I rather expected her to come with you.'

'She's pregnant, again, the foolish girl. Spitting out children like grape seeds. Heaven knows why Justin wants so many children; he has three sons already.'

Justin, who had come back into the room, stiffened, but kept a courteous tone. 'Your sister and I long for a little girl this time, Quintus, and the boys are wildly excited, of course. Lucilla was set on travelling with us, but I insisted she stay at home on the farm. It's too hot for her to travel in her condition. She'll come to see you and Julia in Rome, when you're settled.'

Hortensia curled her lip, as if at the thought of any Roman noblewoman finding travel too taxing, pregnant or otherwise. Quintus steered her firmly back to the subject.

'Well, Mother, how is it we meet here?' He poured her a little wine, watering it well before passing the glass to her. She took a sip, folding her legs elegantly and settling into her chair.

THE CARNELIAN PHOENIX

'*You* have driven me here, Quintus. My concern for my beloved son would not allow me rest or stay, once I had heard the dreadful news from Lucilla.' Quintus felt the sinking in his stomach that had accompanied so many of their conversations over the years. He stood quickly, determined that she would not see his apprehension.

'What dreadful news, Mother?'

'About this concubine of yours, this Briton you've seen fit to bring with you. As if it wasn't enough for you to reject Calpurnia, the well-connected wife I took so much trouble to find for you. Why couldn't you follow the honourable customs? It was good enough for your grandparents to select me, a respectable girl from Patavium, for your father, so why couldn't you stay married to the high-class Roman lady chosen by your mother? Now you have to bring further shame on us with this woman and her illegitimate child. I don't call her *your* child — I believe it's a girl? In Rome, we've heard about the crude polygamous behaviour of these blue-painted northerners —'

Hortensia halted abruptly as Justin stepped towards them in time to stop Quintus exploding into response.

'Hortensia, you haven't met the Lady Julia yet,' he said gently. He turned to Quintus. 'Is Julia here at the inn? I'm so looking forward to seeing her, and Lucilla was most disappointed she wouldn't be with me to greet your lady.' It was meant to mollify, and Quintus tried to squash down his rising bile for Justin's sake.

Female voices spoke beyond the door. Tiro for once was ahead of the game. He darted out, and spoke low and quick outside. It was a wasted effort. Julia came in, dressed in her best and evidently making an effort. Quintus hurried to her.

'Julia, should you be out of bed?'

Julia looked with silent enquiry at Hortensia. Quintus felt his gut clench. He wondered bitterly how much of the conversation Julia had already overhead.

'Mother, this is Lady Julia Aureliana of the Durotriges. Julia, my mother, Hortensia Martial.' Julia said nothing, standing tall and very pale. Quintus could not read her expression, making him even more apprehensive.

Hortensia remained seated. She nevertheless rose to the occasion with all the frosty arrogance of a Roman patrician addressing a barbarian. 'A little early in the day for a whore to be paying visits, even a cheap British one, isn't it?'

Julia glanced at Quintus, her face giving away less than a Londinium merchant in bargaining mode. Then she dipped her head in the slightest of inclinations and left the room. Justin looked horrified, and quickly followed Julia out with Tiro. Tiro could be heard urging Julia to take his arm to go up to her room.

Quintus, caught between incandescent anger at his mother and outraged hurt for Julia, quivered as he kept his control. The blood was thumping in his head. He was reminded of his shock months ago back in Britannia, when his friend Governor Gaius Trebonius revealed himself to be a traitor. The memory of that feeling, how the sneers and threats of Trebonius had somehow pushed him to recover his poise and think more clearly, flooded back. His mother took a sip of her wine, looking collected. There was triumph in her expression. Quintus eyed her, this stranger with her inscrutable grey eyes and air of self-possession so like his own. He'd passed the point of no return with her. He felt a sense of liberation.

'Mother, what you just said to Julia was unforgivable. She is a woman of rank and great respect in her own country. Britannia, I remind you, may be distant, but it's been a settled Roman province for generations. Julia is well-educated, held in high regard by all who know her, and is a skilled healer. Our daughter, Aurelia, who I happily acknowledge as mine, is wealthy in her own right and is being educated as befits a Roman noblewoman and future leader of her tribe. But even if none of that meant anything to you, you should at least respect Julia for my sake. She is my great love, and will, I hope, be my wife soon —'

'No, Quintus, not that! Have you no shame? I shall not allow it!'

Quintus clenched his teeth, and held his breath till the clamour of blood in his ears became deafening. Then he let the air hiss out of his lungs, waiting till his heartbeat slowed before he dared speak. He would not lose his *gravitas* in front of this woman, who he no longer thought of as his mother.

'Nothing you can say or do will alter my feelings or intentions, Mother. I will leave you to consider your words. You will be more comfortable in your own bedchamber, and I will send your maid to attend you there.' He stood, keeping his eyes averted and left the room, calling for Tiro

Chapter Seven

Massilia, Gaul

Next to the dining room was a salon, where guests of the *mansio* could entertain, or relax between meals with drinks and snacks. Justin emerged as Quintus was passing, and pulled his brother-in-law inside.

'Not now!' snapped Quintus. But one look at his unhappy friend's face changed his mind. He sighed and sat, rubbing his leg where the old war scars were prickling. Justin poured him wine, not watered this time. They drank in silence.

Justin leaned forward, brow furrowed. 'I'm sorry, Quintus. I should have warned you, but there was no opportunity. Lucilla and I tried to stop Hortensia travelling to Gaul to intercept you. She would not be swayed.' He lapsed into silence, looking so uncomfortable that Quintus found a short laugh forcing its way out of him, despite his hurt and anger.

'Mother always was determined to have her own way, regardless of anyone else. Look how long she made you and Lucilla wait to be married.'

'Yes... But there's something more, Quintus.'

Quintus crooked an eyebrow and waited. Justin, being tied to Rome until a few months ago by his service in the Praetorians, had been forced to spend far more time with Hortensia than Quintus, who had escaped into his career

THE CARNELIAN PHOENIX

in the east before settling in Britannia. Justin looked awkward. 'I'm not sure what's going on, Quintus. As you say, Hortensia has always been proud, and well, prickly. Ever since your father…'

'Became unpopular?'

'Yes. When I came back from Britannia with the legions, while you were still so close to death yourself in Eboracum, I knew then something had happened. Something at Lucilla's home — your old home on the Quirinal, I mean. Your parents had never been close, Lucilla told me, but matters between them became icy. I suppose I was distracted by the troubles in Rome under Emperor Caracalla. Such a dangerous time for anyone with connections to his brother Geta. I just kept my nose clean, and went on persuading Hortensia to allow my marriage to Lucilla so I could keep your sister safe. Instead, she sent Lucilla to Faustus in Etruria. Then your father died. That was a terrible time.'

'And then?'

'Then she suddenly allowed us to marry. She must have realised what was best for Lucilla. Although she insisted on staying in Rome herself, in a little house Faustus gave her. The big house was empty till your wedding to Calpurnia, but…'

'Yes.' Quintus could hear the strain in his own voice, and managed a tight grin.

'Anyway,' Justin went on hastily, 'I didn't see much of your mother after that, of course. But whenever she did come to Etruria, or Lucilla visited her in Rome, she seemed more relaxed. Less worried about being widowed than we expected. I have to say she rose well to the challenge of having been the wife of a man on Caracalla's proscribed list, even when most of your family's money and estates went too. She mentioned having new friends. It was odd, really.'

His voice trailed off. Quintus was puzzled; he had never known his mother to be relaxed or even remotely happy. As he was wondering how to express this doubt, there was a discreet knock. Hortensia's maid came in.

'Dominus,' she addressed Justin, 'the mistress wishes to speak to you about arrangements for her return to Rome.' She dipped a salute, and left Justin to smile resignedly at Quintus and follow her out.

No sooner had they left than Vibia slipped in. She closed the door quietly.

'Quintus, I must speak to you urgently.'

'By all means.' Internally he groaned. This could only be to do with Hortensia's arrival. Vibia had named no names, but it had already occurred to Quintus that the "new owner" of Faustus's estate had to be a member of his own family. Faustus had died childless, having never married after his fiancée succumbed to the Antonine plague. Who but Hortensia would be ruthless enough to sell an unknown young girl without checking her status?

It was worse than he thought. As he listened to Vibia's urgent words, he felt anger and horror growing again.

'I didn't know at the time, but when I saw your mother arrive here I recognised her as the heiress of Uncle Faustus' estate, the new owner who sold me to the brothel. She must have known about Mother and me.' Vibia was anxious, head turned towards the door as she spoke.

Quintus made her sit, and pressed some wine on his half-sister.

'But how? Father was dead, and Uncle Faustus would never betray his trust. Was it one of the servants who found out? Had Fabiola confided in someone?'

'No. Mother knew all too well how dangerous our position would become if anyone knew about our connection with Father, or about our faith in Christ. She kept those secrets until she died. Somehow your mother *did* find out, and took the earliest opportunity to get her revenge. She was the first to arrive when Uncle Faustus died, and immediately went against his dying wishes. Perhaps she found his will, and decided to get rid of me before your sister Lucilla could get there.'

'But Lucilla sent me Father's letter and the phoenix ring, which she had found among Faustus's affairs.' Quintus was puzzled.

'Your mother was in a terrible hurry. I think she was so set on destroying me, having missed her chance of revenge against Mother, that she sold me off even before the main auction of the estate and the real slaves. I was a free woman after all, so she would have to sell me to a criminal such as a crooked brothel keeper. She didn't seem to much care about anything else, not even the money. But, Quintus, she'll find me here. I can't go through that again. What am I to do?'

Vibia was right. Hortensia couldn't be allowed to cause any more damage to his half-sister.

'That won't happen, Vibia. I wish we'd found each other years ago. You are under my care now, and I will protect you from the world, including my mother.'

Vibia's eyes welled up with tears. She sobbed as he gathered her up in his arms. 'Thank you, dear Quintus. I will never forget what you've done for me. Your support means the world.'

Neither of them, caught up in emotion and regret, heard the faint creak outside the door as someone went past.

A few minutes later Justin came back to announce Hortensia had demanded passage on the next available ship back to Rome.

'I can't persuade her to wait, Quintus,' he said, rubbing his hands over his troubled face as Vibia quietly slipped away upstairs to check on Julia. 'What shall we do?'

Quintus thought.

'Right, we'll play a holding game.' He told Justin about the dead prisoner escort party at Lugdunum. 'That had already changed my mission well beyond anything in my original orders. Let me call in Tiro — he needs to be in on this.'

The three men talked and drank well-watered local wine, as the hot southern sun climbed to its zenith and the hubbub of the *mansio* rose and fell around them. Fortunately Quintus had sufficient rank to guarantee they were left undisturbed in the salon.

Quintus began. 'I've been thinking about what we found at the ambush scene, Tiro. Trebonius left dead, Labienus missing. I think Trebonius was killed to shut him up, and Labienus was taken either as hostage, or in a rescue. But why?'

'I've been thinking too, boss. What if Trebonius knew too much about the wider plot, and the plotters in Rome didn't trust him not to spill the beans under torture?'

'Perhaps. But then why keep Labienus?'

Justin weighed in. 'Maybe he's been taken as surety. His family are influential and have powerful friends, even at court I hear.'

'Go on,' Quintus prompted. 'Who are these powerful friends?' But Justin had no names to offer, only vague stories circulating in that premier rumour-mill, the Praetorian *castra*.

THE CARNELIAN PHOENIX

Tiro interrupted, 'Sir, the Labienus brothers came from Rome in the first place, to help Trebonius raise his insurrection in Britannia.'

Justin looked puzzled. 'Meaning what, Tiro?'

Tiro blushed, and rubbed his chin. Quintus smiled; Tiro wasn't used to debating with the upper classes, even with Quintus himself.

'Well, here's how I work it out, Tribune. Gaius Trebonius was sent out as governor to Britannia from Rome right enough — could have been part of a plot laid well before he arrived. But he already had long form in Britannia, having been the legate of the Second Augusta legion, as well as having served under Emperor Septimius Severus in the Caledonian wars. All that made him popular in the province, and acceptable to the British tribes. But the Labieni — well, they had no previous connections with our province. No reason to be there —'

Quintus leapt up.

'— except to take advantage of Trebonius and his secure position in Britannia, keep him on the straight and narrow, while *their* orders came from the real masterminds in Rome. Tiro, you're a genius!' Quintus thumped his *optio* on the back, making Tiro cough.

'Where does that leave us, then?' asked Justin.

Quintus strode up and down, talking as ideas came to him.

'For my money, if Tiro is right, it must mean Cassius Labienus has been rescued by the Praetorians —'

'What!' Justin also rose, looking troubled.

'Ah, yes, you don't know. Sit down, Justin, you won't like this.' Quintus explained how Felix Antonius had borne witness to the scorpion emblems on his attacker's shields. He watched his brother-in-law for a moment, saying gently, 'It wouldn't be the first time the

Praetorians have taken it upon themselves to act beyond their role in safeguarding the imperial family. Even as far away as Gaul.'

Justin sighed, and let his head drop into his hands. 'There had been rumours, Quintus, even before the two Praetorian prefects were …removed. I heard the odd thing or two myself before I left, but I didn't want to know. To be honest, I've been getting quite uneasy. That's why I brought forward my retirement.'

'Well, your suspicions might just be right.'

Quintus looked grim. He returned to the subject of their immediate plans. He had decided to continue to Rome forthwith, but needed to talk through his thinking, wanting to be sure he was being objective.

'So, we have Cassius Labienus being taken to Rome by the Praetorians. We don't yet know why, but we can be sure we need to follow as fast as possible.'

'What about Lucius and Fulminata, sir?'

Justin cocked an interrogative eyebrow. Quintus explained.

'British collaborators of the would-be usurper Trebonius. Lucius Claudius helped to raise money, silver stolen from the Emperor's British mines in Mendip, to bribe the officers of the Second Augusta legion to rebel. Fulminata is more shadowy: a British actress who somehow got involved with Antoninus Labienus in Londinium, and turned her hand to murder as needed in the Summer Country. A very nasty piece of work, but she was caught and branded by the Sisterhood of Wise Women in Aquae Sulis. They sent her into exile. Among the Sisters is my Julia, who is a healer, as well as a tribal leader.'

He saw that Justin was looking thoroughly confused. Quintus grinned briefly.

THE CARNELIAN PHOENIX

'All conventional stuff in Britannia, brother. Anyway, I doubt either Lucius or Fulminata have much weight in Rome. The second, more important part of our mission has now come into play, and I hope Governor Rufinus will forgive me for including you, Justin, in our counsels. We urgently need to follow Cassius to try to reveal what my governor suspects, threats to Chief Minister Ulpian. Plus it is our duty to uncover the murderers of our Londinium colleagues at Lugdunum. We may find one or both of the British traitors with Cassius. Fulminata for one won't miss the chance to swan around Rome with her new lover, where her punishment brand won't mean as much. Lucius — I'm not so sure. Tiro, you remember he told Drusus back in Britannia that Fulminata was his lover? But it seems clear she had already tied her fortunes to the star of Antoninus Labienus until his death in Lindinis.'

Quintus paused, thinking. He needed Tiro away for a moment. ' Tiro, would you mind checking on Julia? We really need to know when we can depart for Rome.'

He waited till Tiro had left the room, looking long at his brother-in-law. 'Justin, I need your advice. I am beginning to fear the British rebellion was only part of a bigger plot that could affect the chief minister, and even the throne itself. You were a serving Praetorian officer, and I won't ask you to betray your old comrades. But I believe there are deep roots to this, stretching right back to my father's death. I can't tell you all my fears — I have promised someone close to me to keep an old secret. But if I'm on the right track, none of our family is safe, not even Lucilla and the boys. I think it more important than ever that you go home, to Etruria. Mother may not like it, but your responsibility to her can be handed over to me.

But while I have you with us, I hope you can give me your counsel in strict confidence.'

Justin crossed the room to his brother-in-law, grasping his arm in the age-old salute of comrades in war.

'You need not ask where my loyalties lie, Quintus. You and I, we've been friends since we spent our afternoons together after school, playing in the street behind your house. We served in the Guard, fought side by side in Caledonia, and for many years we've had ties of blood, as well as brotherhood. Of course I'll help wherever I can, and keep your secrets.'

Quintus returned the warm pressure of his friend's arm, pleased and relieved. But something Justin said had distracted him, reviving the shades of a fleeting memory or dream.

Boys playing harpastum, in teams. That's right…it was in the street behind his old house, tossing or kicking the small hard ball between the three of them — Justin, Quintus, and his younger brother Flavius. Flavius complaining that the older two kicked too hard, never let him get the ball, and Quintus calling to him to toss the ball his way, to stop it crossing the line in the dirt. There were other boys, another team of three, brothers from a nearby patrician house. Two tall and blond, the third smaller, darker, younger. The little one would rush around behind them, so eager to sweep up the ball…

A sudden crash heralded Tiro barrelling through the door.

'Sir, sir! She's gone!'

Justin looked startled; Quintus, more used to Tiro, merely asked, 'Who's gone?'

'Lady Julia, sir! I found Vibia sitting in your room, looking upset. She says Julia sent her out on some errand. She had to walk to the main market in the forum, took her

THE CARNELIAN PHOENIX

a while. When she got back, she found the room empty of Julia and her pack.'

Before Quintus could react, he heard swift little feet run down the stairs. By the time he'd opened the door, whoever it was had left the *mansio*. Quintus dashed up the stairs, *pugio* in hand, while Tiro and Justin each took the passages to the main entrance and the small slaves' door at the back of the inn.

'What is all this commotion?'

It was Hortensia, leaning over the internal balcony on the first floor landing. Quintus thought for a moment she had just come out of the room he shared with Julia, but his mother went on, 'I've been woken from my nap to find this place in chaos. People dashing up and down stairs, making a complete din. That sulky Briton of yours, I suppose, no notion of how to behave like a lady.'

Quintus ignored her, thrusting his way past her into their bedroom. Tiro was right; Julia was gone, with all her belongings. Except her turquoise mantle, lying unnoticed on the floor behind a basket chair. Quintus picked it up, raising the fine wool to his face and breathing in the faint lingering scent of rosewater. His mother opened her mouth, but he forestalled her.

'If I ever discover, Mother, that Julia's leaving had anything to do with you, our relationship ends that day.' He turned on his heel and clattered down the stairs, dagger still loose in his hand, while Hortensia stared after him.

Tiro rushed back into the passage, saw Quintus, and panted out, 'She's disappeared too. Julia's maid, Vibia, I mean. She must have gone with the mistress.'

Chapter Eight

Gades, Hispania

Julia woke. She was lying in a narrow bed by the wall. The bed, strangely, was swaying. She thought for a while, not really very interested. She must be on a boat. She lay still, listening to the lapping of water and enjoying the muted play of dawning sunlight as she closed her eyes. It was quiet here, apart from the call of seabirds, gulls she supposed. She had no idea why or how long she had been here, and cared less. She was comfortable, sleepy and at ease. She slept again.

She woke later, feeling enormously hungry. Sunlight was rippling up and down the walls of the wooden cabin. She was at Bol, she supposed. She and her brother Marcus had travelled to the big port on the southern coast of the Durotriges' territory several times as children. Or perhaps she had come to the docks in Glevum, accompanying their father on a business trip. But no — it was too warm here for either British port, and the sunlight was too bright, more fiery silver than soft gold. Stretching, she ran her hands over her body, to discover she was dressed in her undertunic, with her hair tied back. Through the linen of the tunic her ribs and hips felt sharp. She felt further, making a discovery.

THE CARNELIAN PHOENIX

'Oh!' She rolled onto her side, noticing that she wore a gold chain round her neck. It was her own chain, but she did not think she had been wearing it when she —

'Oh!' she said again.

A woman she had not previously noticed stood up from a lightweight wicker chair, smiling. It was a beaming smile, offsetting an astonishingly bright personage. Julia blinked. She had never seen such strident auburn hair, so much makeup, nor such a hoard of blazing jewellery hung on one person before.

'Well, Julia, I am very glad to see you awake, and not being sick for once. I was right that dressing you in your gold chain would protect you from the risks of the sea.' The woman was deep-bosomed, with muscular, rounded arms and solid shoulders under a gauzy gown of the very best silk. No doubt all the way from Cathay. Her fingers — even her thumbs — bore flashing rings with large gems, and so many clanking golden bangles adorned her wrists that she made a continuous jangling sound as she moved around the cabin, pouring water into a fine glass, and adjusting pillows to help Julia sit up.

A cascade of questions flooded Julia's mind. *Where am I? Who are you?* were prominent among them. The woman smiled again, revealing a single gold tooth in her otherwise immaculate mouth.

'You're wondering who I am.' Julia nodded gratefully, sipping the water. 'I am Fulvia Pompeia, shipowner of Massilia. And we have just arrived in Gades in Hispania Baetica, aboard my flagship *Athena*.' Fulvia paused, apparently happy to let that sink in before continuing.

Julia gaped at her, provoking Fulvia into a burst of laughter. 'Just sit back, my dear. Here, eat these grapes. The doctor says you need feeding up after a week of constant vomiting. I'll explain while you eat.'

It seemed Fulvia was the only child of an extremely wealthy but dead Massilian shipping magnate, and the youngish widow of another. *Athena* was just one of her fleet of trading vessels, the largest and most comfortable. It also benefited from being captained by one Artemidorus, who was apparently talented in more ways than just seamanship.

'I found after my husband died and left me *loaded*, darling, that life ashore as a childless widow was so dull! And then I hired Artemidorus to skipper my flagship, this *gorgeous* trader, queen of the Roman merchant marine. Wait till you see the figure of the goddess Athena I had set at the prow, all gilded. I spend most of my time at sea. I might as well conduct all the business myself, instead of being cheated by those lazy scum my late husband so foolishly trusted. I soon put a stop to that, I can tell you.' The woman's face darkened momentarily, then brightened again.

Julia found herself liking Fulvia.

Next came an account of how Julia came to be aboard the ship. It seemed *Athena's* crew had been readying for sea at their homeport of Massilia, and had just completed the ritual of sacrifice on the poop to please and propitiate Neptune — and, of course, any other gods who took it into their heads to be interested.

'For I make it my business in this trade to know whom to please!'

They were about to pull in the gangplank and were preparing the anchor and mooring lines to be taken aboard, when Fulvia spotted Julia.

'Lying in a heap you were, my dear, crumpled onto the quayside in all your prettiness. Fortunately your saddle bag was there with your clothes inside when you dropped down in a faint, otherwise we would have had to dress

THE CARNELIAN PHOENIX

you in seaman's roughs!' Fulvia laughed heartily. 'I tried to speak to you, but at first all you would say was that you must get away. You gripped my arm, wouldn't let me go. Eventually you told me your name was Julia and you were lost, you couldn't go back, you must get home. Then you collapsed into a deep stupor. I guessed you had run away from something, or someone. And your accent tells me you are a long way from home. Britannia, or Germania, I think?'

Julia had to concede Fulvia's shrewd guesses. She still felt terribly weak; she had clearly been very ill and in need of a doctor, which Fulvia had apparently provided.

'Always dock in ports with good doctors, my dear. It pays in the long run, you've no notion how many plagues and fevers we meet on our voyages.'

The Massilian doctor had pronounced Julia badly dehydrated and run down with protracted food poisoning. He prescribed careful nursing, light food and a long rest. In her few waking moments, Julia had become so distressed at the suggestion of looking for her travelling companions that Fulvia dropped the subject. Instead, with the cargo laden and wind and tides being favourable, the *Athena* slipped her anchorage and made for sea, heading west for Hispania.

'And now,' Fulvia added, 'I'm going into Gades city to see my agent, order some supplies, and do a little shopping. I wonder if you would like me to get anything for you, Julia? Perhaps from the herbalist?' There was a sympathetic light in Fulvia's clever eyes while she waited for a response. 'My dear, we both know what ails you. Apart from the food poisoning, which was real enough but is on its way out. You are with child. I have myself suffered the same sickness, many times over. If you want a confidante, I can keep secrets very well.'

Julia was astonished. 'How did you know? You said you had no children!'

'That isn't the same as never having been pregnant. I have conceived and lost many children. The Goddess Juno never blessed me with carrying a baby beyond three months — I don't know why. During my marriage, my husband blamed me and made me seek remedies from every quack and charlatan up and down the seven seas. None worked and then he died, releasing me from the obligation of an heir. But no matter. I have a happy life now, and widowhood suits me. I just ensure my beloved Arti sets no seed in me. I couldn't bear the loss of his child, too. And when I'm gone, my distant cousins can squabble over my vast estate.'

Julia said nothing, feeling sad for her new friend. She had never considered what being barren would be like. Her whole adult life had been taken up with concern for Aurelia. And there was the emerging possibility of a new child.

Fulvia took Julia's hand, her gold rings rattling, and squeezed it.

'I don't ask for your confidences, Julia. But I think you have choices to make, and Gades will be your last chance to act for some time. Once we weigh anchor here, we will be at sea for weeks. How far gone are you?'

Julia drew breath, reluctant to admit the truth she had been hiding even from herself. She had not noticed that her courses never arrived while they'd been travelling through Gaul. The sudden illness striking at Lugdunum, associated with the massacre of the British soldiers, had distracted her. By the time she began to wonder, she had felt so ill and low she couldn't face telling Quintus. She counted back in her mind.

THE CARNELIAN PHOENIX

'I think this baby must have been conceived in April, before I left Britannia. I should have known the signs, being a healer myself, but perhaps I didn't want to. You're right, Fulvia, I do need to make decisions. But it's so difficult.' She leaned back against the pillows, feeling exhausted suddenly.

Fulvia furrowed her brow. 'Well, Julia, you have a little time yet. Do you want to carry this child?'

Julia turned her head to the wall, eyes closed. She wished it would all go away. She didn't want to think about Quintus, about the agonising betrayal that had driven her from him. Before their arrival in Massilia, she would have been delighted to be pregnant. To have another child with the man she loved seemed all she could have desired.

Then Hortensia came. Her brutal rejection had sent Julia spinning into doubt and renewed sickness. Worse, Julia had emerged from her sickroom just in time for Quintus to cut her heart out. She heard it with her own ears, the committal of himself and his love to Vibia. Clear as if she was in the room, she'd heard him say he wished he had found Vibia years ago. *Before he came back to Britannia, he meant. Before he discovered he had a daughter, and took on the duty of being Aurelia's father. Always that damned Roman sense of duty!*

There was no choice, really. Quintus had found the woman he truly wanted, and in Julia's own hearing had promised to protect Vibia against the world. Even from his hateful mother.

But no protection for me. Not the inconvenient "British whore". A little Roman slave girl is more acceptable than I am to the man who I thought loved me.

She'd managed to control the immediate return of nausea, while she gathered together her scattered clothes and scribbled and addressed a brief note on a sheet of the papyrus provided by the *mansio*. A new pain came on suddenly. A stabbing pain, creeping in waves across her belly. She'd drawn a hissing breath, quickly folded the note addressed to Quintus, and left it in view before closing the door and creeping downstairs. Her pride and the anxiety not to be seen had kept her upright and moving all the way to the docks. Then, as she scanned the bustle of ships from everywhere across the empire, the realisation of what she'd done and what lay before her overwhelmed her. She remembered sinking down onto her knees on the hot paving flags, retching, while dreadful cramps folded her in half.

She did not remember falling into blackness.

***

'We'll be moored in Gades overnight. Tell me which herbs are best and I will go myself to the apothecary to buy them for you. No one else will know, I promise, not even Artemidorus.'

'Thank you, Fulvia. You're so kind. I've made my decision. About… the baby. Please, could you try to buy bark of guelder rose, *viburnum opulus*?'

Fulvia looked at her soberly, and held out her arms to Julia. Julia's tears fell in earnest, and she sobbed while the scented woman gathered her into an embrace before leaving the cabin.

The *Athena* lay at anchor all through that hot still day. Julia could hear screaming gulls rocking on the softened sea, and smelt the exotic warmth of southern plants, but the effort to rise from her bunk was too enormous to be contemplated. The painful spasms continued, and she wondered with dull resignation whether she was miscarrying anyway, and the choice thus made for her. At times she wished she could just slip away, not have to

THE CARNELIAN PHOENIX

bear the pain of so much loss. As evening fell, bringing blessed cool, Fulvia returned with the herbs. She sat by Julia's bunk and took her hand.

'Julia, I've picked up some useful whispers from our agents here, and talked to Arti about our route. We were already due to head to Aquitania to take on a cargo of local wine. Now, I want to consult some associates there, to look into a new trade possibility further north. So, my dear, tomorrow we will sail for Burdigala on the morning tide. Sea and winds are set fair, bless Neptune and Athena, and once we arrive in that port of great trade and even greater gossip, we shall know more. But it may be that we can take you further than that.'

Julia wept again, this time from relief. Fulvia pressed her shoulder lightly, and left her exhausted passenger to sleep.

Chapter Nine

Massilia, Gaul

It was useless, even with Justin's help. Julia and Vibia were not to be found. The three men scoured the port of Massilia fruitlessly, till the lingering shades of evening dropped into a deep warm night. No one had seen two unescorted women seeking passage. Tiro was last back to the *mansio*, determined to bring news — any news — to his boss.

He had not seen Quintus with such a desperate white face since the battle at Corinium last spring. Then, the odds against them had been stacked as high as heaven, and Tiro had known they were going to their deaths against the usurper Trebonius and his bribed legion. *But we bloody-well came out of that scrap in one piece, sort of, if you discount the broken ribs and blistered arm. We were the heroes of Britannia. We'll win out again.*

But Tiro knew in his heart this was a different kind of disaster. Women — well, what could you do? He thought briefly of Britta, and then wished he hadn't. Julia and Vibia had gone off together, Jupiter knew why or where, leaving Hortensia stalking the inn with a look of such disdain on her well-bred face — it was enough to make you sick. He certainly wouldn't think about the fragrant Britta either.

THE CARNELIAN PHOENIX

The why of it was the worst, Tiro reflected, as the men gathered over an early breakfast before resuming the search again.

'I don't understand, boss. Why would they leave like that?'

Quintus was staring at the morsel of bread in his hand, oil dripping from it unnoticed onto the table. Then he lifted his head.

'They had every reason to leave. Both of them because of my mother. Julia — well, you witnessed yourself the way my mother spoke to her. Unforgivable! And Vibia…' He glanced at Justin and Tiro. 'I suppose you'll have to know. Vibia is not who she seems. Yesterday, she gave me absolute proof that she is the daughter of my father Bassianus. My half-sister.' He held up his little finger to show them his new intaglio. 'This was his ring. The stone bears the symbol of Christos, the risen phoenix. Before he died, my father secretly converted to the cult of Christos. Many years ago he met and fell in love with a Christian lady, Fabiola. She bore him a daughter, Vibia, and he sent them in secrecy to live with Uncle Faustus at the family estate in Etruria. Father left me the ring with an explanatory letter, though I have only recently received his legacy. When Faustus died, my mother discovered Vibia. She took her revenge…' Quintus stopped. He gripped the edge of the table, his knuckles translucent.

'By Jupiter and Mars! I don't believe it!' Tiro was filled with sudden rage. He pushed back so hard from the table that his chair fell over as he leapt to his feet. 'Hortensia *sold* Vibia? To a crooked brothel keeper in Rome? What kind of woman would do such a terrible thing to an innocent young girl?'

Justin broke in, his level voice calming the other two.

'Hortensia is capable of much under her genteel exterior. She has set ideas of how the world should be, and her place in it. That is why Lucilla insisted I accompany her here to meet you, Quintus. It was clear to both of us that she would never welcome Julia into the family, no matter how noble and worthy Julia Aureliana obviously is. I wish I had prevented Hortensia from travelling. She has caused such damage and pain.'

'You could not have stopped her, Justin.' Quintus added in a voice of exhausted bitterness, 'Mother always gets her way.'

Tiro rubbed his chin, feeling irresolute and upset. 'Bugger this! What can we do?'

Quintus stood, his face turning hard. 'Right. I'll go to the harbour master as soon as his office opens, check which ships left last night and those due to sail today. He'll have a list of all passengers with exit permits. Could you two make enquiries with ships along the quayside as well?'

Justin grabbed his arm. 'Of course, brother. We'll split up and search as quickly as we can. Don't worry — we'll find them.'

***

Tiro had forgotten his hat, and as the unforgiving southern sun burned down on him, sweat soon began to coat his face and slicked the inside of his tunic with prickles. A pounding headache kept him company as he dashed along the wharfs, searching and calling. His shouts produced no results, only coarse jokes as to why he couldn't find a girl on land; there were plenty available in the taverns.

Trouble was, Massilia was such a popular port, being well protected from currents and prevailing winds. Ships came and went to and from destinations all round Mare

THE CARNELIAN PHOENIX

Nostrum: shipping olive oil, rich Gallic wine, the pungent *garum* sauce so beloved of Romans, grain to be baked into the empire's daily bread. There were too many ships to search: tramp ships, fast naval vessels with double banks of trained oarsmen, cargo ships of all sizes and arrays. He doubted he'd find the two women.

'Last call for boarding! Final call to passengers for Portus!' a bow-legged sailor bellowed behind Tiro. He turned to see dock slaves who had been loading sacks onto a fast galley on the next jetty, threading their way back between late passengers making haste to board. As he watched, the gangplank was pulled up onto the galley behind the final passenger, a tall man. He caught a glimpse of a slight young girl with the tall man, adjusting her mantle to tug it off her head. He couldn't see her face, but something in the way she moved shocked him into recognition. The sun burnished the gold threads in her soft brown hair. She leaned over the side waving, apparently to catch the attention of the stevedores below. There was something in her outreached hand, something light that moved in the sea breeze, perhaps a sheet of papyrus. She called out again to the workers below, but her words were snatched away by the breeze and drowned in the noise of the bustling port.

Tiro gaped as the tall man swung a vivid green cloak off his shoulders to wrap the girl into a tight embrace. She tilted her head up, turning away from Tiro as he raised both arms to wave frantically at her. He shouted her name, running along the wharf around the intervening jetty to reach her ship. But the captain's bellowed orders cut across Tiro's yells. Before he could attract her attention, the sheet of papyrus blew out of her hand unnoticed and flapped slowly to the sea, floating for an instant before sinking.

Tiro stared in disbelief as the galley oars creaked, the main sail bellied out, and Vibia departed Massilia in the arms of Cassius Labienus.

***

Justin was slumped alone in the salon with a jug of wine before him when Tiro walked in. Justin shook his head wearily, not speaking. Tiro trudged up the wooden stairs to find his boss. He felt hot, exhausted, and miserable.

Quintus looked much worse. The Governor's Man was sitting on the edge of his bed, the bed he had shared with Julia. That he had passed from the normal world into a realm of suffering was obvious even to Tiro, who would cheerfully acknowledge he wasn't always the most intuitive man in the room.

The *beneficiarius* was holding a mantle made of the finest British wool and dyed the same shifting blue-green as the sea outside the window. His eyes were closed as he held the shawl to his face, inhaling the scent. He rubbed his fingers across the fine weave. Tiro was stricken into immobility. If he had thought his own heart broken by Britta's rejection, and then Vibia's choices …

'Julia's left me, Tiro. I knew she would. She was always too good for me. All I did was break her heart, ruin her life, and leave her. She needed a much better man than I can ever be.' Tiro stood useless, watching the rigid white face and those restless hands, stroking and stroking the turquoise *palla* until the delicate fabric ripped. Quintus's eyes sprang open at the shock of the sudden sound in the silent bedchamber.

Tiro remembered he had more bad news to pass on, and left the room to fetch Justin. He would need all the support he could get, because they had to decide quickly where to go, and who to try to follow — Julia; Vibia and Cassius; or Lucius and Fulminata.

THE CARNELIAN PHOENIX

***

The three men made another trip to the harbour master, consulting his lists again. Julia was not on the manifest for the galley Tiro had seen departing for Portus. Vibia *was* listed, together with Cassius Labienus, having booked only shortly before departure at an extra fee. They were obviously travelling to Rome by the fastest available craft. That was where the trails ended: they could find no trace of Lucius Claudius or Fulminata, or of Julia.

'Who else?' demanded Quintus, white-faced as a cadaver still, but speaking, thinking and acting now with controlled energy.

'Your honour?' The man was slow on the uptake.

'Who else was added to your departure manifests, either yesterday or today?'

Several people, it seemed, but none answering to Julia's name or description. 'No sir, I never had a British lady — not lately, anyhow.' The man sucked the end of his stylus reflectively. 'We get all sorts coming and going here in Massilia, of course, but I would have remembered your lady for sure.'

Quintus was silent, the hard look back on his face.

'Which ships left during that time, then?' asked Justin.

'Well, sir, how long have you got for me to look? Let's see…there was the *Isis,* setting sail for Egypt of course, with oil, equipment for water pumps, and a party of slaves for the new procurator there. And I've got written here the *Concordia*, good ship that one, she plies regular to Sicilia, mostly ceramics and wine, but quite a few passengers at this time of year. Then there was the *Athena,* making for Gades with oil and fish sauce to trade for minerals; the *Hercules,* tramping along the Gallic coast…' And on and on. It was an impossible hunt.

Justin put his hand on Quintus's shoulder. 'Come, brother, a little wine, a rest in a cool taverna, and we'll decide what to do next.'

Tiro had never been so glad to have Justin around as he was now. His calm ways and affection for his brother-in-law was just what was needed as they sat round a little table in a nearby inn. Tiro went to the bar to order wine, water, olives and hot snacks while Justin continued to talk good sense. By the time the food arrived they had made concrete plans, focusing on Julia to begin with. They would call on the temples and hospital, in case she had been taken ill and was being cared for; ask at the gate out of town, checking whether she had left Massilia by road; and register her description with the local authorities. They'd book passage on to Rome for themselves then, going after Cassius and Vibia. Quintus still had his mission from Governor Rufinus, as well as the obligation to capture the killers of Felix Antonius and the Londinium escort party. And as Justin reminded them, there was Hortensia to see home.

Tiro felt weary. *To get rid of, he means. The boss will never forgive his mother for driving Lady Julia away, but there's nothing more we can do here. Clearly Julia has gone. After all, she does have money, connections, and a good head on her.* But Tiro, looking at the Governor's Man, knew they were both worrying about Julia: ill, alone, unhappy, forced into a long journey back to Britannia.

He knew that Quintus would bear it. Because he *was* the Governor's Man, and he still had his duty.

Bloody Ulpian better be worth saving, is all I can say. For two sestertii, if I were the boss, I'd be going home the other way faster than a race in the Circus Maximus.

THE CARNELIAN PHOENIX

Tiro rubbed his hands through his flaxen hair, unable to shake off the picture of Vibia with Cassius Labienus.

***

A week later, the voyage having been delayed by a tear in the mainsail, their ship was rowed into the enormous artificial harbour at Portus in Italia. They passed beyond the four-layered lighthouse to dock at a wharf, lined by a colonnade containing agents' offices. Quintus took Hortensia and her maid off for a drink and a seat in the shade. His body language was stiff and correct, but his mother's demanding voice made no concessions until he had found a place that satisfied her. As he left them to make enquiries at the customs office, Tiro heard Hortensia's carrying voice demanding a basket of ripe figs from the barmaid: 'Make sure you bring only the sweetest figs, girl!'

Tiro looked around, squinting against the bright light. Great arcaded warehouses stretched as far as the eye could see. Justin pointed out the Praetorian Guard patrols marching along the docks.

'Must be valuable goods stored in there,' said Tiro, impressed, and at the same time, irritated by the noise of thousands of dockworkers and ships' crew, the constant din of carts and carriages rattling past, and the heat radiating off the massive white-washed buildings. *Why was everywhere so hot and bright?* he wondered. He hoped Rome itself would be easier to bear. Probably nice and shady, with all those tall buildings.

'Valuable? I should say so. These soldiers are guarding the daily bread of Rome, Tiro. In those granaries are the harvests brought from Egypt, enough to feed all the hungry bellies of our great capital. Without that grain there would soon be riots and starvation. There's even a firemen's barracks here in the port, in case of fire.'

Quintus came back, frowning.

'No word of Julia. But the customs agent says Vibia and Cassius disembarked yesterday. So they'll be long gone, I'm afraid.' Quintus betrayed his frustration, rubbing the scars on his right thigh.

'Labienus gave an address, almost certainly false. I am sure the Labienii do not live anywhere near the Aventine, that area's too commercial for such a patrician family.'

Justin broke in.

'Well, we knew that, Quintus. Don't you remember? When we were boys, playing with Flavius in the back streets near your old house on the Quirinal? There were those other local boys, a gang we sometimes came across, fought with even. Two blond brothers, arrogant we thought them, especially the elder. The Labieni boys. Remember the time we had a proper fight with them, and you gave the elder boy a black eye. Your father made us go to the Labienus house to apologise. It was just in the next block to your home.'

Quintus frowned more, evidently searching for a slippery memory. Then he shook his head, saying, 'You may be right, Justin. I'm too tired to remember.' He beckoned to his mother to join them, as a carriage pulled up to take them on to Rome. Outwardly he seemed calm and focussed, but Tiro recognised the hard face of a worried Quintus. He guessed that anxiety about the womenfolk — Julia, Vibia, and even Hortensia in her own damaging way — was eating him up.

Chapter Ten

Rome, the Forum

The carriage off-loaded them before they reached the centre of the city. Quintus said that they'd move faster on foot through the congested streets. He engaged a litter and some slaves to take Hortensia, her maid and the luggage on to his mother's pretty, little townhouse. It had been made over to her by Faustus on the death of Bassianus. She complained to any who would listen about its modest size and old-fashioned appearance, but in truth it suited her very well, being small enough to be manageable, and in a quiet neighbourhood lower down the Quirinal than the rambling old Valerius mansion.

Quintus was relieved when her cortège departed across the forum. It was all he could do to keep his manners around his mother, and his mood was foul after reining in his anger and disgust the whole way from Massilia. Only his careful breeding and innate revulsion at making a scene had stopped him unleashing his anger at Hortensia.

Julia will be proud of me when I tell her, he thought, before recalling that he did not know if she would ever speak to him again. His mood darkened further as they passed through the arch of Septimius Severus, recalling his brother Flavius, dead in Caledonia. Memories of that war led on to remembering his first meeting with Julia at Eboracum, while he was being treated for leg wounds.

And so his thoughts dug a deeper circle as they chased each other round, until Justin arrested them by saying with forced cheerfulness, 'Here we are! Hortensia's house. And here's Silenus and Drusilla to greet us, with chilled wine no doubt on hand.'

The elderly freed couple bowed as they entered, clearly delighted to see Quintus and Justin.

'My optio, Tiro,' Quintus announced in brief introduction. 'Make sure he's given a shady room, Silenus, would you? He's British, not used to sunlight and heat.'

Tiro acknowledged the poor joke with a fleeting grin, and followed Drusilla and Justin across the little atrium towards the bedchambers.

'Has my mother arrived?'

'Yes, sir, and gone to lie down in her room.'

'Good.'

Quintus made no comment about the matron of the house disappearing without looking to her guests' comfort. Not for the first time, he wondered how Bassianus had borne living with Hortensia. Small surprise he had sought affection elsewhere. The image of Vibia came to him. He sighed, wondering whether it would in all conscience be right to seek her out here in Rome. On the one hand, she had apparently been taken away by a sought criminal complicit in the British rebellion, and quite possibly a murderer too. And even if they did find her here in this vast city, he could hardly bring her back home to Hortensia. On the other hand, Tiro had seen her appearing to acquiesce in Cassius's embrace.

And Julia? Alone briefly for the first time since she had disappeared, he couldn't repress the pain. His precious Julia, who had left him, to flee — who knew where? He

THE CARNELIAN PHOENIX

clapped his hands angrily. When a young house slave hurried in, he asked abruptly for writing materials, a flask of wine and three glasses to be brought out, and went to wait for his friends in the shade of the little garden at the back of the house.

***

Justin and Tiro, bathed and wearing fresh tunics, joined him. There were three letters lying bound and stacked neatly on the table in front of Quintus. He poured wine, offering water which both men refused.

'Right. As I see it, we have several problems we are honour-bound to solve. I'll outline those, and see what you both think. But first, Justin, have you heard from Lucilla? Is she in Rome?'

Justin looked rueful, holding out a note from his wife. It had been sent hastily in reply to the warning he'd written from Massilia. Lucilla wrote she was so enraged at her mother's behaviour, and so hurt for Quintus and Julia, that she could not bring herself to come to her mother's house. She would await them at the farm in Etruria, and hoped to greet her beloved brother soon, when his business allowed him to visit. She was very worried for Julia and asked to be told when Quintus heard anything more. She was also anxious to have her husband back at home.

'I told her nothing of your other business here, with Ulpian,' Justin added in a lowered voice. 'Nor of Vibia, or your father's secrets. Lucilla has not been quite as well as usual with this babe, and the heat in Rome is too intense for her wellbeing. I really don't want her travelling, or being upset by more bad news.'

'Good man. Much better that way,' said Quintus, though he felt torn. He and his younger sister had been especially close since they lost their brother Flavius. He missed her, and had been longing to introduce her to Julia.

'Of course you must go home, Justin. But let me have your counsel tonight. I see three problems: the big one first. It's evident from the ambush at Lugdunum that Cassius Labienus, and possibly Lucius Claudius and Fulminata too, have been rescued or at least taken in charge by the Praetorian Guard. We don't know why, or at whose behest, but it seems likely to me that the Praetorians are back at their favourite past time: power-broking.' He tapped the letters. 'I'm sending an initial report here to Governor Rufinus in Londinium. Our task as witnesses at the trial of Trebonius has turned into a murder investigation, one we believe involves the Praetorians. That won't be easy. Nevertheless, these are the murders of British soldiers, crimes Tiro and I have a duty to investigate. So: how to proceed with pursuing the Lugdunum ambushers, while keeping our proceedings secret?

'Problem two: I still have the responsibility laid on me by our governor to try to protect his cousin, Praetorian Prefect Ulpian. That will require me to dig into motives and moods in the Guard to uncover possible antagonism, and is allied to the first task. I'll make a start by talking to Ulpian. My second letter asks for a private meeting with him.

'Problem three: should we pursue Vibia? We know she's in the company of a dangerous man, willingly or not. Her situation also looks likely to become part of a bigger scenario. We might *have* to find her, to be able to solve problems one and two.'

Tiro had been shuffling his feet under the table and rubbing his chin, a sure sign he wanted to say something.

'Well, Tiro?'

THE CARNELIAN PHOENIX

'Sir, I know you are putting your duty as a Roman officer ahead of all else — but what about Lady Julia? Aren't we going to try to follow her?'

Quintus couldn't bring himself to reply. He picked up the third letter, and showed Tiro the address.

To Marcellus Crispus, Commandant of the Beneficiarius Station, Aquae Sulis.

Tiro nodded in silent understanding. When Julia reached Britannia, Marcellus would find her and let Quintus know.

'Justin — your thoughts. I assume now you've heard from Lucilla you'll want to head home?'

Justin sighed, and stretched his long legs out before him. 'Yes, I think I should, first thing tomorrow. I promised Lucilla I'd be with her when the baby comes. But I do have something, or someone, to offer you instead of my poor services. I told you earlier I had heard rumours inside the Praetorians. I had a reliable colleague, Centurion Martinus Lucretius, who may well know more. He's an intelligence gatherer from your old outfit, Quintus, at the special service in the Castra Peregrina. He was seconded to us when Ulpian took over as Praetorian Prefect. He acts as liaison between Commandant Licinius Pomponius at the Castra Peregrina, and the Praetorian Guard command. He's nominally attached to my old cohort, and is a tiptop officer. I trust and value him.'

'Good. I'll ask Licinius about making contact with Martinus, on the quiet.'

Justin glanced meaningfully at Tiro; clearly he had something to say that needed to remain between him and his brother-in-law. Tiro took the hint, escorted by his wine. 'I'll go and chase up some snacks from Drusilla.'

With Tiro gone, Justin continued, 'Getting in discreet touch with the commandant is easily done. Today is the day of the Sun, sacred to Mithras. There will be a Mithraic rite this afternoon in the cave temple of the Castra Peregrina. Licinius Pomponius is sure to be there.'

Quintus stood, shaking out his cramped right leg. 'That will save me another messenger at least.' He summoned Silenus, who had obviously been waiting nearby in case he was wanted. 'Ah, Silenus, two letters to go urgently, please, by the official post to Britannia: one to Commandant Marcellus Crispus at the *beneficiarius* station in Aquae Sulis, the other to Governor Aradius Rufinus at his palace in Londinium. Then a note by messenger to the home of Praetorian Prefect Ulpian.'

Justin said, 'Ulpian lives in a suite of rooms at the imperial palace on the Palatine, Quintus.'

He glanced at the returning Tiro, who had come back carrying a mostly empty platter. They both grinned while Tiro explained through a full mouth that Drusilla had insisted he taste the snacks. He choked in mid-sentence, laughing a crumb down the wrong way, but Quintus felt better for the moment of lightness.

'Never mind, Tiro. I hope we may later dine even better than on Drusilla's treats. Come on, we've got work to do.'

***

Quintus managed to negotiate the strange familiarity of the Castra Peregrina with his feelings in check. The last time he had been here in his old headquarters — it felt an aeon ago — he had been expecting nothing more than the standard assignment, probably to the eastern provinces where he had spent so many years investigating. He recalled that visit with some shame. He had been dismissive of his groom, poor Gnaeus, and icy to the Commandant, Licinius Pomponius. His commanding officer was a good man, and had tried once more to offer Quintus promotion as a staff officer in Rome. Quintus had barely listened, so caught up in the lingering miasma of shame and depression he'd inhabited back then. He'd taken little notice of the kind intent. But now, even with the sharp anxiety of their mission and the worse pain of Julia leaving him, he realised he no longer felt the numbness that had wrapped him round so long. He still had his father's death to avenge as well as a myriad of heavy burdens, but he had people to fight for, too. Life was worth living in spite of everything. He was still smiling ruefully as they approached the descending entrance to the Temple of Mithras, built under one of the barracks blocks inside the Castra. Here Tiro departed, not being an initiate in the mystery religion. His job was to wander round the forum and up to the Palatine, playing the näive provincial, but with a practised ear to the ground.

***

The dark room of the cave was a long aisle lined with broad stone benches. Lamplight flickered over the cult image of the Invincible Sun God Mithras, glittering in high relief. The god's face was gilded, his Phrygian cap glowing violet-red, his sleeved tunic the same scarlet as the sacrificial blood streaming down the neck of the painted bull.

Some ten or so other worshippers had already gathered. The Pater, in his white tunic, baggy red trousers and scarlet cloak, was about to begin the service. Quintus made his way to a welcome familiar figure, upright and strong-jawed. He nodded to Commandant Licinius Pomponius, taking the seat next to him.

'Quintus Valerius! I had not heard you were back in Rome. It's a pleasure to see you here at the temple.'

Quintus smiled with genuine regard. Now he no longer worked for him, he could see Pomponius as his equal, someone he trusted.

'And mine, to see you looking so well, Licinius Pomponius.' The two men grasped hands. The man sitting nearest on the stone bench had moved along to make room. He was a broad young man with ruddy hair and an eager face, who inclined his head to the commandant.

'*Beneficiarius,* this is Centurion Martinus Lucretius.' Quintus saluted him, then sat back as the service began.

He allowed the beloved rites to wash over him, stilling his busy mind into calm. As he slid into meditation, he wondered briefly about his father's acceptance of Christianity. Was the Christian god — some sort of confusing merger of three gods in one, he'd been told — really so alluring, compared to the benevolent Lord of Light, Mithras, with his promise of eternal salvation on the final judgement day when the dead shall rise again?

After the ceremony was complete, another man masked as the Lion set up the ritual meal. With no initiate gradings taking place that day, it was a simple snack of bread and wine. Quintus explained softly and briefly to Licinius Pomponius why he was in Rome, noting that he was following up crimes in Britannia which had bled over into Gaul and prevented the route to justice of a treacherous usurper. Licinius looked serious.

'Brother, you are always welcome, both here in the cave, and in the Castra Peregrina. If you need any help, anything at all, you can call on me and my men.'

'My man Tiro and I could do with accommodation, sir,' he began. 'My mother's home is small; we are inconveniencing her.'

THE CARNELIAN PHOENIX

Licinius nodded. They were interrupted by the Father, a tall man with curly hair and a well-grown beard. He introduced himself to Quintus as Ulpian. His proud bearing and deep voice were distinctive, and marked him out as more than the standard Father. Quintus felt a sense of dread as he saluted the Praetorian Prefect. He decided not to beat about the bush.

'I am the senior Governor's Man from Britannia, sir, and bring greetings from your cousin, Governor Aradius Rufinus,' he said. 'I have urgent news for you, and beg the time to speak to you more privately.'

Ulpian inclined his head. 'I would be most honoured if you and the commandant would both come to a light supper tonight. I have rooms at the Palace; Pomponius can show you.' He nodded once, then moved on to help the Lion distribute the meal round the cave.

***

Quintus left the Mithraeum with Licinius and Martinus, pondering how the word "brother" could have so many meanings. They almost tripped over an eager Tiro, hopping from foot to foot in the barracks courtyard beyond.

'Sir! Sir! I've found her!'

Quintus grabbed him hard by the arm, his face lighting up.

'Julia? Where is she? Is she safe, well?'

Tiro's face collapsed into dismay so suddenly, it would have been comical any other time.

'No, sir. Sorry — I meant Vibia. I know where Vibia is. I heard her singing. I can show you the house!'

Quintus said to the commandant, 'My half-sister, sir. We found her unexpectedly in Massilia, in distress, and are hoping to locate her again in Rome. Tiro, let's go somewhere quieter to discuss this. Perhaps we can fetch our belongings from Mother's house first, and set ourselves up in the officers' quarters here at the Castra, as the commandant suggests?'

'But, boss — Vibia!'

'Tiro, if Vibia is singing, she must be happy and safe, at least for now. I'm invited to dine with Ulpian tonight, so we'll need to shift ourselves.'

'Yes sir. Umm, I err, wouldn't feel comfortable at the palace…'

Licinius Pomponius smiled. 'Tiro, can I introduce Centurion Martinus Lucretius? He's Roman-born and knows the city well. He'll help you find your way around. Perhaps you could have a bite to eat together? There are plenty of good wine bars and hot food stalls round the Castra that Martinus can show you.'

The ruddy centurion looked encouragingly at Tiro. 'It's true, I'm a native Roman. Though Pa came with Septimius Severus from the Pannonia legions, and later went home to fetch Ma. Let's find this girl of yours,' — Tiro blushed deeply —'and then grab something tasty and a few jars.'

Quintus saw the look of relief on his colleague's face, and silently blessed Commandant Pomponius for his tact as the commandant headed off to his headquarters.

'Good plan; I'll leave you to find Vibia. I'll go back to Mother's and collect our belongings. Meanwhile, Tiro, can you try to make arrangements for me to go back with you to meet Vibia in secret? If you're right about what you saw at Massilia, she probably won't be able to speak openly. Use your charm, won't you? And, Martinus — see what the word on the street is. Whether any particular trouble is brewing.'

Quintus spoke lightly but his heart sank at the soft look on Tiro's face, with the prospect of seeing Vibia again.

He'd seen that look before, in Aquae Sulis and Bo Gwelt, when Tiro was convinced he was in love with Britta.

Why, oh why, did Tiro fall in love so easily? Quintus foresaw more heartbreak ahead.

Chapter Eleven

Rome, Quirinal Hill

Bless you, Lord of Light, thought Quintus, when he discreetly entered Hortensia's house to be told she was out. Quintus explained to the old retainers that he was leaving, having been offered more convenient accommodation at the Castra Peregrina. Silenus's shoulders sagged a little. Quintus caught a glint of moisture in the old man's eyes, and felt irritated, then sorry. He said quickly, 'Of course we'll be back to visit Mother from time to time. We'll make sure we drop into the kitchen to see you and Drusilla too.' He grasped Silenus's hand in farewell.

'Oh, Dominus! I nearly forgot.' Drusilla held out a note to Quintus. 'The mistress must have meant to give you this; it's addressed to you. I found it when I was polishing her dresser.' He tucked the note away without looking; it was a fair bet he would not enjoy the reading. He hugged Drusilla, remembering the many times he and Flavius had sat in her kitchen domain as boys, filling up on her warming food and having scratches and bruises treated. It was time to go. He made a clean getaway through the servants' entrance. But Quintus knew he was only postponing more conflict with his mother.

***

THE CARNELIAN PHOENIX

As a youngster growing up in Rome, Quintus had often gazed at the imperial palace. He had always regarded the vast sprawl on the Palatine Hill as part of the landscape, just the other side of the city from his home on the Quirinal. As the long summer evening held sway, parties of early revellers emerged accompanied by slaves bearing fluttering torches. Carts full of farm produce, banned during the day, began to clatter into the city.

Quintus walked to the palace with Licinius Pomponius, a regular at Ulpian's gatherings. He looked more closely at their destination. When he was a child, his father had taken him to see the huge building site on the old Palatine, where Emperor Septimius Severus was adding a new palace. The structure hung out from the hillside, held up on enormous arches. It was a mighty achievement, impressing the little boy who would later go on to fight for that same emperor beyond the sundering British seas.

Quintus shook his head as he entered the palace with Licinius, ridding himself of poignant childhood memories of his father.

***

The famed jurist Ulpian greeted Quintus and Licinius cordially in his elegant receiving rooms. Freed from the Pater's cap, his was a noble visage: a high forehead, a mass of curling hair, and a magnificent beard to complement his impressive features. His posture was imposing and welcoming, as if accepting the homage of those around him in a generous spirit. He was an exceptionally gifted and high-achieving lawyer, who had recently reached the apogee of his career when appointed by Augusta Mamaea to head the imperial council, advising young Emperor Alexander Severus. He didn't seem to mind who knew it.

Quintus was glad Tiro was gainfully occupied elsewhere; this was not an evening he would have enjoyed. It was a small, but nonetheless intimidating, gathering: several senators, one of them an old friend of Bassianus Valerius; a famous female poet, who was holding forth to two young and impressionable scions of great families dressed in blinding new togas; and a few high officials, including the Prefect of the Annona whose job was to ensure the daily flow of grain to the citizens of Rome. A flutter of beautiful women, mostly young and dressed in gorgeous silks, had been cornered by various colleagues of Ulpian.

Quintus's heart sank. How was he to have a confidential meeting with Ulpian in this crowd?

The conversation flowed in highbrow Latin and Greek, the host at ease in either language. Well-trained slaves brought round glass carafes of wine and an array of delicious titbits on trays, followed by others presenting hand basins and napkins. Couches were provided, but most guests stood, the better to circulate.

Quintus and Licinius remained on the edge of the room, outnumbered by the high-powered gathering. Quintus turned quickly when a dry little voice spoke from behind.

'Quintus Valerius?'

It was his father's long-standing colleague in the senate, Proculus Caecilius. The old man, small and pot-bellied, beamed at him and Quintus felt a swoop of nostalgia at the sight of his father's dearest friend. They grasped hands, gazing at each other in silence till Licinius coughed.

'I beg your pardon, Senator. My colleague and former commandant from the Castra Peregrina, Licinius Pomponius.'

THE CARNELIAN PHOENIX

'Dear boy, the commandant and I know each other of old. I make it my business to keep in touch with your career, despite your mother's best endeavours.' This was said in a neutral tone, but Quintus remembered how fond his father had been of this perspicacious and loyal friend. 'But tell me, Quintus, what brings *you* here to the residence of our Praetorian Prefect?'

Quintus gave the easy version: how he had transferred to work for the British Governor, and had travelled to Rome to visit his family and to bring news and greetings from Governor Rufinus to his distinguished cousin Ulpian.

Proculus chuckled. 'The true story, please. I know Aradius Rufinus, and have heard something of your recent adventures in Britannia. I'm an old man and my time is precious, so come on, let's have the real reasons.' As he said this, the stooped senator led the way into an empty side room. Seemingly by magic, he had also caught the eye of their host, who made his excuses and crossed the room to join them. Licinius shut the door behind them.

Quintus gave Ulpian the letter of introduction from his governor. They stood in silence while he read it, once swiftly, the second time more slowly. The Praetorian Prefect raised his leonine head, seeming to look into the distance.

'What do you know of this letter and my cousin's concerns, Quintus Valerius?'

'Only what Governor Rufinus told me. That you were recently appointed Senior Praetorian Prefect and head of the emperor's council, that your subordinate Praetorian Prefects Flavianus and Chrestus have since…died, and that my governor is worried for your personal safety as a consequence, believing you to have enemies in Rome at high levels. Governor Rufinus suspects, and I agree, that an attempted coup in Britannia this past spring was connected to an ongoing plot here in the city.'

The jurist's quick legal mind seized on the important point. 'What evidence do you have of such possible linked plots, *Beneficiarius*?'

'The usurper in Britannia, the former British Governor Gaius Trebonius, was supported by two Roman brothers, Antoninus and Cassius Labienus of a prominent patrician family. Antoninus died in Britannia when we prevented the coup, and his younger brother was captured. Together with Trebonius, the two were being brought to Rome for Senate trial when their prisoner escort party was ambushed in Gaul. Only Labienus escaped being killed. I have good reason to believe the attackers were Praetorian Guards. There is further evidence that at least one of the British co-conspirators, who had also escaped from Britannia, had joined the ambush. What's more, Cassius Labienus was seen by my man Tiro taking ship from Massilia to Portus, and was registered as disembarking within the past week.'

Ulpian frowned, an expression that changed his demeanour from assured nobility to something more vulnerable. Behind the stern intellect, Quintus caught a glimpse of an uneasy man.

The little senator coughed. 'Councillor Ulpian, if I may…?'

'By all means, Senator Caecilius.'

'I respectfully suggest that the *beneficiarius* be given whatever clearance and resources he needs to pursue his quarry. His track record in finding criminals and murderers is impeccable; he has the confidence of your cousin; and he comes with experience in both the Praetorian Guard and our estimable secret service at the

THE CARNELIAN PHOENIX

Castra Peregrina. If you wish, the Governor's Man can keep me, as representative of the senate, informed of his progress.'

Ulpian moved to a window, staring into the far distance across the glorious city before speaking. 'There are other threats to Rome, from further away. Recently I heard that Ardashir the Sassanid has defeated the King of Parthia. I fear he is casting envious eyes west towards our eastern provinces. And only yesterday a courier from our governor in Noricum reported rumours of the Germans massing across the great rivers, poised to strike at our northern boundaries. Rome has always had mighty enemies, but right now, with our Emperor still so young, is a time of special peril.'

He turned away from the balmy night air and the massed glow of street lanterns below the palace walls. 'I have no doubt my cousin Aradius chose his messenger wisely. Uncover this domestic plot for me, Quintus Valerius. Reveal these enemies before their actions bring more danger to our great city and our emperor. I am merely the servant of Alexander Severus, but while I can be of value to him and his mother, as Aradius reminds me, I must look to my own safety. You are my best tool in that.'

Quintus dared one further warning. 'Sir, my men and I will do our utmost to secure justice, and ensure you continue your service to the imperial family. But I beg you — be careful! Too often the great and mighty of Rome are felled by those unsuspected, those nearest to them.'

Ulpian nodded, and crossed the room as the door burst open. A gaggle of well-heeled and well-oiled young men came in, laughing loudly with their dancing girl companions.

'I think we'll leave this room to others. Time to rejoin the party,' said Ulpian. 'Let me introduce you to some colleagues, Quintus Valerius.'

Back in the main salon, a group quickly gathered around the chief minister. Given Ulpian's formal position as Praetorian Prefect it was hardly surprising there were several senior officers of the Guard present, some of whom Quintus recognised from his younger days. Licinius, who seemed to know everyone as befitted his job as head of the secret service, introduced a pair of his fellow tribunes to Quintus. He managed not to mention why exactly the British officer was back in Rome. Ulpian crooked a beckoning finger at a tall man, lingering by the door with a faint smile on his face.

'Paul, this is my cousin Aradius's righthand man, come all the way from Britannia to spend time with his family. Quintus Valerius, my legal colleague Paul. He's very able, the sort of man who serves the court well.' By chance Quintus was looking directly at Paul as Ulpian spoke, and was sure — almost sure — he saw a flash of emotion cross Paul's mild face. Which emotion, he couldn't say, and it was soon forgotten when another man, nondescript, shorter and younger, also joined them.

'Ah, Aurelius Epegathus! *Beneficiarius,* may I make known to you my successor as the Prefect of the Annona? His is now the responsibility to keep Rome fed.' Ulpian laughed, deep-voiced, and moved on, his attention demanded elsewhere.

Quintus took stock of the two newcomers, who seemed inclined to linger.

'The Annona, sir?' he enquired of Epegathus. 'A heavy burden, I have no doubt.' The Prefect held his gaze, and Quintus thought he had never seen a colder pair of eyes. Icy eyes, and something about them felt familiar. *Had*

THE CARNELIAN PHOENIX

they run across each other before? But then the shorter man smiled, holding out his hand, and Quintus thought perhaps he had been hasty. That quick smile transformed the man's face. Quintus remembered that the name Aurelius was often associated with freedmen, and wondered if this was indeed a man whose forebears had come from slavery. A freedman could have mixed feelings about these other privileged party-goers.

Epegathus had a strong grip. He held Quintus's hand for a long moment, commenting in a quick light voice, 'As the poet Lucan tells us, "reverence is purchased when rulers feed the mob: a hungry populace knows no fear." My job is to keep the populace nourished and happy.'

Paul, a lean greying man of calm appearance and friendly manner, was watching with apparent approval. He too took Quintus's hand, leaning towards him with a pleasant smile. His hand was bony and caught for a moment on Quintus's signet ring as he released his grip.

'My senior colleague, Ulpian, has told me a little of your visit to Rome as representative of his cousin, the British Governor. My field of expertise is the law. I am also honoured to sit on the imperial council. If I can help in your investigations in any way, please just ask.'

Paul and Epegathus were soon reclaimed by their host, leaving Quintus, Licinius and little Proculus Caecilius alone. The senator led them gratefully to a nest of couches. With the break in conversation Quintus had a moment to reflect. Despite his patrician background he felt smothered by the atmosphere of this party. There was something feral in the air. He suddenly wished they could leave. He'd much rather be in a wine bar, drinking and joking with Tiro and Martinus. He looked around the room, his gaze catching that of a fleshy-faced man with a cleft chin and deep-set eyes. The man nodded, and the little senator nodded back.

'Quintus, here's someone you'll enjoy meeting. Our noted historian, Senator Cassius Dio.' Caecilius led the way, adding, ' Be warned, Cassius takes his vocation very seriously. He'll bend your ears about his historical writings all night, if you let him.'

Licinius drifted away, his soldier's sharp eye caught by some potentially useful acquaintances. A pleasant few minutes followed. Cassius Dio was erudite, with a tendency towards scurrilous gossip that lightened the talk. He had known Quintus's father, and said a few words of condolence and regard about the long-deceased Senator Bassianus Valerius. Quintus was beginning to relax with an glass of excellent wine in his hand, when Cassius Dio looked round carefully. Quintus saw the gimlet sharpness in his look.

'I must mingle. A final word for you, *Beneficiarius*. I don't know your business here at the palace, and I don't want to know. Not yet. You can write and tell me all about it at a safe distance, if you survive. I warn you, though — get rid of that ring.' He nodded at the carnelian signet ring on Quintus's little finger.

Before Quintus could respond, Dio grasped his senatorial colleague Caecilius on the shoulder briefly in farewell. He moved away, on the hunt for more explosive nuggets to be added later to his writings.

Caecilius sighed, an amusing sight as the little man raised his shoulders and shook all the way down to his potbelly. But the expression on his face was entirely serious.

'Dio is right, you know. There is no one here you can trust. Ulpian has no real idea how near the sharks are circling. And there are those in power at court who hold with the old Emperor Septimius in matters of religion. Not everyone has the tolerance and respect of eastern cults that young Alexander Severus shows. Keep your sword sharp and your friends close, Quintus. Get your job here done, then go home to your governor. My best advice is to stay in Britannia.'

The senator glanced across the room, and Quintus saw him looking at the company of officials surrounding Ulpian. 'Call me a snob, but I have observed that a freedman often has no loyalty to any but himself.'

'What do you mean? Isn't the emperor tolerant of all faiths, as I had heard?'

Caecilius shrugged. 'Not everyone at court is as liberal-minded. Some who began their careers under Emperor Septimius still reject the eastern mystery religions.' A short silence fell between them. Then Caecilius added, his eyes softened and tone sotto voce, 'If there is an afterlife, Quintus Valerius, Bassianus will be aware of the man you have become. Believe me, he would approve. But you may be venturing into dangerous waters here. Your life is in Britannia now. Get back there.'

It sounded like golden advice, and Quintus wished he could take it. Instead, Licinius having rejoined them, they made their way back to their host. They found the chief councillor in conversation with Epegathus. The younger man had his face turned to one side, slightly downwards as if in consideration.

Right at that moment, as if visited on him by some truculent god or evil spirit, a scene slotted into Quintus's mind. He remembered again the boys who had played in the street behind his house, the two golden brothers. Two golden brothers who had grown up to become dangerous usurpers. In a flash of over-late recognition, he realised that he had known the Labieni brothers then— not from Britannia but as young boys in Rome over twenty years ago. And always part of their childhood gang was a younger lad, tagging behind. Little Dog, they called him then. A year or two younger than Cassius, brown-haired, bit of a runt really. He was the son of Labienus Senior's trusted freedman. Less forthcoming than his foster brothers, with their overbearing pride and sneering confidence, he was inclined to hang back in their street games — perhaps physically shy, perhaps just more calculating. And, as it had turned out, much cleverer. A survivor who had risen to the top. Looking closely at Aurelius Epegathus, Quintus was sure that this man was the childhood friend of the traitor Cassius Labienus, standing nearby and listening intently to the Emperor's chief minister.

Sharks, circling.

Quintus felt icy cold. He turned to his companions. Licinius was chatting in his assured way to Caecilius; neither of them seemed to have noticed anything. Quintus looked back at Ulpian and saw that he was momentarily alone. Seizing his opportunity, Quintus pushed his way across the salon to reach Ulpian before he could move on. He grasped the councillor's arm, splashing wine over the brim of his glass. Ulpian looked annoyed, then seeing Quintus's expression, demanded, 'What is it?'

But as Quintus faltered, not quite knowing how to put into words his sudden suspicions, another voice spoke. A gentle voice with a familiar regional accent.

'Colleague, could we beg a moment of your time? Prefect Epegathus has been speaking of his concerns about the safety of the grain warehouses at Portus. We would appreciate your advice as to what can be done to increase security.'

Quintus watched with resignation as Ulpian's pride was appealed to. His moment was lost, the opportunity snatched away. He felt suddenly tired. Tomorrow would bring its own chances; for tonight, he was done.

Chapter Twelve

Rome, the Caelian Hill

The crowded noisy bar near the Castra had a low ceiling, rickety tables and a smoky atmosphere redolent of fried food. Tiro loved it. They were on their third round of drinks — cheap whites from Germania. Tiro gulped and swilled noisily.

'Well?' demanded Martinus. 'Better than *mulsum*?'

'Hmm,' said Tiro, swishing the wine between his molars until Martinus thumped him on the back. He sent a cloud of amber spraying across the table. 'Oof, what was that for?'

'It's not exactly Falernian, is it? Just get it down your neck, and we'll order some more. And Tiro, while you're up at the bar, get that armful to bring some more snacks, will you?'

The 'armful' alluded to, a plump young barmaid whose tunica was sliding further off one rounded shoulder as the evening progressed, winked at Tiro and sashayed off to the kitchen.

'Anyway,' offered Martinus when Tiro came back with a fresh flask of peppery wine, 'if you want the real stuff, you should come to my home town, Carnuntum.'

'In Pannonia? I thought you were born here in Rome.'

'Yes, but my Pa came here with the old Emperor. He sent for Ma from his own village, and never stopped

THE CARNELIAN PHOENIX

raving about the wonderful booze they make there till he died.'

'In battle?' asked Tiro, preparing to be entertained by a long martial story.

'Nope. In bed, with his *caligae* on, after too much eating and drinking at my sister's wedding.' Both men burst out laughing, and time was spent swapping increasingly raucous and profane tales of soldiers, women, and wine shops they had known and loved. Eventually Tiro remembered, as he poured coins out onto the bar to buy more drinks, that Quintus had supplied the funds with a commission: to cruise around, keeping his ear to the ground and collecting intelligence. Especially intelligence derived from drunk uniformed men off-duty: vigiles, local guards, Praetorians. He also remembered that he was supposed to look for Vibia before the getting-pretend-drunk part of the evening. *Best drink this jug up quick, then. Martinus is a good lad with hollow legs. We'll be out the door and on the prowl in no time.*

***

It wasn't that much later, really, when they left the wineshop to a farewell chorus of good wishes and the smiles of the disappointed barmaid.

'Fancy the cat-house?' Martinus looked hopeful. There was a brothel conveniently located next door. Tiro thought, *When in Rome*, not much caring either way. Britta didn't want him, and Vibia had run off with a fancy toff. Why not?

A little later he wished he hadn't bothered. The girl he chose, young and pale, wasn't Vibia, and the brothel was grubby and lacked privacy. It was over quickly, and he was glad to get out of there.

Darkness had dropped, but the air was warm still. Warm, and suffused with gutter vomit, burnt take-away food, and the odd whiff of sewers. Martinus had stolen a torch off a slave, who was propped up asleep against a wall while awaiting his master. They could almost see their way, and there were regular passers-by also bearing lights, so they didn't trip up much.

'This bird of yours, Tiro, where is she supposed to be?'

Tiro, whose mind was still running on women, replied absently.

'Britta? She's in the Summer Country, south-west Britannia.'

'Britannia! I'm not bloody walking that far tonight. Not in these boots; they're half worn out. I thought she was here, with some dodgy rich bloke. Didn't you say you heard her singing in the garden of a posh house?'

'Oh, that girl. Vibia.' Tiro felt his face heat up unseen in the shadows.

'Yes, Vibia. Pretty name.' Martinus peered at Tiro, holding the smoking torch dangerously close. His face was smeared with soot and sweat from the overheated little bar. 'You drunk or something?'

'Don't be ridiculous! I never drink on duty.'

'Oh. What were we doing in that bar then?'

'Being off-duty. Now we're back on duty.'

'Right.'

They sauntered on, Martinus wondering exactly when duty rosters began and ended for British soldiers, and Tiro hot and bothered at getting lost amid the filthy alleys leading away from the Caelian Hill. He called a silent blessing on Dionysus as they stumbled towards the well-lit expanse of the Forum. Even Tiro knew where he was. He promised himself he would pour a grateful libation to the patron god of drunkards, and with any luck Dionysus would soon expedite Tiro's return home to Britannia.

THE CARNELIAN PHOENIX

Home to simpler cities, clean barmaids, and decent weather. But where had he heard Vibia singing?

'Tiro?'

'What? Can't you shut up and let me think about where we're going?'

'There's some low-lives following us.'

'What kind of low-lives? Soldiers on the spree, or street muggers?'

'Both.'

'Both? What kind of stupid answer is that —'

Martinus dropped the torch and summarily dragged Tiro into a dark crevice of the alley. 'Ssh!' They watched as a bunch of men with hard faces and the bedraggled tunics favoured by urban labourers trotted past. Their boots were surprisingly robust and well-cared for, and each of them had bulges under their tunics suggestive of the daggers authorised only to Praetorians or vigiles while inside the pomerium. The Forum was the heart of the city, and the alleys around it were definitely inside Rome's old sacred boundary

Tiro was delighted. The evening just kept getting better and better. First his stomach had been pleasantly lined with booze and greasy fast-food; followed by a bit of banter with a pub full of likely lads, and his new best friend Martinus; and — oh joy! — the prospect of a dustup. He stepped confidently into the street, and was immediately whacked from behind, high and hard.

The rough-looking bunch had broken up into two parties. This was not playing fair. Had Tiro been blessed with more height, he might have been laid out by an impact over his kidneys. As it was, he was knocked clean off his feet by the blow landing on his shoulder blade. He lay there for an instant, hoping he hadn't been stabbed. He couldn't see Martinus, but he heard him yell, 'To me,

Juno, protector of Rome!' as the young centurion launched himself at their attackers.

Tiro was in that optimal state of inebriation when reckless aggression peaks before ebbing into sleepy miscalculation. That was fortunate, as he discovered two things on getting to his feet: first, that he hadn't been stabbed; second, that he was flaming angry, and dying to have a pop at these Roman slime balls. He wished fleetingly that he hadn't decided to leave his *pugio* back in his quarters. But what the hell — Tiro rarely won fights using a dagger, mainly because he loved to get stuck in with fist and boot. Leave the swordsmanship to the boss, he thought, as he sized up the nearest combatant.

There were at least seven or eight of the ruffians surrounding them, he concluded. Poor odds to some, but Martinus, while quite a modest sort, had told enough revealing stories over the wine to convince Tiro he could hold his own. Hopefully he could hold his wine as well. In the flickering light of wall-mounted cressets, he saw that Martinus, good lad, had not left his *pugio* at home. He was using it to considerable effect, and already two ruffians were lying on the ground, one rolling around swearing faintly, the other ominously still.

Tiro wondered how many bones there were in the human body. He reckoned he could have a good go at breaking a few. His fondness for the mixed martial arts known as *pancratium* tempted him to begin with kicks and throws, but the need to rid the world of these thugs decided him to use his fearsome punches. The first man stepped in, blessedly short himself. Tiro's straight right to the throat crushed something, and the man dropped with a gurgle. The second attacker was a tall skinny type, so Tiro feinted and dodged to tempt the fool to rush past him waving his dagger uselessly. Tiro swept his legs from under him, then jumped hard on his lower back. That crack really was a most satisfactory noise. The next idiot tried to pull a sword, getting it caught up in the tatty cloak he'd worn to hide it. Too slow, too late.

The least eager of the pack, at the back and evidently able to count, turned to run, calling to his mate, 'Leave it, Sextus! We're not paid enough for this.' Sextus slid round Martinus, and shoved him backwards hard against a wall. The centurion's head made an audible connection with brickwork; his knees buckled and he sagged momentarily. Not for long. Sextus wasn't as quick-witted or fleet of foot as his friend. Tiro rushed him, knocked him off his feet and threw him onto his back, wrestling-style, smashing his head comprehensively on the cobbles. He knelt on the unconscious man, lifting and dropping the head one more time just for luck.

When Tiro looked up, Martinus had already picked himself up and was polishing off the last of the gang, wiping blood off his long knife before sheathing it.

They stood a moment, panting.

'I thought we weren't allowed to carry weapons inside the old Roman city boundaries?' said Tiro, as they turned over the bodies looking for identifying features.

'That rule is only for fucking idiots. Surely you didn't come out without your dagger?'

'Umm, must have forgotten it.'

Martinus laughed, and raised his hand as if to clap Tiro on the shoulder. He thought better of it, suddenly swearing and clutching the back of his head. His hand came away with blood from where he'd had the altercation with the wall.

'Problem?'

'No, just a cut on the bonce, and a blinder of a headache starting.'

'Shouldn't drink so much. Or headbutt walls.'

Martinus wrinkled his brow. 'Yeah, yeah. Should we collect up the weapons, and report the bodies to someone official?'

'Weapons yes; reports, no. I'm pretty sure the *beneficiarius* would want this little incident kept confidential, at least till we know who authorised it.'

They wasted no more time. Full darkness had fallen, and they still had to locate Vibia.

***

For once in his life, Tiro had planned ahead. When they knocked up the door porter at the grand townhouse of Cassius Labienus, Tiro had a cover letter from Quintus addressed to Vibia, a smart smooth tablet bound round with official-looking red thread. He saluted the doubtful attendant, allowing Martinus to do the talking. As Quintus said drily, Tiro's distinctive Londinium accent might just give the game away. They were left waiting outside in the street for a worrying time, until Tiro began to wonder if they had the wrong house after all. Then a shutter on a ground floor window swung open, and a soft pretty voice that made his heartbeat accelerate begged Tiro to come in through the window, but quietly.

In the flickering light of the candle she carried, Vibia looked disconcerted to see Tiro. She held a finger to her lips, leading them down a narrow corridor and into a small room in the servant's wing, a storeroom to judge by the smell of spices. She looked both eager and scared, her hands shaking slightly as she took the letter from Tiro. She moved her candle closer to read, and cried out softly as she noticed blood on Tiro's clothes.

'Are you hurt, Tiro? What have they done to you?'

THE CARNELIAN PHOENIX

'It's fine, miss. We were attacked, but we saw them off, no problem. You could look at Martinus's head. He's got a scratch .'

Vibia hurried to bind the head graze with cloth torn off a pile of folded linen on a shelf. She tutted domestically, and Tiro felt his chest filling with proprietorial pleasure.

Vibia returned her attention to the letter, which was a short message giving Vibia greetings from her unnamed brother, and asking when he could visit. She looked at them in dismay. 'But why have you come? This house isn't safe, there are people who visit my… who visit here. They mustn't know you are here.'

'We're here to rescue you, Vibia. I saw you on the dockside at Massilia. I know who it is who took you — that rebel and murderer Cassius Labienus. I've come to escort you back to the boss. Quintus Valerius will protect you. And I will, too.'

She looked pale. He saw she was shivering a little and put his arm round her, without thinking. She glanced once at his arm. He dropped it awkwardly.

'Tiro, you misunderstand. I'm not here as a prisoner, not held against my will at all. I came with Cassius because …because I love him.'

Tiro wobbled as the floor sucked out from under him. Another woman was rejecting him. He felt an ache in his chest that had nothing to do with the recent street brawl.

'What? No, that can't be right. He's a monster, a traitor. How can you even know this man? How can you love him?'

Vibia turned her soft young face to his. 'I can't tell you the whole story, Tiro, but you've got it all wrong. Cassius isn't a monster. He's mixed up with some wicked people, dragged into it all by his brother. But he knows now that they *are* bad, and he told me he wishes —'

She sobbed. Tears slid over her cheekbones. Despite his hurt and anger, he was distracted by her rose-petal face and the faint scent of pomegranate oil in her hair.

Martinus cleared his throat, dragging back Tiro's attention. 'So you think your lover has regrets, miss? Would he be willing to help us with information, do you think?'

Vibia hesitated, perhaps turning words round in her mind before answering. Her hand wandered up to her throat, grasping the small silver pendant sitting in the folds of her pink *stola.*

'I think he might. If a way could be found… But I know he is very concerned for me, being a Christian. He says one of the plotters, who was a favourite of Emperor Caracalla, particularly hates Christians. If they find out about me, we'll be in terrible trouble.'

Tiro was distracted again, his eyes caught by the silver fish. He knew nothing of this Christian business, and cared less. But he had heard that the sect was very resistant to acknowledging the Roman pantheon, and that generally ended badly. You didn't mess with the Roman gods.

Martinus spoke instead. 'Tiro, do you think Quintus Valerius might be able to help? Help both of them, I mean — his sister and her…'

Vibia broke in. 'Oh, yes. Tiro, you must beg Quintus to help us. I can't leave without Cassius, and Cassius will only go if he believes he is doing the right thing. Quintus can persuade him, I know he can!'

Tiro was doubtful, remembering the deadly encounters with the two Labienus brothers in Britannia. Both Cassius and Antoninus had been in the attempted British coup not so long ago — in it right up to their necks. What were the

THE CARNELIAN PHOENIX

chances that Quintus would forgive and forget just like that?

He looked again at Vibia, her pleading eyes and tear-wet face, and threw caution to the winds.

'Leave it to me. I'll get him to come back with us, to talk to you. I'm sure —'

A smart rapping at the front door was followed by a shout. 'Doorward! Boy! Where is that lazy slave? Let us in!'

Vibia looked anxious. 'It's Cassius, with some friends. Wait here! Stay very quiet.' She left the storeroom silently, turning the key in the lock outside. Tiro was immensely grateful she'd chosen the spices storeroom to hide them in, with its solid lock. Then immediately worried at being locked in the home of the man at the top of the *beneficiarius's* most-wanted list. Martinus shrugged and grinned, swaying a little. Damn his eyes, he *was* drunk!

Tiro heard Vibia's sweet voice intercepting the host and his unidentified visitors — what Tiro would have given to see through the storeroom door — and the sounds of voices and feet soon faded away. They'd probably go into the triclinium, safely away from the servants' quarters. A few minutes later Vibia unlocked the door and summoned them, finger to lips again, to follow her. They were not seen; all the staff were presumably serving the master and his guests.

Before they departed through the same low window, Tiro turned to say farewell. Vibia suddenly reached up to put her arms around his neck, and kissed him on his cheek. He was stunned; for a mad moment he wanted to insist on staying. But he knew her heart would never be his.

She said quickly, 'Tell my brother to come urgently when I send for him. There is great danger coming, I fear. He must help me get my Cassius out of this plot. I don't know what they are planning, but I know it's deadly.'

Before Tiro could respond she was gone, shutters closed gently behind her. The two soldiers were left in the moonlit street, one swaying and grinning still, the other rubbing his cheek where the warm kiss lingered.

Chapter Thirteen

Burdigala, Gaul

The *Athena* made an easy passage north, with favourable winds pushing her to best speed. Even so, they had been sailing across the huge Mare Cantabricum for nearly four weeks before they entered the wide estuary of the Garunna river in western Gaul. As the ship swept upstream towards the port on the south bank, Julia thought how charming the gently sloping vineyards looked. Being at sea in good weather had transformed her looks and mood. The drugs Fulvia bought in Gades had taken effect, and she felt better. The tasty rations supplied by the ship's cook had rounded out her concave belly and left her feeling well at ease.

'You're getting quite brown for a Briton,' Fulvia commented. They were relaxing on deck in the slanted shade of the mainsail, nibbling on nuts and dried grapes and sipping well-watered wine. Burdigala, dead ahead, was famed for its Biturica wine, one of the main reasons Fulvia traded there; but the *Athena* had also taken on a cargo of acceptable Hispanic wine at Gades. Fulvia and her cheerful captain Artemidorus shared a flagon of wine most evenings when duty allowed. Julia contented herself with a small cup now and again, watered by three parts.

She suspected that most of the crew's wine supply was consumed by the owner and her captain, while they were curled up together on the deck at night.

The first time Julia had woken to leave her cabin to pass water, she had been taken aback to see the pair thus: the wealthy sophisticated Fulvia, swathed in blankets and held snug in the arms of her swarthy mariner with their backs to the mast, talking quietly together. Having offered the ship's single cabin back to them many times, Julia accepted their unusual relationship and gave it no more heed. As did the crew. It worked, the gods approved, and *Athena* continued to be a happy and prosperous ship.

'I do love the sunshine, Fulvia,' Julia admitted. 'But we quite often have lovely summers where I live. We even have our own vineyards.' Fulvia cocked a disbelieving eyebrow, and Julia added hastily, 'Nothing as good as the wines you ship, of course. But we enjoy our British wine, mixed with our own honey.' She fell silent, watching the wading birds — herons, she thought — catching small silvery fish on the edges of the estuary as they beat upstream.

'Tell me about your home, dearest girl,' said Fulvia, settling back with her eyes closed.

So Julia told her about the Summer Country, with its watery meres, low-ranging hills, silty coasts and rich lovely farmland. She spoke about her home, Bo Gwelt, where she and her elder brother Marcus had passed such happy childhoods. Her voice faltered as she described how Marcus had died during the fire that swept Bo Gwelt the previous spring, destroying much of the old villa. 'But we've rebuilt most of it, in local honey-coloured stone, more beautiful than ever. Only the west wing is still in ruins…' Her voice faded, as she pictured again the black

THE CARNELIAN PHOENIX

wreck of that wing. That was where the fire had started, after Marcus had been killed by a crushing head blow as he worked late one night in his estate office. She failed to blot out the memory of her own return that same evening from Lindinis. Representing her sick brother, she'd gone to save her tribe from incited rebellion by that wicked pair, the actress Fulminata and her patrician lover Antoninus Labienus. With Quintus and Tiro, she'd returned to find her home ablaze and her brother missing.

Fulvia opened her eyes. 'My dear, I'm sorry. I didn't mean to cause you pain. Forgive me. I feel we've become close friends during this voyage, but that doesn't excuse my inveterate snoopiness.'

'No, Fulvia, I want you to know. Talking about Bo Gwelt, about Marcus, makes it easier for me to remember the good things still left to me.' And suddenly Julia found herself telling Fulvia everything, emptying her heart to this clever, kind woman. She spoke of Aurelia, her adored headstrong daughter, who loved riding her horses around their large estate in the Polden Hills. How Aurelia had been adopted by her late brother, and was now herself the wealthy owner of the property. How the neighbouring landowner's son, Drusus Sorio, had a crush on the leggy, dark-haired Aurelia. But the girl hadn't noticed yet, seeing Drusus only as her horse-mad friend.

She spoke about her own medical training by Demetrios, the Greek doctor-turned-tutor at Bo Gwelt, and her work with the military surgeon at the Aquae Sulis clinic. It was while she was reminiscing about her time with the Wise Women of Eboracum, learning about herbalism at the Temple of Serapis, that Fulvia asked, 'Is that where you met Aurelia's father?' Julia nodded, lost in a stream of remembrance; then stopped, looking at her friend in chagrin. Fulvia held her hands up, smiling. 'I warned you — snoopy.'

Julia sighed. 'Quintus. Praetorian Quintus Valerius. He was so young — we both were. He came in the army of old Emperor Septimius Severus to fight the Caledonian tribes in the far north of Britannia. His brother Flavius died on the battlefield right in front of him, and Quintus was badly wounded, evacuated south to the base hospital at Eboracum. It all happened so fast. I suppose very young people often fall in love suddenly, like we did.' She paused, back in that long golden spring, remembering the pale sun-kissed stones of the northern city. Emperor Septimius had recently died there and the new Emperor Caracalla and his co-ruler Geta had left, so Eboracum was no longer the temporary capital of the Roman world. But the citizens still carried their heads high as they bustled around the enlarged forum. Julia and Quintus passed the afternoons hand in hand, locked together in oblivious disregard.

'And then he left.'

'Just like that?'

'His mother wrote to tell him his father had died suddenly, and the family was shamed and driven out of imperial favour. He felt he had to go home. I thought — I thought his passage would take some time to arrange. He hadn't even been signed off by the surgeons, he was still limping. I imagined I had time to tell him. I tried to tell him…'

'He never came back?'

'Yes, he did. Early this year he suddenly crashed back into my life. I was so angry, still bitter about him leaving, even after all those years. I had made my own life without him, a good life. But when I saw him with Aurelia — they're so alike, Fulvia, same dark hair, same grey eyes, same vitality — I knew I couldn't just dismiss him. And then he rescued Aurelia from the fire, and somehow we found ourselves working together, with Decurion Agrippa Sorio and Centurion Marcellus Crispus of the Aquae Sulis cohort, to prevent the British coup, and…'

'And you found you hadn't stopped loving him?'

Julia couldn't speak, just nodded silently as she fought her emotions. It never got any easier.

'Ah, Julia, even the most level-headed of us can fall for a man and wake up to find our lives have changed for ever.'

Fulvia stood, stretching and shading her eyes in search of her own man. Artemidorus turned from giving the steersman instructions and smiled at his flame-headed lover. Deep lines fanned out from his dark eyes as his face lit up. Fulvia hurried to join him, her bracelets jangling and her exotic silks billowing round her ankles.

***

The next morning Julia awoke to a bright hot day, feeling restless. Fulvia and most of the crew had already gone ashore, and the bustling wharfs of Burdigala were packed with stevedores, merchants, passengers, farmers and traders of all descriptions. Artemidorus waved at her, teeth glinting against his deeply tanned skin, as Julia weaved her way cautiously down the gangplank. It was the first time she'd been on dry land since leaving Massilia, and her feet were trying to walk in several directions at once.

She walked past some of the many warehouses at Burdigala storing the region's famous wine, ready for export. A delicious scent of blackcurrant and plum, overlaid with the odd hint of lead, exuded from the stacked wine barrels and amphorae. She sniffed appreciatively, grateful to enjoy the smell now her stomach was more settled. She found Fulvia sitting in the shade outside her shipping agent's office. Her friend waved her over, and introduced the agent, a shy elderly man who was clearly in awe of his exuberant female patron. Fulvia showed her to a seat under the awning.

'Julia, the gossip I've just heard here has prompted me to think further about opening up a new trade route. How would you feel about going on with us direct to Britannia?'

The mention of her home province certainly piqued Julia's interest. She sat up, delighted.

Fulvia smiled. 'I thought that might please you. It's the tin, you see. The tin mines of Hispania are running dry, but the need for bronze around the empire is as much as ever. No tin to alloy with copper: no bronze. I've been pondering that ebbing market for some time. As it happens,' Fulvia preened a little, running her jewelled hand through her highly coloured locks, 'I am the direct descendant — the great, great, great-something granddaughter — of the unrivalled Massilian explorer, Pytheas the Greek. Pytheas is long gone and his achievements often forgotten, alas, but our family treasured his maps and records. I have them still, and so I know where the fabled tin mines of Belerion are.' She paused in triumph, having captured Julia's entire attention. Being a well-educated native of south-west Britannia, Julia knew of the tin mines of the British ancients in Kernow, and their claims of sea-trade with dark-haired men in strange ships in the long ago, before Rome ever came to Britannia.

The agent turned to Julia. 'Mistress, do you know the nearest anchorage to Belerion?'

Julia had to admit she didn't. 'But I can provide directions to the safest harbours in south-west Britannia,'

THE CARNELIAN PHOENIX

she said. 'The coast of Kernow is craggy and dangerous. The tides can be deadly, and there are many uncharted rocks and reefs, I've been told.'

A bench was pulled out next to her, and she turned to see Fulvia's captain sliding his muscular thighs beneath the table.

'Just in time, my love,' said his mistress. 'Julia was about to explain the best anchorage for the *Athena*, if we want to resurrect the tin trade with Britannia.'

After Julia had told all she could remember of the vast deepwater harbour at Bol, and the fast military road that led from nearby Durnovaria direct to Kernow, Fulvia nodded in satisfaction. Julia added she had good connections with the southern Durotriges, and could easily supply a guide and interpreter to take them on from Bol by road, a lot safer than risking the big Roman merchant ship in Cornish waters.

She left them to enjoy an intimate lunch together, and set off to stroll along the riverside quay to see the sights of this big bustling city. Behind the docks rose an impressive three-storey amphitheatre, and in the distance was a massive white temple on a hillside. Certainly Burdigala was determined to show off its prosperity and heritage.

Julia was getting hungry, still a sensation she welcomed after the months of sickness. She found a respectable tavern in a quiet street behind the docks, and enjoyed a small meal of honeyed mushrooms with slivers of duck breast. The inn-keeper's son who served her was clearly intrigued. As she was settling the bill, he asked shyly if she was British.

'Yes,' said Julia, smiling at him. 'Was it my accent, or my looks?'

'Well, Domina, it's true we don't get many ladies like you in Burdigala. But you do talk like 'im, the crazy boy what's been living on the wharf, so I ventured to ask.'

'The crazy boy?'

The serving lad shuffled his feet, and hitched his tunic away from a freckled shoulder. 'My father says not to trouble folks, or mess with loons struck by the gods. Only I feel sorry for him. He've been living on the docks, in fair weather and foul, for weeks. I sometimes sneak him bits of scraps, leftovers from the kitchen and that. When Father's not looking.' He looked around, ducking his head when the barmaid came out to serve drinks at the adjoining table.

Julia felt sorry for the serving lad. He clearly felt the poor mad stranger should be helped by a fellow Briton, and Julia may have been the first to come by in some time. She shrugged. She was free till evening, and perhaps her money and healing skills might help this unfortunate traveller.

'Have you got time to show me?'

'Yes'm. I have a break now, if you could come?'

***

Julia did not recognise the sick boy at first. He crouched, back turned, under a tarpaulin in the partial shade of a stack of rotting timbers piled at the back of a wharf. He was rocking and crooning. The waiter was right, though. His words were crazy, but fluent and in a British accent.

He was speaking earnestly, as if to a group of friends.

'But you see, she did love me. Yes, yes,' he nodded vigorously to thin air, 'she loved me. I loved her. I still love her, though she has betrayed me. Jupiter, Juno and Minerva gave her to me. In Londinium, my friend. It was the greatest love of all time. We were like Hero and

THE CARNELIAN PHOENIX

Leander, or Orpheus and his Eurydice.' The boy's thin frame shook as he spoke, the soiled remnants of what had been an expensive yellow tunic shivering across his prominent ribs.

Reluctantly, Julia made herself look properly at this demented beggar despite a flash of nausea. Loath though she was to accept it, here he was: Lucius Claudius, nephew of her dead brother's widow Claudia, son of Claudius Bulbo who had died so horribly in the fire at Bo Gwelt. Lucius Claudius, who she had overheard plotting with Claudia to recover the silver he stole from the Mendip mines to fund the attempted coup by Gaius Trebonius. Lucius Claudius, the killer of her beloved brother, Marcus Aurelianus.

Lucius Claudius, who had fled Britannia with the branded, exiled Fulminata, and was here, apparently abandoned and alone in Gaul.

She approached him slowly, gently, touching him on the shoulder to attract his attention without scaring him.

'Lucius?'

He seemed at first not to hear her. Then he turned his thin face towards her, and started back, apparently horrified at the sight of Julia.

'The Wise Woman!' He tried to scrabble to his feet, staring at an invisible circle of witnesses. 'Do you see her, the Wise Woman? She's come to claim her vengeance, to curse me and cast me into the shades of Hades.'

'No, no, Lucius, I want to help you. You're ill, and in need of food and shelter. Come with me, I will get you help, take you home.'

While Julia heard herself saying these things to Lucius, part of her remained distanced, astonished that she could offer help to this lunatic who had taken her brother away so brutally. But the healer in her overcame the disgust of an angry grieving sister. She held her hand out. Other people approached, apparently seeing her efforts with the boy, but she took no notice. She moved closer to Lucius, who was holding his face averted. He made a sudden movement, springing to his feet and bolting past, pushing her over hard onto the ground. She lay prone with grazed hands, momentarily stunned and out of breath. The young waiter was still there. He came forward quickly to help her.

'Domina! Are you hurt?'

She brushed him aside, looking for the escaping Lucius. Erratic footfalls moved away along the wharf. Before she could locate the sound, she glimpsed Lucius passing out of sight behind a moored ship. There was a splash, followed some time later by another, louder one. Fulvia suddenly came into view, running with her fine skirts clutched above her knees.

'Julia! What's going on here?'

Before Julia could answer, Fulvia turned to stare at a man swimming strongly in the harbour, holding a bundle of rags up in his arms. Fulvia shouted, 'Arti!' and ran — surprisingly lightly for such a sizeable woman — along the jetty. She helped the soaking Artemidorus tug and tussle the lifeless body of Lucius out of the water.

All of this had happened so quickly that Julia was still brushing herself down and reassuring the boy from the bar that she was not hurt. She joined the other two, kneeling down on the rough wood to check whether Lucius was breathing. The captain gently pushed her away.

'Let me see to the lad.' He lifted Lucius easily, turning him over with his head to one side. He pressed firmly and rhythmically on the boy's bony back, and Julia saw water begin to pump in trickles out of the boy's mouth. He didn't move, though, and Julia began to despair. Lucius must be drowned. She emptied her mind, preparing to dedicate his unfortunate spirit to the goddess Minerva in her merciful wisdom, when Lucius came abruptly back to life, spluttering and choking.

Artemidorus picked him up, supporting the boy in a sitting position while he spewed more seawater and fought to catch his breath.

It seemed they had saved Lucius — but what were they to do with him?

Chapter Fourteen

Rome, Castra Peregrina

Quintus was tired and troubled when he and Licinius returned to the Castra. His mind was full of the threat to Ulpian, and his own suspicions about Epegathus. But then he considered. He might be wrong: it was many years since he'd seen that little lad playing on the Quirinal with the Labieni boys. What could he actually say to Ulpian? That he thought Aurelius Epegathus looked like a boyhood friend of the escaped criminal Cassius Labienus? Ulpian was a lawyer, and was bound to ask for evidence. Quintus's suppositions were based on what — hazy recollections from his own past? Epegathus, as Prefect of the Annona in charge of the daily bread for millions, was a powerful man who had gained his position through cultivating the trust of the empress, no doubt. He would have friends with their own power bases too, likely enough inside the Guard.

No. Quintus had nothing to back up what was still merely a hunch, and likely a hunch prejudiced by his own boyhood memories. It would take more than that to counter two such powerful men as Epegathus and Cassius Labienus.

He glanced at the note Drusilla had given him, and set it aside till the morning. He needed no more anxiety or resentment that night.

THE CARNELIAN PHOENIX

***

He slept badly anyway. Justin had risen at dawn, and already departed for his home in Etruria. At their table in the officers' refectory, Tiro looked hungover. He told Quintus about the attack in the streets the previous evening.

'A stray mugging?'

'No, sir. It felt more like we were set on by thugs who knew about us, and had followed us.' Martinus, who had been formally seconded to them, came in looking the worse for wear with his head freshly bandaged.

'I see you had some fun last night,' Quintus nodded at the unhappy centurion. 'Come to my quarters with Tiro when you've breakfasted.'

Back in his room, Quintus picked up Hortensia's letter. Only then did he realise the familiar handwriting on the papyrus was not his mother's. His heart lurched sideways in his chest.

Tiro, who had just come in with Martinus, looked at him curiously. 'Something wrong, boss?'

Quintus sat heavily. 'What did Drusilla say about this letter? Do you remember?'

'Just that Hortensia had left it on her dresser, addressed to you.'

'Right.'

He was silent for a long time, while rage and disgust surged through him. His hands were shaking. He glanced up at Tiro before smoothing back the folded sheet, and saw his junior colleague's concerned eyes fixed on him.

At Massilia.
Quintus Valerius, from Julia Aureliana, greetings.
I heard you speaking to Vibia, and so I understand I have lost you. I am leaving here quietly so that we need

not see each other again. I realise that I am not your true and only love, but still I could not leave without writing to you. For the sake of what was between us, and the great love I bear you, despite everything, I needed to say farewell properly.

You must not be concerned about me. I am used to being alone; indeed, I never looked to have you back in Britannia at all, and it was a miracle from blessed Minerva to spend these few months in your arms. I must return to being who I was, an independent woman with my work, my home, our daughter and my people to care for.

Please don't worry about Aurelia. She will be upset at first — she was becoming very fond of you — but she is tough and resourceful, and also surrounded by people who love her. We will both be fine…

Quintus dropped the letter, letting the fine sheet slide to his lap. Martinus cleared his throat.

'I'll step outside, shall I?' He stood clumsily and lurched, touching the door frame for support as he left the room.

Quintus took up the letter again, scanning the rest. He sank his head into his hands.

'The letter is from Julia. She overheard and misunderstood my conversation with Vibia in Massilia. She thinks — hold on… she writes that she heard me commit my love to Vibia. And so I did, as Vibia's brother! She adds that she knows Hortensia will never accept her, and so she does not want to cause a breach with my family. She must have left the letter for me in Massilia, and my mother — *deodamnatus!* — found it.'

'Sir, Quintus, this is…is —'

THE CARNELIAN PHOENIX

Quintus nodded. He knew what it was. The end of his duty as a son. As far as he was concerned, he no longer had a parent. It was also the beginning of what might be a long hard quest to find Julia and win back her trust. But that was a quest he would honour, no matter if it took the rest of his life.

'She writes, "I will go home the quickest way, Quintus. I will be safe, I have money and connections. Don't try to follow or find me. Best to have a clean break."'

Quintus read the final lines to himself, swallowed, and tucked the letter carefully into his belt pouch. He sat in silence, staring at his booted feet. There was nothing to say. The greatest joy of his life had been smashed into pieces by the deliberate actions of his mother.

Martinus knocked and stuck his head, bandage rather askew, round the door. 'Come on, Tiro. Let's get a drink.' Tiro cast a downbeat glance at Quintus and followed Martinus out.

Some time later — Quintus had no idea how much later, but the sun was pouring its heat at full height through the high south windows of the fort — he stirred, pushed his *gladius* firmly into its scabbard, and left the Castra barracks. He walked quickly towards the Quirinal.

***

Silenus hurried to greet Quintus after the door porter had admitted him into Hortensia's little house.

His mother called from upstairs, 'Silenus! Who is that?'

Quintus pressed his finger to his lips. Hortensia's voice echoed as it penetrated down the stairs and into the atrium. Instantly recognisable: her tone, her cadence, her timbre. Her accent. An uncommon accent here in Rome, but one he had heard recently somewhere.

Quintus hated coincidences. In fact, he did not believe in them. If two items of concern to him seemed to be related there was every chance, in his extensive experience, that they *were* related. He reached back mentally, trying to remember. Where had he heard that accent in the past few days?

His mother came downstairs, trailing a diaphanous rose-coloured *palla* and wearing a sour face.

'Oh, it's you, Quintus. You'd better come into the salon.' She clicked her fingers at Silenus, and turned away, her pointed red slippers clacking on the mosaic floor.

'I suppose you've come to apologise.' Hortensia settled herself on a couch, her legs elegantly tucked away. 'Well, I'm waiting.'

I will not let anger defeat me. Lord Mithras, give me the poise and strength of will to overcome this woman. He focused on his breath, watching each come and go as he had been taught in the east as a younger man. His mother did indeed wait, seeming baffled. Not until Quintus pulled out Julia's letter did she react.

'Mother, did you hide this letter from me?'

' Of course I did! What kind of mother would I be, not to want your best interests? I can't allow you to marry that British nobody. How could such an alliance advance your family?'

'Even though you knew she was my choice, the woman I love?'

'Love?' Hortensia practically spat the word, her beringed hands held tightly together. 'What does love matter? I loved someone, once. A man I knew when we were young, who asked most properly to marry me. A wholly respectable boy of my own city of Patavium, who, I might add, has since come a long way in the world. But my family deemed the match unsuitable. They said he wasn't good enough. I was torn away from my love, and made to marry your father.'

Quintus looked at Hortensia in surprise. A faint current of sympathy momentarily swirled against the torrent of his resentment and anger. So his mother too had loved and lost?

She spoke again, instantly destroying the frail bridge between them. 'What was good enough for me must be good for you too. I was made to marry to suit my family. Married to a man who betrayed me with a common woman; worse, a Christian! I found out about his mistress, and his daughter. Once I knew, I made sure of her!' She paused, staring at Quintus. 'I overcame the shame of my husband's suicide, the end of my standing and wealth. I even survived his profound betrayal of me. And now I have saved you, my son, from your own weakness. I've freed you to make a better match, as a good mother should. A match here in Rome, with a proper Roman family. I still have connections — better than ever. I've finally shaken off the burden of your father's disgrace, and we as a family can reclaim our place in society.'

Quintus looked with disgust at this woman who shared his blood. The same woman who had given birth to his dead brother Flavius and his beloved sister Lucilla. There was nothing in her he recognised. He thought briefly of his father, a strong generous man who had loved his city. Who had given everything for his *Romanitas* and to save the woman and daughter who mattered even more.

He stood, preparing to leave.

'I have not given you permission to go, Quintus. You have yet to apologise to me.' She looked disdainful rather than angry, but he found he no longer cared.

'I do not need your permission for anything, Hortensia Martial. I disown you as my mother. I heard what you said in Massilia, to drive away Julia. Now I know what you did to my sister Vibia. The gods also know of your vile actions. But I will find Julia, marry her and keep her safe, a long way from you. I will do whatever I can for my half-sister too.'

He walked to the door, turning to give her a final look.

'If I find that you had anything, anything at all, to do with my father's death, I will not wait for the justice of the gods. I will hunt you down and kill you myself.' As he turned away he caught a flash of fear on her face.

He nodded to Silenus and Drusilla as he left the house. He headed downhill back to the Castra Peregrina and found Tiro hurtling towards him.

'She's sent for us! Your sister, sir — I mean Vibia. She says she has information, but you must come quickly.'

'Martinus?'

'He's gone to meet an informant, sir, says he'll see us back at the Castra.'

'Lead on then!' Quintus followed at a run, feeling the afternoon heat rising off the streets to hit him in the face as they turned about. His bad leg itched in the tormenting haze. He tucked grimly in behind his eager *optio,* who was dashing on ahead.

***

Vibia was seated when Quintus and Tiro entered the reception room of Cassius's elegant house. They were greeted at the main door by her personal slave, and led through the silent cool house to the back. Vibia's shoulders were hunched, and her face was swollen by recent tears.

'Vibia?'

THE CARNELIAN PHOENIX

She raised her face. Tiro looked awkward. 'Would you like me to wait outside?'

She shook her head, holding out her hands to him. Tiro sat next to her, watching her with a look of intense longing, but he took care not to touch more than her hands.

'You know you can trust us,' Quintus said gently.

She gave a long slow sigh. 'I've sent the servants out for the afternoon. There are things you need to know. It's just…there's something personal I must say first. About… about my time in the brothel.'

Quintus glanced at Tiro. 'Are you sure you want to share this?'

She nodded; Tiro looked down at his knees.

'You see, there was a child. Or at least, there should have been. I…lost it.'

Quintus waited, feeling intense pain. He also felt angry, and desperately upset that his sister had such things she felt she had to hide. His heart bumped into a faster pace, and it was all he could do to sit quietly until she spoke again.

'There was a man — a client at the brothel. He came again, and again. He seemed at first to be like all the others, but then he began to linger after coming into my cubicle before we… I was surprised, because he clearly came from a wealthy home, and would have slaves there to meet his needs. He talked to me. He asked what I preferred. Sometimes, he came just to sit with me. The madam got angry and demanded to know if I displeased him.

'And then…it changed for me, too. He was the only one who didn't hurt me. I began to long for his visits. I would kiss him, and mean it. Sometimes, he seemed angry when he arrived. I would wait while he seemed to turn over matters in his mind. His anger would leave, he would grow gentle and lie with me like a lover.'

She paused, but Quintus didn't interrupt her, knowing she was coming to the distressing part of her confession and needed to draw on her remaining strength to continue. Tiro sat rigid by her side.

'One day, I discovered I was pregnant. If I told the madam she would make me get rid of it. But I knew it was his child, my lover's. He came to me that same day. I was in agony, not knowing whether to tell him or not. He was eager, excited.

'Vibia, I have decided. I want you to be only mine. I love you. Let me take you to my home, straight away.' I gazed at him, not believing what I was hearing. It was so wonderful — we would be together, our child would have a safe, happy home. The only man I could ever love was proposing marriage to me. I was so, so happy.' Vibia stopped, choking. Fresh tears pressed out from under her swollen eyelids.

'Quintus, he asked me to go away with him — as his concubine. An acknowledged mistress, with all I could desire.'

Vibia raised her head, looking Quintus straight in the eyes. 'I refused him. I said I loved him, that he was the only man I would ever love. But to live with him in sin would anger the one I loved even more, Lord Jesus, my Messiah. I told him it was forbidden to me, a Christian, to live with a man outside marriage. He laughed. It was a bitter sound, and I knew I had hurt and angered him.

"You're nothing but a whore. I offer you a wonderful life of luxury and security, and you refuse me. No Labienus would marry a slave, especially one despoiled in the brothels. And how could I marry a Christian, even if you were a pure girl of good standing? My family would be humiliated and shamed."

'It was the hardest thing I have ever done, like cutting off my arm. I told him, "At least I am an honest whore. If I were to become your mistress, I would be lying to my dead parents, to myself …and worst of all, to my God."

'And that was the end of it, or so I thought. He never knew about his child. He left; I didn't see him again. One of the other girls spitefully told the madam I was pregnant. She beat me till I lost the baby. Then she sold me. But the merciful God intervened. I came to Massilia, to you, and there he found me. He told me he still loved me, and then, I fear, I sinned grievously. I told him I couldn't bear to live without him, and would be whatever he wanted, only to be with him.

'I tried to let you know, Quintus. I wrote a note, had it all ready, telling you that I was leaving with Cassius, and thanking you and Tiro. But the ship's captain wouldn't wait, and the stevedores didn't see me. The note fell in the sea. I'm sorry!

'Anyway, that's how I came here. And now I need to tell you the rest: what I have discovered in this house. About the plot that threatens the city, the Emperor, and my love, Cassius.'

Quintus felt exhausted. The effort to remain still, to hold himself in check while Vibia recounted her terrible tale, had taken all his strength. Despite the toll, he must lay his feelings to one side and listen to what more she had to say. It would be important. He took her hand, and held it gently until she was ready to speak again.

Chapter Fifteen

Burdigala, Gaul

'What's to do, my love?' Artemidorus asked Fulvia, when they had persuaded Lucius into Julia's cabin, and Julia had coaxed him to eat and drink a little, and settled him to sleep. She refused to tie him up, saying he had suffered enough.

'I don't know. Julia, what do you wish?'

Julia shook her head, feeling torn. She wasn't sure herself. The part of her that mourned her brother wanted revenge, to throw the boy into the deepest part of the ocean. This was, after all, the wicked Lucius Claudius who had smashed her brother's head in at Bo Gwelt, and then set fire to the estate office to cover up his crimes of theft and murder.

But another part of Julia was stronger: the healer in her. She recognised from her studies with Demetrios of the great Roman doctor, Galen, that Lucius was ill: ill in his brain and his soul. She had helped *Medicus* Anicius Piso at the Aquae Sulis hospital treat sufferers from the same disorder. Galen discarded the old ideas that such illnesses were due to possession by demons. He taught that illness affecting the brain was caused by distortion of the rational mental functions, not by affliction from the gods. Anicius had shown her Galen's gently effective approach to treatment of illnesses of the mind: correct diet, moderate

THE CARNELIAN PHOENIX

exercise, enough sleep, and most of all the attention and care of an understanding physician.

Many would say Lucius must be punished by the gods, and certainly his sins and crimes deserved punishment. But Julia had seen this pattern of suffering before, in which mania was followed by intense depression. She had witnessed how daily care and attention to the body, together with donatives and prayers to Sulis Minerva, had helped such sick people much more than restraint or punishment.

She explained as much to Fulvia and her captain. Fulvia was doubtful, Artemidorus frankly sceptical. Julia told them plainly that as well as it being her duty as a trained healer, she was impelled by the need to discover what more Lucius knew about the British rebellion and its links with the plot in Rome.

'I saw myself the deaths of twenty or more British soldiers at Lugdunum by Praetorians sent from Rome, by whoever commanded the silencing of the traitor Gaius Trebonius. Lucius may be our only living witness.'

'Who cares about Rome?' asked Fulvia, shrugging. Being the descendant of Greeks settled for centuries in Massilia, Fulvia was content to enjoy the trading advantages of being a Roman citizen, but didn't feel much innate loyalty to the city of Rome. Neither did her captain, whose whole being was bound up with sea-faring and the love of his mistress. Even Julia was more concerned about the security of her own island of Britannia, but she knew from Quintus that the fate of the British provinces was closely connected to the stability of the empire.

'We thought the British coup was over when Gaius Trebonius and Cassius Labienus were taken captive at Corinium. But we know from the ambush at Lugdunum that the plot continues, and has spread. Quintus is convinced that Rome itself is in danger. It is clear someone high up is pulling the strings that freed Labienus, and maybe had Trebonius killed. Whatever has passed between the *beneficiarius* and me, I owe it to Quintus and Tiro and my people at home, to do what I can to uncover the wider plot. We know Lucius Claudius and his former companion Fulminata were involved. If I can tease any more information out of this poor boy, I must try.'

So the *Athena* sat in port while Julia nursed Lucius carefully, sleeping next to him in the ship's cabin, persuading his capricious appetite, encouraging him to take walks with her up and down the quaysides of Burdigala. All the time she listened carefully, hoping for clues, something to reveal the masterplan; some glimmer of the truth that she could send to Quintus. Her resentment and despair at being rejected by Hortensia, and again by Quintus, faded into the background in her new purpose.

At first it seemed hopeless. Lucius remained low and lethargic, barely eating, sleeping only in snatches. He did not refuse to speak, but seemed to remember very little. No matter how often she gently alluded to his life in the Summer Country: home at Iscalis with his wealthy father; riding the Polden hills with his friend Drusus Sorio; trips to Londinium and his first meeting with the sloe-eyed actress Fulminata, he could tell her nothing of any sense. He would look at her blankly, and she could see his attention drift away.

On the day before the *Athena* was to set off north on her resumed voyage, she asked him if he remembered her daughter, Aurelia.

THE CARNELIAN PHOENIX

He looked at her. 'Aurelia? Aurelia?' His eyes changed focus, went wide. 'I'm sorry! I didn't mean it. I didn't mean to kill the fox, or insult you.' The boy sobbed as if heart-broken. 'I didn't mean to kill your father. He found me trying to take the money, and I — I panicked and picked up the first thing I found. I hit him with it, Aurelia. Forgive me, it was a terrible mistake.'

He stood suddenly, the first energetic movement he had made for days. Fearing to startle him, Julia got up too, slowly and smoothly. She saw Artemidorus crook a finger to a sailor. Julia shook her head slightly, and the man stepped away, keeping watch from a distance.

'Come, Lucius, let's go for a walk. You can tell me all about it.'

Julia held out her hand, hardly daring to hope, but the moment of energy seemed sustained, and Lucius grasped her hand and followed her down the gangplank.

They headed up from the port towards the great hillside temple to the local goddess Tutela, white stone blocks gleaming in the full heat of the summer day. Suddenly, Lucius began to speak in time with his steps, the words tumbling out as if he was heaving a great weight off his chest.

'Lucky Aurelia, so blessed. Everyone loves her. Her pony Milo, her dog too. Even Drusus, my best friend Drusus, loves Aurelia. I was…upset — no, angry — when she wouldn't like me. Always disappearing to the stables whenever I visited Bo Gwelt. Aunt Claudia said, 'Just wait, she'll be yours one day, and this vast estate, all of it will be yours.' So I waited, though it burned my bones to be ignored, excluded. But she took up with Drusus, always wanting to be riding around with that young fool. And still my aunt and father counselled patience.

'Then I met Fulminata. A real woman, older, experienced, someone with hot blood in her veins and a passionate vision of a better life.' His eyes moved away, focussing on something in the distance.

'Come here, my love. Come back to me. I will give you anything you want. Forget that little girl at Bo Gwelt, come with me to power, fame and fortune.' His eyes lit up, his face was transformed, eager and mobile. 'Fulminata, my beloved! Don't heed those deadly brothers. I have riches, silver enough to bathe in. Stay with me, come back to the Summer Country. Be my wife, my beautiful pampered wife.'

His face twisted, and suddenly he looked bereft. Julia realised she was watching a re-enactment of sorts, a charade playing out in Lucius's fragile mind, summoning back the melodrama of his obsessions.

'I know where the silver is, Fulminata. I'll bring it to you; don't leave me for Cassius. Don't leave me, Fulminata!'

Lucius seemed to falter as they gained the top of the hill, stumbling at the foot of the tall grey marble altar in front of the temple. He lay down in the grass, saying he was tired. Julia seized the chance. She found the attendant priest and pressed money on him. The priest dutifully lit charcoal piled onto the altar, placing fragrant frankincense atop the smouldering coals to release the sweet smoky offering so beloved of the goddess. Julia sank to her knees in prayer. She did not know the Goddess Tutela, but was well accustomed to worshipping her own patron goddess, Sulis Minerva. She retreated into reverie, emptying her mind whilst retaining awareness of Lucius, lying asleep by her side.

Afterwards, when he woke they sat together almost in a kind of companionship. The westering sun was still pouring out intense heat, so they settled comfortably in the shade with their backs to a Corinthian pillar. Julia bought some watered wine to share from a passing street vendor.

Lucius's voice was calm and steady.

'After we lost the battle at Corinium, I knew we had to flee. Fulminata returned after…after her punishment in Aquae Sulis. With Antoninus Labienus dead, she came to me, desperate. I still loved her. I even thought her disfigurement would make her mine. We needed each other — I was a criminal, a fleeing traitor, and she had been banished for her part in the murders and insurrection. We took ship together, hoping we'd be safe in Gaul. But at Augustodunum she somehow heard of the Praetorian plan to set up an ambush at Lugdunum, to rescue Cassius and Gaius from their prisoner escort party. She changed, becoming hard and impatient. I could see she no longer wanted me. I… I began to feel ill again. I am plagued, you know, by low spirits. Always after a time of busy happiness, my spirits droop. So low sometimes, so low… I wish I was dead.'

He nearly whispered this last sentence. Julia said nothing, but took his trembling sweaty hand, and squeezed it. After a moment, he wiped his eyes and continued.

'She was eager for us to join Cassius, sure of her welcome with him. The ambush was over when we rode up. So many bodies! Cassius had been freed by a man he called "Brother" and "Little Dog". It seemed to be a boyhood nickname, as they embraced warmly. Then the man, Little Dog — he seemed to be the leader although he wore no uniform amongst all those soldiers — he raised Trebonius to his feet, intending, I think, to free him too.

'I knew she always carried a knife, but…I had no idea what she was planning. When she suddenly stabbed Trebonius in the back, twice, I was shocked and terrified. He was manacled, helpless, he didn't see it coming. None of us did. I couldn't seem to move, to stop her, even to cry out. I think she did it to please Cassius, to prove her love.'

Lucius stopped, taking a deep breath and holding it before letting it out slowly, reflectively. 'She was so wrong. Cassius Labienus looked at her as if she was the lowest worm in the dirt.

'"He was already dead of his guilt, you fool," Labienus said. "But we needed his trial to prove it. Now the world will wonder. You are reckless, damaged goods. I felt sorry for you, I suppose, after my brother died. Pah! You disgust me. Get away, take your lapdog. I never want to see you again."

'He turned his back on both of us. The other man, Little Dog, shrugged, and waved his armed men back. They rode away, leaving the dead soldiers, leaving us to make our own path. When we finally got here there was only enough money for one passage to Britannia. She boarded a ship and left me here with nothing.

'I've been so ill, Aurelia. So ill, for so long. Please, please, don't you leave me too!'

Julia's heart melted; she took the shivering young man into her arms and held him long while the heat leached out of the ancient temple stones.

When they got back to the *Athena*, still followed by the faithful sailor, Julia wrote two letters. A short urgent note to Centurion Marcellus at the Aquae Sulis station, warning him to watch the roads of the Summer Country; and a second, longer letter. This one caused her much trouble and heartache, and the night was well advanced before she had sealed and despatched the letters, and lain down in the cabin to snatch a short sleep before the evening tide took the *Athena* out to sea.

Chapter Sixteen

Rome, the house of the Labieni

The salon was beginning to grow darker. Vibia paused her account as a knock came at the door. Slaves entered to light the candles and oil lamps scattered around the room, and then left silently.

She pushed back a wing of her golden-brown hair.

'Quintus, what I have to say saddens me because it means Cassius and I must leave Rome in secret. But it also makes my heart sing as we begin a new life together, just the two of us. You know that Cassius had two brothers? The elder was called Antoninus.'

'Antoninus — yes, we knew him.' Quintus did not add that Antoninus had died of a sword thrust through the heart, inflicted in front of them at Lindinis. They had not killed him — that had been his ill-fated associate Caesulanus — but they might as well have done. There was a flicker of chagrin on Tiro's face, perhaps from shame at losing that witness, or irritation that justice had not been served.

'He also had a younger foster brother. All three boys adored each other. Cassius and his foster brother are still close.' She paused, and Quintus held himself still; but his hands trembled slightly as he spoke.

'Do you know his full name, Vibia, this younger brother?'

THE CARNELIAN PHOENIX

She shook her head. 'No. Cassius calls him Marcus. They were so close as children. Sometimes Cassius calls him by his childhood nickname.'

Quintus held up his hand. He had that horrible sensation one has when jumping off a high cliff into deep water.

'Do you know the nickname?' He managed to keep his voice calm.

'Why, "Little Dog",' she said, looking surprised. 'Does it matter? I think they called him that because he was always eager to take part in their ball games as a youngster. Cassius recalls those childhood days so kindly, playing together in the streets of the Quirinal.'

Quintus sighed. He had been right all along, but it did not please him a jot to know that.

'I think I know who the foster brother is, Vibia. My brother Flavius and I, and Justin, we all knew the Labienus boys when we were lads. They played with us in the street where we grew up. Antoninus, Cassius — and the little one, Marcus.'

'Marcus?'

'Marcus Aurelius Epegathus. Now Prefect of the Annona. Minister of state, and very close to the emperor's councils.'

'Ah!' They sat in silence for a long moment. Then Vibia stirred, her slight movement causing the silver chain round her neck to flicker in the candle light.

'I said that the brothers are still close. That *was* true, till Cassius brought me back from Massilia with him. Marcus — Aurelius Epegathus — came to see us when he heard Cassius had returned. He had become a great man, awarded high office as you say. Cassius says his brother has plans which are wrapped up with the same plot you uncovered in Britannia.

'And then Marcus saw me wearing this.' Her hand wrapped itself tight around the silver fish. 'He seemed not to be surprised, though he knew it for what it is, a symbol of my undying faith.

'I thought at first Marcus just disapproved of me, of my background as a slave prostitute. But now I know that he has long hated Christians. He once told Cassius he considers Christians to be impious as we deny the old gods of Rome. During his service under the previous emperor, Elagabalus, he began to push for the persecution of my fellow-religionists. I don't know how he found out about me, but he has threatened Cassius. I told Cassius to give me up, to let me go into hiding somewhere, but he won't.'

Quintus's heart sank. Everything Vibia said confirmed that Marcus Aurelius Epegathus was determined to root out Christianity, even if it meant toppling the dynasty with its moderate views on religion. He understood that his sister was in terrible trouble. Dio's warning had not been about Mithraism at all. He, and possibly others at Ulpian's party, must have observed the carnelian phoenix and understood its significance.

Vibia nodded. She seemed calm, almost resigned. 'Yes, Marcus knows I am a Christian and has become my enemy. I heard him say to Cassius, "That girl must go! Set aside your feelings, and remember our bond, our mission. If you fail in this, brother, I cannot vouch for your own safety. We are a tight group of powerful men, right at the top, with a plan to restore Rome to her former greatness. You of all people know this. We have both lost a brother already — I will not hesitate to sacrifice my only living brother to save Rome, if I must.

"Rome is failing, Cassius, and do you know why? It's because we've gone soft on religion, soft on spreading

THE CARNELIAN PHOENIX

citizenship to the undeserving, soft on the values that once raised Rome above all other powers in the world. Noble men, in the ancient pattern of Brutus and your Republican namesake Cassius, are striving to end this regime of women and weak boys. We will bring back respect for Rome's old gods, and the ways of strong men, firm rules, true values. We will not stop, no matter the sacrifice, to do our duty to Rome and our forebears. You must do your part, too."

'Marcus left then, but he sent a message today asking about me, pretending concern that I was being safely escorted away from Rome and was provided for. But the look on his face, Quintus, when he saw me — it was implacable hatred. He will not stop till I am dead. I fear this house is being watched. As long as I live and remain Christian, I am a danger to Cassius."

Quintus turned to Tiro, thinking fast in his agitation.

'I already had my suspicions. Now, I'm sure that the ringleader of the plot against Ulpian is Aurelius Epegathus. I also believe that it's not just Ulpian in danger: Emperor Alexander could be his target too. We need to warn the Augusta and Ulpian, as soon as possible. Epegathus will stop at nothing short of regime change, I fear.'

He pressed Vibia's hand once more. 'Here, Vibia, take this.'

He tugged the carnelian signet ring off his little finger, and gave it to her. 'Use this as a secret signal. You must get away, go into hiding. There will be other Christians here in Rome. You may already know some. The young Emperor is sympathetic; they say he even has a shrine to the god Christos in his palace. Use what connections you can, and make yourself safe, even if you have to leave Cassius to his fate. Then send me word, with the ring.'

She shook her head, resolute. 'I will never leave him, not now. We are reconciled for better or worse. He repents his actions, repents his involvement with his brother's plots. I will persuade him to come with me, and start a new quiet life elsewhere.'

Quintus was troubled by this, and he wasn't alone. Tiro, who had kept silent so far, broke in.

'Let us help you, Vibia! I'm sure we can find you safe passage. Come to Britannia with us — your brother and I will make sure you are safe.'

Quintus watched, helpless, as Tiro exposed his heart to Vibia. She smiled, but he saw a tear crushed between her eyelids as she shook her head.

'Thank you, Tiro, I will never forget your kindness. But I can't leave Cassius.'

Quintus considered. He looked at his sister, feeling torn. The rebel he had fought at Corinium, the Cassius Labienus he considered his enemy, was here at his mercy. But this dear newly-discovered sister must not be hurt any more. How was he to reconcile these two urges?

He made up his mind, saying to Vibia. 'My dear, I understand you love Cassius, and trust him. I will trust you too in this. But if we are to get both of you to safety, you must do something for me first. I need hard evidence: names, timings, methods of this plot. Only Cassius can give me this information. Will you arrange a meeting for us with him, as soon as possible? Send the ring to me as token. Don't delay leaving home. Get away, hide with your Christian community if you can, and I will arrange safe passage for both of you once I've spoken to Cassius. Then, and only then. From what you have told me, it's clear that whatever Cassius knows is my best hope of convincing the chief minister and the Augusta to take the threat seriously. Will you do that, my brave little sister?'

THE CARNELIAN PHOENIX

She nodded, and came close to hug her brother. He held her very tight, feeling with all his heart the need to protect her, and fearing equally that the task was already beyond him.

They left quietly then, Quintus deeply troubled and Tiro unwontedly silent.

'Sir, surely we could take Vibia with us into safe custody right away? We could guard her in the Castra, and make sure she finds sanctuary somewhere safe.'

'No,' said Quintus steadily, though his heart felt like a lead lump as he condemned his young sister to more danger. 'No, we must find out what more Cassius Labienus knows. He has been at the centre of this insurrection all along; I can't believe he doesn't know who all the instigators are. Until I have those names, I cannot properly protect the emperor or his chief councillor, which I am sworn to do.'

The two men walked on in silence, each lost in private thought.

***

The guard at the Castra entrance gates saluted smartly.

'*Beneficiarius* Quintus Valerius! Letter arrived for you, sir, marked urgent.'

Quintus dismissed Tiro, stepping quickly over to the Castra offices where he was given two letters. Back in their quarters, he unwrapped the thread and broke the seal on the first, a letter from Britannia. It was dated less than two weeks earlier, and had clearly been despatched by the fastest possible post:

To Quintus Valerius, Senior Beneficiarius, at the Castra Peregrina, Rome.
Hail and greetings, brother,

JACQUIE ROGERS

I write in haste to inform you that Claudia, widow of Magistrate Marcus Aurelianus, is dead. I am sorry to have to tell you it was murder, dear brother, no doubt about it. Surgeon Piso of the hospital here has certified she died of loss of blood after her throat was cut. She was attacked in her own home, in Iscalis. I have had all the slaves there interviewed, but with no evidence forthcoming against any of them, I have taken no further action against the household. The culprit has not yet been apprehended.

Could you kindly inform Lady Julia Aureliana that suitable arrangements for obsequies are being made on behalf of Lady Aurelia, Domina Claudia's stepdaughter? The funeral will take place here at Bo Gwelt, as the widow's only living blood relative, her nephew Lucius, remains at large and missing. He is also posted as prime suspect in the case, given his past criminal record, and we have conducted searches for him in case he has returned to Britannia. No trace of him has been found.

One last item to report, and it is a strange one. Demetrios and Britta have kept in touch while you and Lady Julia have been away. Last week they came to see me, with a strange story to share. It appears the ghost of Lady Julia's brother, Magistrate Marcus Aurelianus, has been seen at Bo Gwelt. He seems to be haunting the deserted west wing; several of the servants have seen him. This seems impious and unexpected to me. I always understood that ghosts appeared only when they had not been correctly buried. So Pliny tells us, says Demetrios. I attended the funeral rites of Marcus myself, as you know, and would vouch nothing could have caused his ghost any distress.

Being cautious in view of the recent killing of Domina Claudia, I have made arrangements to safeguard Bo

THE CARNELIAN PHOENIX

Gwelt. Two of my best men are posted there to watch, and to accompany your daughter when she is abroad on business. She often spends time at Bawdrip, so I have alerted Decurion Agrippa Sorio of the sad events too.

I hope these interventions meet with your approval, Quintus.

Till your return to the Summer Country, I remain your friend and brother officer.

From Centurion Marcellus Crispus, Aquae Sulis cohort.

An addendum had been written by the secretary of the governor, who had clearly expedited the post to speed this news:

Quintus, I fear this further death may have links to the rebellion last spring, and possibly to your enquiries in Rome. I leave it to you to decide on suitable action. I will support you in whatever you decide. Perhaps Lady Julia should return, although she will miss the funeral.

Aradius Rufinus,
Governor of Britannia Superior

Quintus rubbed his forehead, thinking. What could this mean? The Claudii had certainly all been born under unlucky stars: Bulbo dead in the inferno at Bo Gwelt; his only son Lucius missing under suspicion of fraud, rebellion and murder; and now Claudia, Julia's sister-in-law, dead by an unknown attacker.

His own letter to the governor must have crossed this more urgent one, so he must decide alone what to do: to return to Britannia immediately; or stay here to safeguard Ulpian and try to stop what he feared — a long-planned uprising against the throne.

***

Tiro returned from the Castra bathhouse, tousled hair damp, looking all the happier for hot water and a relaxing scrape-down with a strigil. Quintus had opened his second letter, sent more recently from Burdigala on the Gaulish coast. He was re-reading the letter, near bursting with joy and fearful apprehension. Tiro halted in his tracks, whatever banal remarks he'd been about to make clearly swept away by one look at Quintus.

'Sir, you have news? Good news?'

Quintus crossed the room, and amazed even himself: he grabbed Tiro in a bearhug and lifted the surprised optio right off his feet. Tiro yelled in amazement, 'Sir! Let me down! What is it?'

Martinus came in as Quintus released Tiro and sat down heavily on his bunk, laughing and choking together.

'Wine, Martinus, and make it the best this dusty old fort can provide!'

Martinus backed out, looking amused, and could be heard collaring the catering slaves loudly.

'You've heard from Julia, haven't you? That must be it.' Tiro grinned hugely.

Quintus didn't notice the lack of honorific. He was so caught in sudden ecstasy, laced through with extreme anxiety. Not until Martinus had returned with two flagons of rough red wine and three beakers — 'Best I could do at short notice, sir!' — and Tiro had grabbed the wine and poured it out, splashing it down the sides of the beakers, did Quintus manage to calm down and speak.

'Yes, this letter is from Julia. And she's safe — better than safe — but up to her eyeballs in trouble, and heading into worse. Always the same, my dearest, darling girl!'

He read aloud:

THE CARNELIAN PHOENIX

My Quintus,

I seize the chance while docked in Burdigala to write to tell you what is in my heart.

But first, I have news pertaining to your investigation. The actress Fulminata took passage from here, Burdigala, to Britannia, some weeks ago. I had this from Lucius Claudius, who I found here, suffering terribly with illness in his psyche. I have him safe under my care. He is wandering in his mind, and much of what he says is senseless. He went on and on about a little dog; there were no small dogs on the quayside, I checked. But he also told me that Fulminata killed Gaius Trebonius at Lugdunum, and was then rejected by Cassius Labienus. A party of soldiers has freed Cassius and helped him to Rome, as you suspected.

Fulminata knows where the remaining Vebriacum silver is, and may have gone in search of it. Aurelia and all our people at Bo Gwelt are in danger from this woman, who we know will not scruple to kill anyone who stands in her way, or even witnesses her crimes. I fear for them, and am making all haste home.

I am safe with my friend, Fulvia Pompeia, shipowner of Massilia. I have voyaged with her aboard her flagship Athena, *as fast and safe a merchant vessel as one could wish for. We make sail tonight for Bol, on the south coast of my own country. Do not fear for me, my heart; I will take counsel with Centurion Crispus and Decurion Sorio in whatever I do.*

Quintus, I have thought so much about what I overheard you say to Vibia. I was rash to run away in Massilia, just as I did as a stupid young girl in Eboracum. I was ill and insecure; I have now recovered from my illness. But I should have stood my ground, confronted you. Fulvia, who has become a true friend to me, has told me how foolish I was to let pride drive me away from you for the second time. It may be that you do regret your former commitment to me, but I owe you the opportunity to tell me so, face to face.

It may also be that you will never read these words of mine. I fear you may be in great danger in Rome, and only the gods, and especially Minerva the wise and just, can decide your fate. I have prayed for you, and will continue to make offerings for your safety.

This last part is so hard to write: if you wish to marry Vibia, I will not stand in your way. I was foolish indeed to refuse your proposal of marriage in the garden at Bo Gwelt, and I bitterly regret that. But if your heart has changed, know that Aurelia will always be your daughter and, painful though it would be to see you with another love, I wish you all happiness and hope you will continue to visit and care about your daughter.

You carry my heart, always.
Julia Aureliana,
Burdigala, Aquitania

Chapter Seventeen

Rome, Castra Peregrina

Quintus threw the letter up towards the low ceiling, whooping and catching the scroll as it bounced back. Tiro looked delighted; Martinus taken aback.

'She's well, she's aboard ship nearing Britannia, she has Lucius Claudius in her charge. Oh, my foolish Julia!'

His joy lurched into sudden concern as he recalled the letter from Marcellus. He smacked his forehead. 'Ghost! By the Lord of Light, I know who the ghost at Bo Gwelt is. Julia's about to take on the most vicious murderer I have ever encountered. It's not just Lucius, I fear. And this time, Tiro —' he felt his stomach clench and his face harden '— this time, we won't be there to ride to her rescue.'

Tiro had no idea what Quintus was talking about, but it didn't matter. Clearly, what did matter was getting back to Britannia, sharpish. He jumped up and headed for the door. 'Martinus, where in this filthy city of yours do I go to arrange our travel home?'

Martinus looked doubtfully at Quintus, whose excitement had quickly leached away into cold apprehension. Quintus tried to put away the image of Julia sailing so blithely into danger. Well or ill, unless she had support of the armed and deadly kind, her life wouldn't be worth a damn against the dangerous

Fulminata. He thought of Ulpian, and the young Emperor Alexander.

'It's already too late,' he muttered.

'Too late for what, sir?'

'The Castra has its own public travel office, sir,' said Martinus, evidently confused.

Tiro gave a grunt of exasperation.

'He knows that!' he said sharply. Martinus looked hurt and subsided into silence, rubbing the back of his head gingerly.

Tiro stared hard at his boss, lowering his gaze after a few moments. He sat on his bunk, shuffling his boots across the tiled floor. There was an uncomfortable silence, eventually broken by Martinus.

'Will someone tell me what's going on? Please?'

Tiro glanced at Quintus, but the Governor's Man had his own eyes downcast, tight-lipped.

'He won't go back to Britannia, Martinus, that's what this means. Not yet. By all the gods, it's madness!' Tiro cut short what he might have gone on to say. Quintus knew this was quite an effort on Tiro's part, and his face softened.

'Tiro, we can't leave while our mission here is incomplete. No matter how much we want to look after our people back home. My sworn duty is to carry out the commands of Aradius Rufinus. Those were threefold: firstly, to observe and report back that justice had been served when Gaius Trebonius was executed. Well, the man is dead — there can be no further retribution by the living on that traitor. Pluto will ensure he suffers in Hades for what he's done.

'My second task was to warn Chief Minister Ulpian, and protect him as best I could from the plots we fear are woven round him. That task still engages me. My third

THE CARNELIAN PHOENIX

task was to assess the security and stability of the regime in Rome. I am in the process of doing that.

'The second and third tasks are bound together, and my responsibility extends to uncovering the murderers of the British escort and Centurion Felix Antonius. We have a prime suspect, someone we have reason to believe is the ringleader of the plots against the Emperor and his advisor, and behind the murders of our British friends. But I have not arrested him, having as yet insufficient evidence to do so as the law demands. Until Epegathus is in chains, and the throne and the Emperor's councillors are secure, I cannot leave Rome.'

Tiro kept his truculent attitude, scuffing his boots around. 'It can't be right, sir, to leave the family back home to fend for themselves with that bitch Fulminata on the prowl. Think about Britta, little Aurelia, and Morcant and all. Can you really leave Lady Julia to the mercy of the lunatic Lucius? What about that, I'd like to know?'

Quintus levelled a cool look at his *optio.*

'I can hardly swim out to the *Athena* in the midst of the Mare Cantabricum to help Julia. She knows what she's doing when it comes to helping sick people. I hate it too, but I must trust her judgement. And what about Vibia? Would you have me abandon her to her enemies, when she has ventured so much to help us?'

Tiro dropped his head, staring down at his busy boots.

'No, sir.' It was a mumble, but Quintus was satisfied.

'Right. Well, as you know Vibia's testimony supports my suspicions that Aurelius Epegathus is at the centre of a web of intrigue aimed at removing the Empress Mamaea, her son Emperor Alexander Severus, and their senior counsellor Ulpian. With those three gone, the state would be headless and ripe for insurrection. I have to take this to the Augusta herself. But I'll need Ulpian with me, to give my fears credibility. I'll ask him to arrange a private audience with the Empress. I think Senator Proculus Caecilius will be willing to act as go-between, so I'll meet him first. I fear we are running out of time... Martinus, what did you glean from your contacts last night?'

The centurion wrinkled his nose. 'Not as much as I hoped, sir. My usual sources have gone quiet; in fact some of my best street scum seem to have left town. I'll try to find out more from among the military, as you suggested. If we're looking at the Praetorian Guard for suspects, we may have to poke a stick in there.'

Quintus frowned. 'Be cautious where you poke your stick, Martinus. It's a deadly wasp's nest to stir up if their plans are ripening, as I fear they are. Still, we must get what we can, and as quickly as possible if I'm to persuade the chief minister and the Empress. I'd especially like intelligence regarding Cassius Labienus, his foster brother and all his contacts. Off you go.'

Martinus saluted and left. His steps seemed clumsy, weaving a less than straight line.

Quintus looked enquiringly at Tiro. 'Did he get any other injuries last night?'

'Only the head, sir. What's for me to do, Gov?'

'I want you back out on the streets, under cover and keeping a sharp eye out. Watch two places in particular: Mother's house on the Quirinal, and the Labienus house. Make no contact with Vibia this time; just see who comes and goes. She mustn't know you're there. I'll get you some support from Licinius Pomponius, a couple of men so you can cover both sites. Report back to me here at sunset.'

Quintus saw Tiro open his mouth to ask questions and protest at not meeting Vibia. Quintus gave him a cool

THE CARNELIAN PHOENIX

look; the optio coloured in a give-away blush, saluted and left quickly.

Quintus smiled to himself, but it was not a happy smile.

***

Senator Proculus Caecilius bustled out of the little amber-coloured Senate House, his face lighting up when he spotted Quintus waiting for him. He said a quick farewell to the gaggle of senators with him, and hurried over.

'Dear boy, again a pleasure!'

'Senator, I need your counsel.'

'Proculus, please. No formalities. Your father was my oldest friend, and I feel as if you are my son. Come, walk with me, and tell me how I can help you.'

'Thank you, sir.'

They crossed the noisy crowded forum towards the Via Sacra. An earnest man in a shabby toga was addressing a desultory crowd as they passed in front of the rostra, his voice hardly to be heard above the rude ripostes of his audience. An egg soared over their heads, smashing accurately at the speaker's feet and splashing yellow up his toga.

Caecilius twitched a smile, as he ducked and hurried on. 'Poor man. I fear the plebs are little interested in his efforts to promote the worship of the old gods. Rome is a more open society under our young Emperor Alexander Severus, but not all hold with his tolerance.'

As they headed east, the senator glanced at Quintus's hand. 'All the same, I'm glad to see you have put away your ring. Very wise.'

Quintus said nothing. Even to Proculus Caecilius, he thought it best not to mention Vibia or his father's conversion to Christianity. The pair halted once they had reached the shady trees opposite the house of the Vestal

Virgins. Proculus lowered himself onto a marble bench, and breathed out.

'To stretch the legs after a long Senate session is wise; to rest the feet once the havoc of the forum is left behind even wiser.'

Quintus nodded, rubbing his leg absently.

'Proculus, I thank you for your support, and the long friendship you showed my unfortunate father. I have never forgotten how you tried to warn him during the proscriptions of Caracalla. We are again in difficult times, and I need your advice and help. Chief Minister Ulpian is under real threat. My investigations suggest that the source of the threat, who I cannot yet name with confidence, is powerful and well-connected. I don't have enough concrete evidence to bring a charge, but I need to warn the Augusta, as she and her son, our Emperor, are also in danger. As you know, being a mere soldier and from a far province these days, I don't have the connections to access the Augusta. But I believe you do. Could you arrange an audience for me?'

The little senator turned his round bright eyes on Quintus, nodding. 'I think I can do that for you. But the Empress is a proud, brilliant woman, convinced of her son's destiny and her own control over the court and the army. She has achieved many ambitions, and now Alexander Severus is nearing full age, her confidence is unshakeable. I may be able to get you an audience, but I cannot guarantee she will take heed.'

Quintus nodded in understanding. 'I can ask no more. Thank you, sir.'

***

Back at the Castra, Martinus was waiting for Quintus. He looked pale.

'I've news, sir. But Licinius Pomponius has asked to hear my report with you, if you don't mind us joining him in the headquarters building?'

He turned to lead Quintus into the courtyard, and suddenly groaned, collapsing against the wall of the colonnade. Quintus dived in to support him, as Martinus leaned over to vomit.

He looked dazed. 'Sorry, sir, feeling a bit dizzy,' he slurred.

'Straight to the *medicus,* my man. No nonsense, now.' Quintus put his arm around Martinus, supporting the white-faced man as they made their way across the central courtyard of the Castra to the hospital. They staggered into the arms of the head surgeon just as Martinus collapsed into unconsciousness. They lowered him onto the floor.

The surgeon stripped off the bandage round Martinus's head, and frowned.

'It's only a graze. When and how did this happen?'

'I wasn't with him, but my *optio* Tiro was. He said Martinus smashed the back of his head against a wall in a fight. He seemed all right at the time, just the scratch, but he's been complaining of a persistent headache, feeling dizzy, and been sick at least once.'

'Concussion,' decided the surgeon, after looking carefully into the unconscious man's ears. 'No blood or clear fluid there, good. But we must let him rest. When he comes round, if I judge him fit, you may come back to visit. Here, orderly!'

Quintus swore under his breath as two medical orderlies came running, helping the surgeon carry the unconscious centurion into the hospital ward.

***

Licinius Pomponius also swore, loudly.

'By all the Furies! Martinus is one of my best and most loyal investigators; I need him active and alert right now. The worst of it is, I don't know who his sources are, or what he's discovered.'

He raised his hands helplessly. 'I'm sorry, Quintus. The best I can do is send a clerk to sit by Martinus and note down anything he says, and call you when he wakes. We'll have to do without his intelligence for the moment.'

By the time Tiro returned after sunset, Quintus was seething with frustration. He felt completely hamstrung, obliged to wait as calmly as he could for the summons to the palace, unable to put out of his mind the bad luck of the delay in receiving Martinus' intelligence. He was striding round the courtyard looking like thunder when Tiro appeared, coming from the hospital.

'Tell me you at least have discovered something useful, Tiro!'

Tiro looked worried. He was fond of Martinus.

'Martinus is unconscious still, but the surgeon thinks he'll improve soon. He's been bled to remove the evil humours, and they gave him something to make him sleep normally, some sort of weed the *medicus* burned under his nostrils — Lady Julia would know. And I'm sure she would approve of the hospital. Not a speck of dust or dirt in there, and plenty of fresh air and light. Hopefully the slave sitting by Martinus will hear something from him when he wakes.

'Apart from that, I have debriefed the pair I sent to your mother's house. I watched outside the Labienus mansion myself, and have nothing to report. Apart from a delivery by a fishmonger's boy, who has offered to help, no one came or went all day. I've paid the boy, Appius, to watch the house with his street-rat friends and report if they see or hear anything.'

'Did you see anything of Vibia?'

'No, sir.' But Tiro squirmed, a sure sign he was covering something. Quintus waited, letting his expression do the talking. 'Turns out the fishmonger's boy is sweet on Vibia's maid. I, err, I gave him a note to pass on, saying she could relay messages through the pair.'

Quintus closed his eyes briefly. It was all too possible that note would be intercepted, and cause even more trouble for Vibia.

'It's all I could do for her, sir.' The pain and pleading were so transparent; Quintus didn't have the heart to chastise him. Then he thought again.

'Without Martinus' spy network, we're in a corner here, Tiro. You might be on to something with your street-rats. Make sure they know where and what to report, and pay them with something they want.'

Tiro was still squirming. Quintus sighed.

'What *did* you promise them? The governor's purse isn't bottomless.'

'Oh no, boss. They don't want money. They want your hasta.'

'What!'

'I mean — just a hold of it, for a moment when the job's over. There's four or five of the little toe-rags, all mates of Appius. Invisible street boys. They could spread out across the city, loiter a bit, bring us all the street talk. We need this help, with Martinus out for the count. Dead keen to help a real *beneficiarius consularis,* they are.' His face was pleading; suddenly Quintus saw a younger Tiro, a street-rat himself, before he joined the army and found his sponsor Felix Antonius.

'All right. What about the men posted at my mother's? What did they report?'

'Your mother went out late in the morning, in a litter with closed drapes. Her face was veiled, but they heard Silenus address her. She returned a few hours later accompanied by — get this, Gov — a set of bodyguards. They went inside the house with her, and didn't come out again. No ordinary slaves, these. Big boys in clean white togas. Everyone in the street moved aside for them, no question.'

'Any identifying marks? I assume they weren't magistrate's lictors?'

'No, sir. The men reported no fasces, no axes. There was one thing, though: one of them, the leader, brushed right past our man who saw a ring on his hand, a bit unusual for the city he thought. He says he saw it clearly: a bronze ring with the engraving of a full-fleeced ram. But what could that mean?'

Quintus puzzled over it, wondering whether the men were some servants Justin had left with Hortensia. Justin and Lucilla farmed sheep for wool on their estate in Etruria. But why would he keep attendants in Rome, at considerable expense, when he wasn't here himself? And a ram with a heavy fleece had never been the motto of the Valerii, or of the Petrius family.

***

Proculus Caecilius was as good as his word. The summons by the Augusta came within the hour. She would receive the *beneficiarius consularis* from Britannia, and his aide, for a brief audience at sunset. Licinius Pomponius brought the summons himself.

'It appears the Augusta does not invite her commandant of spies to provide escort for the honoured British *beneficiarius*. However, I find myself at a loose end on

THE CARNELIAN PHOENIX

this warm evening and in need of a short off-duty stroll. In the unavoidable absence of Martinus Lucretius, I'll come with you as far as the public entrance to the palace.'

He gave a dry smile, and Quintus felt all the better for knowing his trusted commandant would accompany them partway. The tight sensation between his shoulder blades that seemed to have taken up permanent residence eased a little.

Tiro and Quintus readied themselves for their imperial hosts. Tiro fetched out his cleanest tunic, and rubbed his distinguished conduct *phalera* to a blinding polish. Quintus paced up and down their small barrack room, going over again in his mind the words he would use to persuade the Augusta of the serious threats to the throne. As the sun began to drop behind the low Palatine Hill, they inspected each other for neatness and military propriety. Quintus nodded.

'Britain's finest, Tiro. The Empress will be impressed.'
Tiro looked alarmed.

'I'm not expected to go into the audience room, am I? I mean, we're not in Londinium. I'll just fuck up, not knowing how to behave, or what to say.'

'No one will expect you to say anything. Although the Emperor might want to hear your curious accent.' Tiro looked even more alarmed. 'Just teasing! Keep behind me, do as you're told, you'll be invisible.'

The two soldiers gave their sandals a final rub, and headed out with Commandant Pomponius into the hot, still evening.

Chapter Eighteen

Bol, Britannia
The Athena scudded into an immense bay, all her sails aloft and billowing. The god Auster had blessed them with steady southerly winds since they had lifted anchor at Burdigala, much to the satisfaction of *Athena's* master. Artemidorus called to his mistress from the foredeck, looking smug.

'Britannia, dear heart! I told you sacrificing the black cockerel in Burdigala would do the trick.'

Fulvia smiled, gold tooth glinting, and waved back at her commanding lover. She whispered to Julia, 'That man! If the gods ever do listen to him, we'll be in real trouble. Still, he knows his way about on board a ship. And aboard a woman.' She closed one eye in a lascivious wink, and Julia looked away, laughing.

The crew sprang into action, responding to the captain's quick orders as they sailed past a sand bar at the harbour mouth, threading a path between low-lying mudflat islands. It was the biggest harbour Julia had ever seen, bordered by tidal flats and the estuaries of four rivers. The *Athena* made her way to the east of the Hamworthy peninsula, and then Julia knew where she was: the busy commercial and industrial port of Bol. This was where the famous black burnished pottery of the Durotriges was traded from vast jetties stretching out into the deepwater channel. Even the biggest cargo ships of Greece and

THE CARNELIAN PHOENIX

Rome had been coming into dock here for centuries. As they approached their assigned wharf and the crew fastened the hawsers sent uncoiling onto the deck by the British dockers, Julia looked around her with happy familiarity. The ancient round barrows on the low green hills, the raucous white gulls, the smell from the large pottery kilns, the bustle and noise of her own people in her own tongue, misted her eyes. She had been to Bol before, but never coming in by the sea. She was bursting to disembark, to be back on dry land, to be back home.

'Is it always this cold?'

Fulvia was cocooned in a large mantle that wrapped around her silk skirts and dropped to her feet. Julia smiled at her.

'Fulvia, how much is your heart set on being the first merchant to renew the tin trade in Kernow?'

Fulvia nodded. 'I'll have to get used to it. And maybe get some thicker clothes made, too.'

'Buy yourself a good British *birrus,* with a deep hood. You'll be fine. And now, I must get that lad ready to take home.'

Julia looked about for Lucius. He had emerged from the cabin at increasingly frequent intervals over the past week or two, as one of the kinder-hearted of the crew had taken pity on him. Julia had just spotted the curly-headed young man, talking hesitantly to the fatherly sailor, when she was hailed from the shore.

'Lady Julia! Lady Julia Aureliana!'

It was a familiar and most welcome voice. Julia steered Fulvia by the elbow to the gangplank being lowered to the wharf, before rushing down to the dock as fast as she could. She arrived at the bottom out of breath and mainly upright, and hurled herself into the surprised arms of a young centurion in polished army uniform, auburn hair gleaming in the summer sun.

'Marcellus! How did you know — what are you doing here?'

'My lady! I've had a man on watch for you here ever since Quintus Valerius wrote that you were heading home aboard a Massilian merchantman. I wanted to be here to meet you myself. There is much to tell you.'

'Quintus wrote to you? About me?' Her voice wobbled, and she felt herself losing balance again. Fulvia, who had disembarked more sedately, put out a discreetly supportive arm. Julia wavered a smile at her.

'Fulvia, this is my friend Centurion Marcellus Crispus, commander of the Aquae Sulis station, and close colleague of my… of *Beneficiarius* Consularis Quintus Valerius, of whom I have spoken.'

Marcellus did not need to know of the breach with Quintus. This upright young officer was deputy to Quintus and officer-in-charge at the Aquae Sulis station. He was a worthy officer, his honour and intelligence as bright as his hair. After the near-coup foiled at Corinium by Quintus and his allies, Marcellus had been promoted by the grateful new Governor Rufinus to command the special security service in the southwest of Britannia. It was a senior post for one so young, and Julia knew he fully deserved the responsibility.

Fulvia caught on immediately, with another more subtle wink for Julia's benefit.

'Delighted to meet you, Centurion. I am Fulvia Pompeia, owner of the merchant ship *Athena*. This is my captain,' she added, waving at the muscular mariner approaching, 'Artemidorus. It has been our pleasure to bring Lady Julia home. She has been wonderful company

THE CARNELIAN PHOENIX

for me on the voyage, and very useful in caring for our other passenger.'

Marcellus, looking overcome at the sight of this gaudy, richly-dressed lady with the highly-painted face and jangling gold bangles, knitted his brow. His hand strayed to the pommel of his *spatha*. Lucius Claudius weaved an uncertain path down the gangplank, carefully watching his steps all the way down to the dock.

'Julia? Isn't this Lucius Claudius? Stand aside: I should arrest him immediately.'

'No, Marcellus. Let me explain,' she broke in. 'But first, Fulvia and Artemidorus need a pilot, a local who can advise them how best to reach the tin ports of Kernow. Or someone who can advise appropriate road routes, if it wouldn't be safe to take *Athena* along that coast.'

Distracted by this, Marcellus willingly took Arti to meet the Bol harbourmaster. The tanned mariner flashed his trademark smile at Julia as he walked away with the tall young officer.

Fulvia turned to her friend. 'Will it be all right, Julia? Will you be all right — here, I mean?'

Julia hugged the Massiliote.

'Fulvia, you've been a real friend to me when I needed one. I will be fine, more than fine, with Marcellus to escort me to Bo Gwelt. Thank you for everything. Shall I see you again before you return to Massilia? What are your plans?'

'I hope to come back to Bol before we head home. If my negotiations go well, we may return regularly, Arti and I. And then…who knows, my dear? The world is wide, and adventures beckon. There's new trade to be had, richer even than British tin. I hear there is a country in the far east known as Annam, where the silk we Romans treasure is actually made. Imagine the profits to be had if one could bypass the middlemen in India, and the long Silk Road!'

Her eyes, which had adopted a faraway look, came back into focus sharp as a tack. 'But you, my dearest Julia, I was not asking about the road to your home. Don't try to avoid the question! What are you going to do about your own future? Will it be with the Governor's Man?'

Julia was used to Fulvia's direct ways, and had been thinking of little else anyway. But throughout the long voyage aboard the beautiful ship *Athena*, there had seemed no rush to decide what she wanted. The future had felt distant and dreamlike. But now, with the green hills and grey seas of Britannia around her and the chalky white road to the Summer Country ahead, that distant future had caught her up. She held Fulvia out at arm's length for a long moment before pulling the dark-eyed woman back into a tight hug.

'Julia, you're crushing my silks!' warned her friend, gasping with quick laughter. Julia blinked before replying.

'Quintus wrote to Marcellus from Rome. He is still concerned about me, and so Marcellus came here himself to escort me home. Quintus still cares, Fulvia. I think that makes my mind up for me, don't you? It all depends on whether he comes back just with Tiro, or —'

'Oh ho, my pretty, be in no doubt! I, Fulvia Pompeia, daughter of power, widow of wealth, lover of adventure, I tell you — that man will come back to you. Alone. Before you weep any more tears all over these precious silks of mine, I must insist you depart. Go home, Julia, back to your daughter and your people. Be safe and happy, and be sure we will see each other again when the gods allow it.'

THE CARNELIAN PHOENIX

Fulvia pushed Julia away, as Marcellus returned with Artemidorus. The sea captain smiled in farewell. Marcellus gave the Massilian couple a respectful salute. Julia thought she saw Fulvia wipe a speck from her own eye, but she must have been wrong, for Fulvia turned quickly, grabbing her captain by the hand and holding up her gauzy robes around her plump knees as she ran nimbly up the gangplank. Julia heard her call out to the crew, busy loading provisions and freshwater barrels, 'We're on our way to fame and fortune, my lads! Westward ho!'

***

Marcellus had thoughtfully brought Julia's own white mare from Bo Gwelt, together with a spare mount for Lucius. They left Bol the next morning, and Julia quickly settled back into the familiar routine of travel in Britannia. It was a fine, bright late summer's day, with just a hint of the mellow season about to follow. Marcellus clearly had things on his mind, and cleared his throat several times. Nevertheless he seemed uncomfortable, and unwilling to begin his tale. She let a companionable silence develop between them for several miles, before gently inviting him to begin.

'Tell me all the news of home, Marcellus.'

He shook his head at Lucius, and she realised she would have to be patient a little longer. At midday, they stopped at a small roadside inn between Durnovaria and Lindinis to eat. Lucius was much easier in his mind, but twice she had to ask him to water the horses before he seemed awake to her request. He responded with a shy acquiescence, leading the three horses round to the stables behind the taverna. Julia seized the chance as she settled at a rough wooden table to eat with Marcellus.

'Well, Marcellus, what has happened?'

'Prepare to be shocked, my lady,' the young officer, said solemnly. Julia suppressed a smile; she had forgotten how staid Marcellus could be for such a young man. The cares of office hung heavy on him still. She straightened her face, and waited.

Marcellus drew breath and explained that there had been a murder, in Iscalis.

'Iscalis! Surely not!'

'Indeed. Of one of our most revered citizens, and someone close to you.'

Julia stilled at this, wondering who she knew in Iscalis who could possibly count as being close to her. Little Enica, once kitchen slave in the showy Iscalis villa of Claudius Bulbo, was a safe freedwoman at Bo Gwelt, happy mistress of the kitchens there. The only other person Julia knew in the little mining town of Iscalis was

—

'Domina Claudia, your sister-in-law. I'm sorry to bring you this tragic news, Lady Julia.'

Julia composed her face into something that would pass for shock and sorrow. In truth, she *was* actually shocked. Who could possibly bear animus against the widow of her dead brother Marcus?

'She was found by her slaves, about three weeks ago. It was… quite nasty, and she must have died quickly.'

Julia shrugged an impatient shoulder. 'I'm a healer, Marcellus, and I've seen considerable violence. You can tell me the gory details.'

'Her throat was cut, Julia. There was nothing anyone could have done to help her, even you. Her dresser told me she went to bed as normal the night before, but in the morning she found her mistress lying dead, err, in a pool of her own blood.' Marcellus had a disgusted look on his face, as if this particular way of death was inappropriate for a noted lady; once more Julia had to hold her face still, and remind herself how good an officer this young man was.

'Any clues?'

She blushed, as she realised she sounded like Quintus. Marcellus seemed not to notice.

'No. It was assumed that the killer was her nephew Lucius Claudius, of course. Now I know otherwise, and will have to set fresh enquiries in train.'

'Why suspect Lucius at all?'

'Because he had previously been in league with Claudia to hide the missing Vebriacum silver at Bo Gwelt, and because he was a known criminal still at large. The examining magistrate assumed the motive was to steal what was left of the purloined silver, perhaps removing it and taking it to the Claudius villa in Iscalis.'

'The examining magistrate?'

'Err …Decurion Agrippa Sorio. When your brother Marcus died, he was co-opted as new head by the town council. You may remember?'

Julia pondered. She had forgotten that her neighbour and friend, Agrippa Sorio, had felt it his duty to stand in Marcus's place when her brother had been killed. Julia had a great regard for Sorio's loyalty and valued his generous heart. She had even left the oversight of her own estate, Bo Gwelt, in his hands while she was away. But he was not the learned, thoughtful man Marcus had been, and had a tendency to leap to conclusions. Clearly that had happened here, and the worst of it was that the real culprit, whoever that was, had weeks to cover any tracks and disappear. She furrowed her brow.

'Not much we can do about that now, I suppose. I wish Quintus was at home, he would know how to pick up the case.'

Marcellus coloured, and she added hastily, 'He will of course be grateful that you were here as his deputy during such difficult times.' She added, seeing he looked mollified but still worried, 'Has anything else of concern happened?'

His blush deepened. *Good grief, what?* she wondered, giving him time to gather himself. The silence dragged on until she lost patience.

'You seem upset, Marcellus. Do tell me, I may be able to help.'

'It's just — well, it seems both tragic and silly, my lady. It's …Lady Aurelia saw …actually Drusus Sorio was with her, and then the servants found out and said they wouldn't stay in such a house, I don't mean Britta or Morcant or Demetrios of course, but all the same —'

'Get to the point!' Julia found herself almost shrieking. She was immediately mortified, and begged his pardon, saying, 'I'm so sorry, Marcellus, forgive me. I'm just concerned, of course.' He looked sheepishly down at the taverna table, but then seemed to recall he was a Roman officer with the full confidence of Governor Rufinus himself. He looked up and spoke in a steadier voice.

'Lady Julia, the ghost of your dead brother, Magistrate Marcus Aurelianus, is haunting Bo Gwelt.'

Chapter Nineteen

Rome, the Imperial Palace

The route from the Castra Peregrina to the Palatine was a short one, but with steep enough paths to ensure that Tiro was sweating and red-faced long before they reached the entrance to the palace. Licinius Pomponius waved them farewell outside the walls of the vast complex. They were to be received in the imperial audience hall, but had agreed to meet Senator Caecilius first, in the remarkable gardens built by Emperor Septimius Severus. This was a welcoming outdoor space of shady niches, trickles of cool water, playful fountains, and everywhere, wonderful statues. They found the little senator seated on a marble bench, admiring the exotic fish housed in Septimius Severus's lovely ponds and basins. Caecilius frowned when he saw the *optio*. Tiro's face was gleaming with runnels of perspiration and the underarms of his best tunic already sweat-stained.

Quintus shrugged. 'He's British, Proculus. You'd understand if you'd ever been cursed with spending a winter in that northern isle. Or a summer, come to that.'

Proculus tutted, clearly about to protest, when a small shadow detached itself from the deeper shades of a niche and silently approached.

'*Caratacus*,' the shadow challenged, in a boy's whisper.

Tiro responded with '*Boudica*'. A scrawny youngster, doubtless from the slums of the Subura, emerged into the paler dusk. He grinned, revealing gaps where teeth were missing. Proculus Caecilius looked startled; Quintus merely accepting.

'One of Tiro's street- rats. Rats being a field of expertise for our Londoner,' he said by way of explanation.

Tiro beamed. 'Catch on quick, them boys. Much like the lads I mixed with, growing up.' He went into a huddle with the boy, who looked rattled at seeing the venerable senator with his purple-edged toga. The conversation was soon over, and the boy disappeared as suddenly as he had arrived. Quintus was relieved the boy hadn't asked Tiro for a hold of his staff of office, the famous ceremonial *hasta;* the urchin's hands were grimy in the extreme. That promised reward could wait.

Tiro was looking less happy.

'Sir, the boys watching the Labienus house report that both parties concerned have left.' Quintus noted he spoke circumspectly in front of the senator, trusted old friend or not. It didn't hurt to keep a sharp eye out, Quintus thought, with the weight of years of subterfuge and detection heaped on his own shoulders. But all the same, Proculus Caecilius was an ally in this dangerous city.

'I see. And…?'

'It's not known where they went. No body- slaves, no litter for the lady, no horses, no luggage. One of my boys followed, but lost them. Permission to pick up the hunt, sir?'

Quintus cocked an eyebrow at the senator.

'Proculus? Are there more sharks circling, this time around my half-sister?'

Proculus looked startled.

THE CARNELIAN PHOENIX

'Surely you knew about her, being my father's oldest and closest friend?'

Proculus gave one of his body-length quivering sighs.

'Yes, he did confide in me. At least, he told me he had fallen in love with a Christian lady, and they had a child he was determined to keep safe. We…well, after that there were no more opportunities to exchange confidences.' Profound sorrow crossed the wizened little face; Quintus hadn't the heart to ask more.

He decided. 'Right. Tiro, gather your gutter brats, send them out looking for Vibia.' Tiro's moods were always transparent. His face showed a switch from anxiety to eagerness. 'But, Tiro —'

'Sir?'

'I want that man alive too. We might turn him. There's a chance Cassius Labienus could be the key to unlocking this whole business.'

Tiro looked doubtful; Proculus glanced away.

'A chance worth taking. Off you go.'

Tiro and he were out of time, both of them. The Emperor was waiting. More importantly, so was the Augusta.

***

Quintus and Senator Caecilius were challenged, checked and searched by a tiresome number of Praetorians before being allowed to enter the grand reception halls of the old Domitian palace. Knowing what he did about the Praetorians, Quintus found it hard to keep his temper in check with the guards. He did manage it, though, for the sake of his Emperor and for Ulpian. And most of all for Ulpian's cousin. The pale delicate face of Governor Aradius Rufinus was foremost in his mind; Quintus knew why he'd come here, to the Palatine.

He was attempting to save the empire again; this time for his governor and the future of his own province. It did not occur to him to question his changed loyalties. Later he thought perhaps this was the moment he had ceased to be wholly Roman, and given part of his heart to Britannia. It was the island home of the women he loved, Aurelia and Julia. It was his country, too. As he stalked through the marble and gilt magnificence of the palace built by the young Emperor's famous forebears, he dwelt on the foggy meres and low hills of the Summer Country, the raucous streets and broad, brown river of Londinium, the slow-speaking farmers and woollen-clad tavern keepers of Britannia.

Only let me come home safe to Bo Gwelt, he prayed to the Lord of Light, *let me wake with Julia sleeping next to me, let me watch Aurelia racing her horse with Cerberus splashing mud by her side. I beg you, Lord Mithras.*

***

There were four people awaiting them in the audience chamber.

The Augusta Julia Mamaea, of course--tall, serene, intellectual. A princess in her own right, descendant of an illustrious line of eastern princesses who had dominated the rule of the empire since Septimius Severus of Africa had married Julia Domna of Syria. She stood straight and elegant beside the throne, on which sat her only son, Emperor Alexander Severus. He wore a plain white toga — not just, Quintus thought, because he was as yet too young to don the imperial purple toga with its gilt edging. This boy had a mild expression, a clear soft eye, and a gentle face. He wore white because he wanted to, Quintus judged. What would the army make of this young lad, so different from his warlike, and often corrupt, predecessors?

THE CARNELIAN PHOENIX

As Quintus saluted his Emperor, and Senator Caecilius made his own obeisance, the Augusta spoke.

'Alexianus, this is *Beneficiarius* Quintus Valerius, valued servant of the Governor Aradius Rufinus of Britannia Superior, who is cousin to our beloved Ulpian.'

The Augusta more than made up for her son's simple tastes. She was loaded with gold. Her silk robe was encrusted with gold florets; she wore a wide gold necklet with a round diamond clasped in the centre, and both her arms were swathed in gold armlets. Another diamond hung from a tiara that held her carefully-arranged dark curls under control. Everything about Mamaea was controlled. Her smile was smooth, her voice cultured, clear — and cold as an Alpine glacier. This was not a woman to cross.

As she spoke, a third person advanced to greet them. Ulpian took Quintus by the hand with a warm smile, and brought him to the foot of the throne.

Alexianus, known as Alexander since ascending the imperial throne, stood. He smiled shyly. 'You are welcome to Rome, *Beneficiarius,* and to our home.' He held out his hand. Quintus dropped to one knee, bowing his head, and took the soft warm hand in his. Afterwards he wondered if he had been prescient. As he held that smooth unformed hand in his, he felt a faint sense of sadness and loss. This boy had lost his father far too young, and then his wise and beloved grandmother, Julia Maesa, only a few months ago. Still, he had Ulpian, who was clearly a kind of father figure to him. Quintus looked up to see that the boy was indeed smiling at the commanding bearded man standing before him, no longer looking at Quintus.

The fourth figure didn't become apparent to Quintus till he'd been granted gracious imperial permission to stand.

The other man must have been positioned very close behind the tall-backed throne to escape his notice till then. Ulpian held out a beckoning arm to welcome his close colleague and supporter.

'Come, Paul, renew your acquaintance with Quintus Valerius. I believe you knew his father, during your service to Emperors Septimius Severus and Caracalla?'

'Indeed I did. Senator Bassianus Valerius was a great loss to our city, and to the empire.'

The voice was measured, while conveying warmth. The eyes, too, were measured. Quintus might have noted a hint of humour behind them, had he not been suddenly distracted. Paul's voice was smooth, educated, cultivated: Roman. His slight accent, though, was not of the city This man was from the same region as his own mother, and a similar age. Quintus was minded to enquire whether Paul knew Hortensia, but he held back. Not the time nor place for personal pleasantries.

The Emperor broke in, asking the *beneficiarius* to tell him all about the provinces of Britannia. He was clearly interested, the slight smile on his young mobile face encouraging Quintus. But the Governor's Man was aware that the urgent message he had come to deliver was being side-tracked by protocol.

At length, the Empress cut the conversation short, reminding her son he had other duties. He sighed, and summoning his secretaries and clerks, inclined his head politely to Quintus and Senator Caecilius before leaving the chamber.

The mask of amiability dropped from Mamaea's face like a stone. She seated herself in a wooden armchair inlaid with ivory images of Syrian serpents with gemstone eyes, wrapped round palm trees. She crooked

THE CARNELIAN PHOENIX

an imperious finger at her two counsellors, who approached to flank her.

'Well, *Beneficiarius*? What is the urgent message from our British Governor?'

A familiar heart-sinking sensation assailed Quintus. Aware that he sounded stiff and unpersuasive despite his best intentions, he told the Empress of Governor Rufinus's fears for the Severan regime, of the recent crushed insurrection in Britannia, of the murderous attack on Gaius Trebonius in Lugdunum.

'None of this is news,' she snapped. 'Apart from the suggested involvement of my son's bodyguard in the death of ex-governor Trebonius. And even if that were true, it simply pre-empted what would have been a more painful and protracted death for that traitor once convicted in Rome. Ulpian? You are the Praetorian Prefect. What think you of your cousin's fanciful concerns?' She turned to her senior advisor.

Ulpian frowned a little, looking at Quintus thoughtfully. He paused for a moment while he stroked his luxuriant beard.

'Since my appointment as head of your imperial council, and with your blessing, Augusta, I have been taking steps to create a more just society, using the law. You and I, dear lady, cherish justice, separating the equitable from the inequitable. That has led us to take firm measures, like removing those advanced to positions of power without justification, or who were promoted for their notoriety in crimes during the previous reign. Thus we have begun to undo the excesses of the Praetorian Guard, returning them to their proper role of safeguarding the imperial family, with the loyalty demanded by the great Septimius Severus.'

Quintus took this to be a rehearsed justification for the culling of the previous joint Praetorian Prefects, Flavianus and Chrestus; and indeed he had no issue with this draconian action. The former Prefects were notorious for their corruption, and Rome and the empire were undoubtedly better off without them. That did not mean all the Praetorian cohorts agreed with Ulpian's lofty aims.

Quintus tried again.

'Augusta, I have intelligence that the Prefect of the Annona, who was known to be close to both Flavianus and Chrestus, may also pose a threat to the Praetorian Prefect.' Ulpian cast him a warning look; the Empress rebuffed him.

'Nonsense! Aurelius Epegathus is the son of a talented and trusted freedman who served the Emperor Caracalla with distinction. His army connections are considered a great asset to my son's rule. I fear our time here is up.' She stood, a sign of dismissal.

Quintus stepped backwards as the full force of the Empress's comments struck him. The Achilles heel of Alexander Severus was his youth, combining a lack of martial zeal, and submission to his much stronger mother. Caracalla, despite his despotic and cruel reign, had been admired and defended by the armed forces whose interests he had assiduously courted. Until he was assassinated by them. The mother of the Emperor had just announced in so many words that she would do nothing to endanger the relationship between the Praetorians and her son. Too much was at stake for her to attack or remove Epegathus.

Quintus bowed to the inevitable. The Empress swept out, attended by her bodyguard and personal slaves.

But his head lifted as soon as she had gone.

THE CARNELIAN PHOENIX

'Sir!' he said to Ulpian. 'If the Augusta can't or won't act, I beg that you take every precaution you can to protect yourself. Could you perhaps remove at some distance from the court, at least for a while? Come with me to Britannia, where your cousin would be delighted and honoured to receive you.'

Even as he urged this on Ulpian, Quintus knew it was no good. The older man shook his head gently, a softer look in his eyes. 'You don't understand, *Beneficiarius*. My role here is to prepare our Emperor as best I can for his developing role. He will soon enter his majority, and if he is to rule in the just and enlightened way I know he wishes, he needs my advice and support. Alexander calls me his father. I have a duty to my son in heart, and to the city and empire he rules. I cannot slink away into the provinces, no matter what threats to me.'

Ulpian continued to hold Quintus's gaze, silent for a while. Then he sighed.

'The real danger to Alexander, I believe, is external rather than within Rome. He is much loved by the people, you know. No, my true concern for Alexander is the enemy rising in the east, Artaxerxes the Sassanid. He has just defeated the Parthian king, and is uniting the great peoples of the east against Rome. One day, I very much fear, Alexander will have to fight a major war to keep our eastern provinces. On that day he will need the full-hearted loyalty of every Roman soldier, and that includes the Praetorians. The Augusta is right. We must keep the army and all its friends happy, no matter the cost to any individual.'

Paul entered the conversation then. Quintus had forgotten the councillor was still there. As he spoke, his Patavian accent struck Quintus afresh.

'You must forgive our Praetorian Prefect, Quintus Valerius. He may seem reckless to refuse your excellent advice; but I reiterate what he says. The loyalty of the army to our young Emperor is paramount for the dynasty's future. And the key to the army is the Praetorian Guard. However, if I may, I would like to offer my assistance. As you saw at Prefect Ulpian's party recently, Aurelius Epegathus has some confidence in me. Whether misplaced or not is not for me to say.' The tall man shrugged with self-deprecation and a slight smile.

Proculus Caecilius, listening carefully, nodded in agreement.

Ulpian added, 'Paul is right. At my instigation, he has been cultivating the company of Epegathus: an Italian provincial with a freedman's son. Paul's judgement will be useful, Quintus. Let him see if he can sound out the Prefect of the Annona, establish his real motives, his plans, his networks of influence. If we can uncover hard evidence of him plotting, with verifiable details, the Augusta must then listen.'

Caecilius nodded again, his little round belly wobbling as he did so. But Quintus didn't look at him, or at Ulpian; he had been watching Paul. As Ulpian spoke, the same fleeting look he'd seen at the party passed like Jupiter's thundercloud across the councillor's face. There! And then gone. All in the space of time it had taken Ulpian to say *Italian provincial with a freedman's son.*

Something felt wrong here.

'Quintus?' Proculus was jogging his elbow, as Quintus stood immobile and frowning. He looked up to find all three men looking at him in curiosity.

'I beg your pardon, gentlemen,' he said. 'I was pondering something Augusta Mamaea said.' It wasn't true, but it would deflect suspicion.

THE CARNELIAN PHOENIX

The meeting broke up shortly after. Quintus bade farewell to his father's old friend and made his way to the Castra, anxious to get back to barracks. He was seriously worried, but not sure why.

He needed the company of honest men.

Chapter Twenty

Rome, Castra Peregrina

Quintus met neither Tiro nor Licinius on his way home. But someone else had waited some time for him before going away again. The Castra gate guard informed him an old man had begged to see the foreign *beneficiarius*, and being of no obvious threat had been allowed to wait in Quintus's quarters. Eventually he had given up and gone, leaving a message.

So now I'm the foreign Governor's Man, am I? Quintus wasn't sure he liked this. How could he be a foreigner, born and bred as he had been in Rome?

The message from Silenus was brief and ill-written, whether from lack of writing practice or distress wasn't clear. It merely begged Quintus to call on Hortensia. Something was afoot, and Silenus was deeply concerned for his mistress. Quintus sat a while on his bunk, with the message tablet open in his hands, feeling resentful and full of foreboding. He had been determined not to see Hortensia again, after what she had done to Julia and Vibia. Yet something in the distress of his loyal old servant communicated through the hasty scrawl in the wax. He decided to sleep on it, feeling an intense need to rest. Then he lay awake for hours, failing to settle, wondering what was delaying Tiro until suddenly the Castra cockerels and a flood of dawn light announced that

THE CARNELIAN PHOENIX

morning had come. He sat up in alarm, but Tiro was loudly asleep in his bunk, still wearing street clothes.

After a quick visit to Martinus, who was awake and officially on the mend, but being kept in sick quarters by the cautious medics, he caught up with Tiro over a snatched breakfast of sour watered wine, crumbling cheese and lentil cakes. Tiro looked frowsy, and as lacking a good night's sleep, as Quintus was himself. Their conversation was muted by the cheerful banter of the Castra officers around them, and they ate and drank in silence until Commandant Pomponius sat down at their table, neatly dressed and sharp-eyed.

'Morning, both! You two look cheerful, as lively as dead dogs in the gutter.'

Tiro, chewing slowly, nodded at his boss, giving way to Quintus. Quintus rubbed his face, unhappy.

'I had no luck persuading the Empress to take our concerns seriously. She clearly trusts Prefect Epegathus, and although I think Ulpian was more willing to listen, he is so determined to remain by the Emperor's side, he won't budge from Rome or even leave the palace. And I have been summoned to see my mother this morning.' His face set as he pictured the vicious argument he would likely endure.

Licinius cocked an eye. 'I hear your mother has useful connections. See what you can uncover, Quintus. My men are reporting odd rumours, unease in the streets and jumpiness in the vigiles and city guards. It may just be the August heat,' he passed a hand over his brow. 'But my nerves are jangling too.'

Quintus nodded slowly. He too was feeling that unpleasant tightness in the back muscles that so often preceded danger or unwonted surprise. He wriggled his shoulders in an effort to shake away his concerns.

'Yes, sir, I'll see what I can find out.'

He thought about what Justin had said in Massilia: Hortensia having new friends after his father's death. The tether between his shoulder blades tightened.

Tiro looked up from his mangled breakfast, on the alert.

'Commandant, that's what I heard too.' He turned to Quintus, excited to pass on his news. 'Appius's street-rat told me that the vigiles at Portus have doubled their patrols. Would that be standard procedure, perhaps ahead of the arrival of the Egypt grain fleet?'

Licinius Pomponius stared ahead, scratching his cropped grey hair.

' Sir?' prompted Tiro.

'Er, yes, the fleet arrivals might stir the warehouse night watch to increase patrols, beef up security. I wonder…?'

Quintus waited, knowing his senior colleague would divulge his thoughts after consideration. Licinius looked up, still thoughtful, his eyes hooded under bony brows.

Tiro was less patient. He'd started, so he was going to finish.

'Something else to report, sir,' he nodded to Quintus. 'I didn't catch up with Vibia, but I did get word from her. Back at the Labienus house. She left a message there with her maid, to tell us — you, actually, sir — that she and Cassius would go in secret to the games today. You know, at the Flavian amphitheatre. She asks that we meet them there. She thinks it will be safer amongst the crowds.' His voice was raised in excitement; Quintus smiled faintly, knowing that Tiro longed to see Vibia, and equally longed to witness the games in this famous arena, the greatest in the Roman world.

'I must visit my mother first,' he warned his henchman. Tiro's face fell, so he added quickly, 'I'll come on as soon as I can.'

THE CARNELIAN PHOENIX

Licinius stood, stretching. 'Tiro, come with me. I might be able to get Martinus freed from the surgeon's clutches. I'd like him to accompany you to the games. You'll need a companion, but in that public place a meeting with Vibia should be safe enough till the *beneficiarius* can join you too.'

A wide grin spread across the Briton's face as he jumped up to follow Commandant Pomponius, knocking over the dregs of his watered wine in his enthusiasm. Quintus dodged the drip of the blood-red lees, hoping it was not a bad augur for the day. He made a mental note to pour a quick libation at the shrine of Jupiter Redux, the god who oversaw the safe return of the secret service officers from their missions. Then he tightened the belt of his *gladius* under his tunic, and left the Castra.
***

The morning was well-advanced by the time Quintus arrived at the little house at the foot of the Quirinal. Silenus let him in with a grateful look.

'The Domina is most anxious to see you, sir.'

'Do you know why?' Quintus was reluctant to see his mother unwarned and unprepared; reluctant to see her at all, which he tried to hide from the old man.

'The mistress has said nothing to us, sir, but I can tell you she went out very early this morning, and came back —' Silenus faltered, looking strangely embarrassed.

'Yes?'

'Sir, she went out wearing a bright veil, the colour of flame, over her face and came home unveiled.'

Silenus turned pink, whether at the thought of his middle-aged mistress re-marrying, or at having to be the one to tell her son. Quintus stood stock-still, taking in this new shock. *New friends, new friends.* Well, it seemed one of Hortensia's new friends had become more than that. As he crossed the small atrium with its tiny dripping fountain, Drusilla came out of the servants' quarters. She was carrying a basket of laundry, which she put down at the sight of him. He saw she had a rash on her hands and up her forearms. She scratched one arm while she dipped her head in acknowledgement to him.

'What is wrong with your hands, Drusilla?' he demanded. She looked taken aback, dropping her scratching hand as if she hadn't noticed.

'Why, sir, I don't rightly know. The rash came on after breakfast, and it's just getting itchier and sorer. I'll put a balm on it, soon get rid of it, sir.'

'Show me.'

She came over diffidently and held her arms out for his inspection. There were raised vesicles along the skin, up to elbow height. Not for the first time, he wished Julia was here. With her extensive knowledge of ailments, she would know what had caused this rash and how to treat it.

'I noticed it after I carried in the mistress's gifts.'

'Gifts?' he said sharply, lifting his head to look at Silenus who was following his wife into the atrium.

'Yes, sir, wedding gifts they were, a carriage full of them behind her procession home.'

'I think it was the basket of figs, sir,' continued Drusilla eagerly. 'I noticed as I put them in the mistress's little sitting room. She does love sweet figs so, sir. Only it must be the basket, something on it makes me itch terribly.' She scratched at the raised blisters on her palms, spreading over both sides of her hands.

'Make sure you wash your hands, Drusilla. There must be something on that basket that ails you.' She nodded, moving away, and Quintus walked quickly into the salon,

THE CARNELIAN PHOENIX

resolved to challenge his mother once and for all about Vibia.

His mother sat with her usual poise in her high-backed basket chair, feet in soft orange slippers, her eyes shaded against the morning light. The half-empty fig basket stood at her elbow on a tiny side table.

'Why, Quintus, you're here at last, with your marriage congratulations no doubt.' Her voice was calm, even sleepy, lacking its habitual knifelike edge. He stood close, looking carefully at her. She looked unusually tired. He ignored her opening, hardening himself to say what must be said.

'Mother, I must tell you that I have found my sister Vibia. I know what you did to her, and to her mother Fabiola. I am bitterly ashamed of how you treated them.' He was growing angry again. He paused; he must calm down.

'That girl is a liar, a failed prostitute, the daughter of a treacherous Christian.'

'She's the daughter of my father, by the woman he truly loved!' He saw with satisfaction that Hortensia had gone pale and fallen silent. He made an effort, glancing at the new orange slippers.

'Are you married again, Mother?'

'Why, yes! Wish me joy, Quintus. This morning at dawn I was united with the great love of my life, my Julius.'

'I am happy for you,' he said cautiously. 'Tell me, do I know your new husband? Is he here?' He looked round, knowing there was no-one else in the house apart from the two of them and the servants. There was no sign of the reported lictors.

'Oh, no, he is coming back later to take me to his home as his new bride. It was all so sudden, and I needed time to pack my belongings. He is an important man, with affairs of state that occupy him. We have long loved each other. Very long,' she muttered, her voice fading. She seemed to struggle for breath. Her eyelids drooped, and Quintus felt a new pang. She was looking ghastly, a sheen of perspiration on her face. 'Yes, long, long loved each other, here and in Patavium. He calls me his model of propriety, the perfect woman, my beloved Julius does. This is the happiest day of my life…' Her voice slurred, trailing away. She sat quite still, slumped.

Quintus swallowed the lump in his throat, and moved closer to the basket, searching. He was looking for confirmation of a sudden cold dread, without knowing quite what.

She noticed, frowning slightly. The expression seemed to take some effort.

'Well, my son, are you pleased for me?'

'Yes, Mother. If it is what you have long wanted. But you seem — tired. Are you feeling well?'

'Very well, my dear son. Only a little sleepy; it was an early ceremony, as the sun rose to bless us. But my feet and legs are feeling cold. Could you fetch me a rug, dearest boy?'

'Of course, Mother,' he responded automatically, still peering into the basket. He looked carefully at the sticky figs, finding small seeds sprinkled among the fruit. He was careful not to touch the basket or its contents. He reached for Hortensia's wrist. Her pulse was rapid and shallow. She opened her eyes fully at his touch and he saw that the pupils were strangely enlarged, making her eyes look black instead of grey. A slow dribble ran from the corner of her mouth.

She made an effort to speak again. 'My beloved told me, as he took my hand to make me his wife, that I was the woman of respect and modesty he had longed for since youth. That I must trust him. We… had spoken of so many things that worry him. He was troubled by you, my son. I don't know why. But I am getting so cold, Quintus.' There was a short pause, then she said, in some distress, 'Oh, where is he? Julius my beloved, come quickly!'

Quintus had stopped listening. He called urgently to Drusilla. As soon as she hurried into the salon, he said, 'Drusilla, you must drop everything and immediately wash and scrub your hands and arms. Straight away! And don't touch your fingers to your face,' he added as she turned a look of surprise on him. 'Then bring your mistress a blanket.'

He stayed sitting with Hortensia, still holding her hand. As he felt the beat of her heart slowing, thickening, stopping, he remembered the place in Pliny's letters where a woman of Patavium is described as "a model of propriety". He thought of a ring with the insignia of a heavy-fleeced ram. He stood by his mother's side as she died, recalling a rural accent. When Drusilla came back with the blanket, Hortensia had already slipped away. Drusilla exclaimed and sank to her knees, calling her mistress's name and chafing her hands.

'It's too late, Drusilla. Your mistress has left us, and is at peace,' Quintus tried to comfort the faithful old servant. He still held his mother's cold hand. He thought that after all he had something to be grateful for: she had been in no pain. It was odd, but he found his hatred of Hortensia disappearing, erasing the great hurts she had done to him and others. He thought instead of a young girl from the countryside of northern Italia, ripped away from her youthful lover by ambitious parents. He thought of her unhappy life, and the fleeting joy that had ended it.

He turned blindly from Drusilla, unable to speak. It was Drusilla who wailed, kneeling by her dead mistress and weeping inconsolably. He noticed a veil and a chaplet of roses, crushed and fallen to the floor, and absently picked them up. At the door, he patted the upset Silenus on his shoulder.

'Call the priests to do what is needful. I shall return as soon as I can, to arrange the funeral.' Then he left the room, not noticing where he was going. He was not ready yet to think about what had just taken place — or who had caused it to happen, and why. But he knew that the answers to these questions were knocking on a door in his mind, and when he opened that door, there would be no turning back.

He stepped out of his mother's house into the brutal light of broad day. He squinted at the relentless blue-white glare of the Roman sky, marked only by a low smudge of cloud to the west.

He cursed the city of his birth.

***

Quintus was surprised when some time later — how much later he had no idea — he found himself outside the great Flavian amphitheatre. He was even more surprised to hear Tiro's voice inside, raised in desperate shouts. And then he heard Vibia, screaming.

Chapter Twenty-one

Rome, Castra Peregrina

Martinus was pleased to find himself back at Tiro's side as they left the Castra, and told Tiro so repeatedly. Tiro was just relieved that his friend was alive and had his marbles back. Or had he? Perhaps he'd better check.

'So, Martinus, what did you find out from your snout?'

'What?'

'You know, your informer? The one you went to meet before we got duffed up in the alley the other night.'

'Did we? When?'

Tiro sighed, pointing to the dressing still wound round Martinus's head. It had slipped to a rakish angle.

'The night you got that, bashed into a brick wall by those thugs who were trailing us.'

'Did I? Where was that? You been taking me to dodgy places, you bastard?'

'How could I do that when you're the Roman who knows his way round this heaving city?'

'Oh, right. What snout? What did he tell me?'

'If I knew that I wouldn't be asking you, idiot!'

Tiro gave up. Martinus clearly couldn't remember anything of that night. They might never know what the informer had told him, which worried Tiro. He had a feeling in his water it was important. He shrugged. Next time they passed a temple to Jupiter, or Mars maybe, he'd see what sort of deal he could strike with the god. He strode on, happier now. Tiro found doing business with the gods usually worked out, one way or another. Just had to pick the right god. Or goddess. Perhaps Diana? She had a soft spot for martial lads, they said. Or was that Minerva?

'Tiro, look where you're going!'

They had headed down to the valley between the Caelian Hill and the Palatine, where the Emperor Vespasian and his son Titus had built a colossal amphitheatre upon the abandoned site of Emperor Nero's Golden House. Good job too — what did Rome want with another over-sized palace? Tiro narrowly avoided the plinth of a vast statue outside, raised on a pillar in front of the arena. Originally a self-encomium to Nero, it now presented a more acceptable face as Sol Invictus, the popular sun god.

Martinus navigated them past the plinth to reach an entrance to the amphitheatre. There were a great many numbered arcades providing entry to the auditorium. It was free to get in, but spectators had to present an admission card matching the arcade's number. Tiro and Martinus had no entrance ticket, numbered or otherwise. Tiro wasn't worried — this was Martinus' problem, and he had confidence in his colleague's network of informers and helpers. He stood back to admire the huge travertine building, blindingly bright in the full noon sun. Only the odd streak of pigeon droppings here and there marred the magnificence; he grudgingly conceded that even Londinium had the same problem.

But this place gave him a headache as well as a crick in the neck. Why did Roman buildings have to be so bloody big? It was such a mass of columns, arches and vaults, he could hardly make out the individual people streaming in

THE CARNELIAN PHOENIX

and out. The line was longer going in, as the animal shows were nearing the end and the much-loved gladiatorial displays were about to begin. He noticed that the sun awnings were fully extended across the topmost tier, and hoped they would get seats on the shady side.

Martinus trotted off to chat to a door steward and they were soon admitted with a nod. It felt wonderfully cool inside. They headed along a curving tunnel, dim to Tiro's eyes after the outside glare. Thus he did not immediately notice Vibia's personal slave a little further on, beckoning and hissing to them.

'Come on.' Martinus grabbed Tiro by the arm, and they followed the young girl up two flights of stone steps to the level reserved for the noble elite of Rome. They continued along a corridor, then into a stand partitioned with drapes for privacy. The private booth she showed them to was currently empty, and while they waited for Vibia, Tiro's gaze drifted outward. The view over the sanded floor of the arena was stunning. He'd seen gladiator fights in the Londinium amphitheatre of course, and enjoyed them very much. He'd even had daydreams of training gladiators himself, should he ever need another job — and there had been times when that seemed all too likely. He glanced at the scene below. The beast fights had ended, and the last of the pitiful dead creatures were being dragged away as the bloodied sand was refreshed and raked smooth. Tiro saw approvingly that one of the beast fighters, a young fair-haired giant, was pouring a grateful libation onto a ringside shrine before exiting.

'Fortuna protect them,' murmured Martinus piously.

The curtain moved and Vibia was there, alone. She looked apprehensive.

'Tiro! And Martinus! Thank you for coming.' She looked around, checking the drapes were fully dropped behind her.

'Where is …Cassius Labienus?' Tiro couldn't bring himself to use the words "your lover".

'He is guarding access. We hired a private booth here, but although it should be quiet on this level reserved for patricians there is a risk someone we know may come along at any time.' Vibia looked pale as alabaster, and Tiro longed to comfort her, to hold her little body close.

Martinus spoke respectfully. 'How can we help, miss?'

She sat down on the stone bench, facing the bright oval of sand and inviting them to sit with her. 'We must act normally, and seem to be watching the show.' Then she paused, stiffened, and looked away in distress. 'Oh no! How can this be?'

Tiro turned to look. Out in the arena an elderly man had been dragged to a stake raised in the centre. His hands were bound behind him, and as they watched, he was shackled upright to the stake. His tunic was torn and filthy, and long matted hair partly obscured his face. His back bore the bloody marks of a scourge. But it was obvious that Vibia recognised the bedraggled figure.

'Who is it, Vibia?'

'I don't know…' Her hands shook as she stared at her lap, eyes averted from the horror about to be enacted below. 'We Christians still fear persecution, even under this young, tolerant Emperor. We do not exchange full names at our services. I only know that poor man as Asterius. He was arrested as a thief and condemned to death, but I know his real crime was to recover and bury the body of our previous Pope, Callixtus, who was martyred two years ago.'

THE CARNELIAN PHOENIX

As Vibia spoke, clutching the silver fish on its chain around her slim neck, two animal traps were raised in the floor of the amphitheatre. The crowd had thinned a little after the beast fights, spectators hurrying downstairs with good-natured pushing and shoving to buy snacks and drinks. Those left in their seats had been relaxing in the interval before the gladiators made their appearance. Now they roared with excitement, a massive wave of sound lifting all around the arena. Vibia's eyes filled with tears, and Tiro was torn between wanting to comfort her and remaining transfixed, as a lion and two bears approached the lone staked figure. The elderly prisoner was crossing himself and muttering inaudibly into his beard.

'I thought we would be safe here, for a little while,' Vibia said softly, 'but there is no safety for my people anywhere.'

Tiro raised her from her seat, gently taking her hand and pulling her out of the alcove beyond the curtains, where her anxious maid was waiting.

'You mustn't watch this,' he said. 'And anyway, of course you're going to be safe. You have a —' he swallowed and forced himself to continue, '— strong man of high status and wealth to care for you. Tell me, what are your plans?' He hoped to distract her, but she shook her head.

'You don't understand, Tiro. I asked you to meet me here because we have been warned of great danger, Cassius and I. It seems Marcus is insisting that Cassius give me up. Cassius will not do so, and so we must flee immediately, get away from Rome. Perhaps we could come to Britannia with you?' She smiled faintly as she said this, but Tiro noted the smile did not reach her downcast eyes.

From beyond the curtains came the growls and grunts of the animals, deliberately starved to increase their ferocity. Tiro tried to shut his ears, dreading the pitiful sounds the old man would make as he was torn to pieces.

'Come on, Vibia, let's find Cassius. This is no place for you.'

Martinus followed them out into the corridor, which was still empty.

Vibia looked round. 'He was just there, at the bottom of those stairs, waiting till you came to meet me.' She pointed to the nearest staircase, which was as deserted as the corridor. The shouts of the crowd were rising in pitch, mixing with thin screaming from the arena, and Tiro felt Vibia shudder. He propelled her along towards the next staircase.

'Where would he have gone?' asked Martinus.

'I don't know — he said he would wait here!' Vibia sounded panicky. She tugged herself free, making Tiro stumble, and ran off along the corridor.

'After her, Martinus!' yelled Tiro, catching himself against a wall, and pushing off to follow the distraught girl. He saw her rose-pink palla disappearing round the curve, and flung himself after her.

Right into the arms, or rather onto the swords, of a Praetorian patrol. Four of them: three in standard long-sleeved white tunics with swords out and oval shields bearing the emblem of the scorpion. The leading centurion wore a red tunic and a red-crested helmet. An unarmed civilian in a purple-edged toga, short and nondescript, was some way behind them, but he paused when he saw the imminent confrontation ahead .

Vibia screamed and pressed herself back against a wall. Tiro stepped past her, pulling his dagger from the belt of his tunica. This time he'd remembered what Martinus said about carrying weapons in the city; he'd been sharpening his knife ever since. It gleamed in his hand, eager to bite.

A pant and a thud heralded Martinus, who flanked him. 'Stay behind!' he called to Vibia. Tiro stepped forward and immediately his dagger was knocked out of his hand by the longer sword of the leading Praetorian. It skittered away, and the bearded centurion laughed. That was a mistake; Tiro actually preferred unarmed combat, especially in confined spaces. And he really disliked being laughed at.

He ducked his head, saying in an exaggerated Londinium accent, 'Sorry, Dominus, didn't see you coming.' The bearded one laughed again, which pretty much always happened when Romans heard Tiro's accent. *Perfect,* thought Tiro. *While he's laughing, and his dozy mates too, he's not focused. But I am.*

He glanced at Martinus, who despite his cracked head and memory loss was wide awake. *Good!*

Tiro lifted his sunburnt, provincial face with an apologetic look for the centurion, and at the same moment brought up his bunched left paw in a nasty uppercut, hard to the officer's nose. The man's expression changed abruptly from laughing sneer to pained astonishment as his nose burst into gushes of blood, but Tiro had his next move already covered. Grabbing his opponent's red tunic, he pulled him off-balance, then neatly sidestepped and threw him backwards, sweeping his legs out from under him. The centurion landed on his back, giving Tiro ample opportunity to pick up his dagger and stop him dead, literally, with a brutal thrust up under the man's ribcage. Quite a lot more blood, but quick and quiet. Quiet was always a bonus in public places, Tiro reckoned.

Vibia drew a shocked breath, and this time it was the maid, catching her mistress up, who screamed piercingly.

The corridor was getting crowded. Martinus had bustled past him and was swinging his long sword menacingly at the remaining three soldiers. The space was too narrow for more than two to stand abreast. It was all very awkward for the three Praetorians, who had dropped their shields behind them to gain more space for manoeuvre. None of them seemed keen to engage Martinus just yet. Tiro guessed they were expecting reinforcements.

Yes -- the clatter of hobnails came up the staircase behind the Praetorians. The senator, or whatever the purple-edge civilian was, turned to look, and sang out, 'Brother!' at the sight of the man who bolted up. But Tiro knew the newcomer well, and recognised his tall figure, fluid movements and fine green cloak instantly. He certainly wasn't the little fellow's "brother". Green Cloak's real brother, Antoninus Labienus, had died at Lindinis in Britannia right in front of Tiro. Months ago.

Another man followed up the steps, more contained, less of a clatter, and Tiro was pleased to see his boss. Quintus did not look happy. He had his hard, white-faced look on. Tiro knew this did not bode well for anyone crossing his path.

Vibia called out in a sobbing voice, 'Cassius! I'm here! These men are friends.' Cassius Labienus paused, looking at Tiro and Martinus. The man in the toga said, quite quietly but with real menace, 'Think, Cassius! *The Tarpeian Rock is close to the Capitol*,' as Cassius drew out his impressive sword, fancy-hilted, with a flashing high-grade steel blade. Cassius paused at the spoken threat, but the man in the toga hadn't seen Quintus yet. The three goons stepped over their dead centurion and

THE CARNELIAN PHOENIX

drew together, puzzled, and Tiro guessed they were as nonplussed as he was. There seemed altogether too many people here who knew each other.

Quintus and Cassius exchanged looks, as if weighing each other up.

'Later. We'll settle matters between us later, when Vibia is safe,' Tiro heard the Governor's Man say. Cassius nodded once, and they launched themselves together at the three Praetorians from one direction, while Tiro and Martinus closed the gap from the other side.

It was a dirty fight, just how Tiro liked it, but he hoped Vibia wasn't watching as he tossed his *pugio* from hand to hand, luring one of the squaddies away from his mates. The dagger soon found its way into the throat of the startled soldier, who obligingly slumped down dead, blocking access by their remaining two opponents. Tiro snatched a brief look around while retrieving his knife, and saw Quintus and Cassius engaging the other two soldiers. Quintus and Cassius were both fine swordsmen, and though the Praetorians were willing enough, a savage downward cut from Cassius crunched through one man's shoulder, and immediately disabled him.

Meanwhile, Quintus brought his shorter sword up into his opponent's groin, slicing the femoral artery wide open to release a quick torrent of gore. It was either a lucky stroke, or superb swordsmanship. Tiro shrugged. Either would do.

The civilian took the chance to escape the fracas, shoving the remaining living soldier off-balance towards Quintus. Then the man bolted away along the curving corridor, his long toga gathered in both hands.

The soldier with the gaping shoulder wound lay on the floor, begging Quintus for mercy. Tiro watched as

Quintus closed his eyes briefly, as if considering, before he thrust the point of his *gladius* through the man's heart.

'There is no mercy for anyone who threatens my sister,' he said. Cassius nodded, and turned to look around him.

Still their corridor was empty, thanks to Jupiter and Mars, but from the floor above Tiro could hear what sounded like spectators hurrying down the stairs from the cheaper upper levels. He wondered what was going on – surely the show wasn't over in the arena?

Then he looked away from the sight of Vibia, once again melting into the arms of that damned elegant aristocrat. Tiro shrugged. His heart wasn't broken, not really. He'd had enough of women, anyway. And if Martinus didn't take that look of clumsy sympathy off his gods-damned Pannonian face, he'd get what was coming to him.

'Leave the bodies,' Quintus called abruptly to Martinus, who had begun to move them, 'we need to get outside quickly. We have bigger problems.'

As they left the stadium, Tiro could smell cinders and woodsmoke wafting on the sea breeze through the arches. Something more than woodsmoke — burning bread? He peered west. A wide pall of dense brown smoke was spreading in the sky, lifting from the coast on the moderate breeze and reaching long fingers towards the city. Martinus smacked the hilt of his sword against its scabbard.

'Portus! The granaries are on fire!' He groaned and slumped down to sit on the top step. 'We're really fucked now.'

Tiro looked at him, puzzled, as Quintus joined them.

'Ah, yes. What a busy boy Epegathus has been. I wonder where he's gone now?'

'Epegathus?' Tiro was puzzled.

THE CARNELIAN PHOENIX

'My brother,' said Cassius Labienus. 'My foster brother, and oldest friend. He's in charge of the grain supply feeding the city. No-one knows better than Marcus Epegathus that power over the staple food of Rome is power over Rome itself. If he's firing the granaries, we'll find the city in uproar very soon.'

' *That* bloke, the purple-edge toga — he's Aurelius Epegathus?'

'Marcus,' said Vibia.

'Little Dog,' said Quintus. 'Marcus Aurelius Epegathus, Prefect of the Annona, and sworn enemy of Ulpian. Wake up, Tiro.' But it was kindly said.

Vibia, her tiny frame still tucked in the crook of her lover's arm, turned to Quintus and Tiro.

'And my enemy. Marcus will destroy me if he can catch me.'

Cassius wiped a hand across his forehead. He looked less assured now, not so much the haughty aristocrat.

'He also knows you are the daughter of Senator Bassianus Valerius, and sister to Quintus Valerius, my darling.'

Quintus spun on his heel. 'How?'

Cassius sighed, and his handsome face fell.

'Because I told him.'

Quintus frowned, his face hardening.

'You'd better explain. But first, we need to get out of here before we're overrun by a panicked crowd.'

He jogged down the steps, leading them out and away from the vast stadium. He halted behind a row of fast food stalls where they wouldn't be easily overheard.

'Right. Tell me.'

Tiro knew that hard look, and had to give Cassius credit for standing his ground, looking the boss full in the eye.

This had better be good.

Chapter Twenty-two

Bo Gwelt, Britannia

'My lady! Julia!' Britta ran out of the house as Julia rode into the courtyard at Bo Gwelt. Marcellus nodded to Britta as he passed the gateway, heading on to the stables to hand over his mount for watering and feeding. Julia wearily dismounted. Britta hugged her mistress hard, then stood back with a slight frown. She held Julia out at arm's length to study her.

'Should you be riding, mistress?' she demanded. Nothing missed Julia's sharp-eyed housekeeper and best friend.

Julia chose to ignore this, pretending to misunderstand.

'Hello, Britta. Everything all right here? It's been a long journey from Bol harbour; ask Rufus to look after White Lady, will you? And then I need to talk to Morcant and Demetrios about our resident ghost.'

'Well, you'll save them a trip, then.' Britta continued to eye Julia, pointedly looking her up and down.

'How so?'

'They were both due to go over to Bawdrip this afternoon, to consult with Magistrate Sorio about the goings-on hereabouts. So many of the farmworkers are refusing to come onto the estate, it's a real botheration. And us right in the middle of getting in the harvest! Agrippa Sorio has sent for Optio Senecio to come from the fort at Aquae Sulis, what with Centurion Crispus being away. He asked for someone from Bo Gwelt to go too, so we agreed to send Morcant and Demetrios, not knowing you'd both be here in time. As we had no message from you.'

This was so pointed Julia had to laugh. 'I'm sorry, Britta. I'd quite forgotten, having been away so long, who is mistress in this house! So, could you let your brother and Demetrios know they're off the hook, and ask Rufus to saddle a fresh horse for me? I'll grab something to eat and be off with Marcellus as soon as I can.'

Julia was already feeling tired, and it must have shown. Britta's face softened. She put her arm around Julia and walked her into the kitchen. Enica was there, conjuring something delicious for the evening meal. Julia was so happy to be home, she found she was on the verge of tears amidst her smiles. Enica coloured with delight, and bowed to her mistress.

'Enica, how wonderful to see you! No need for nonsense like bowing from the best cook in Britannia. Could I please just have some of your homemade bread, a little cheese and a draught of the farm cider before I go to Bawdrip?'

'Make that three portions, Enica my dear, and I'll send Narina round with a snack to the stables for the Centurion,. He'll be chatting to Rufus,' added Britta. 'I'll keep Lady Julia company, in case she's forgotten the way to Bawdrip.' This was said with a broad wink, as Julia sat down and began to demolish a platter of cheese, bread chunks and olive oil for dipping.

Julia looked up.

'I'm sure Marcellus will want to come with us to Bawdrip, so I don't really have time to have the carriage put to, Britta,' she said, remembering how askance Britta always looked at the prospect of riding a horse. Britta flushed, and Enica suddenly seemed to remember the cider that needed fetching from the scullery.

'What?'

'Nothing. I've carried on with the horse-riding, that's all, Mistress.'

'You? I don't believe it!'

Britta explained that Tiro, while he might not be the most promising husband material, did have a way with riding lessons. 'I decided to persevere with the horse riding, being as how Miss Aurelia is horse-mad and sometimes needs company on her rides.'

'Sometimes? I hope she's not been riding around the countryside on her own? Anyway,' said Julia, noticing her errant daughter hadn't yet arrived to greet her, 'where *is* Aurelia?'

'Oh, she's over to Bawdrip already.'

Julia quirked an interrogative eyebrow.

' She's there most days after her lessons with Demetrios. Helping with the horses.'

'Really? I can't see Aurelia volunteering to muck out the Bawdrip stables.' Julia was puzzled. Aurelia would so much rather be riding than doing stable work.

'Oh no! I don't mean that — course, you don't know. She's helping the Sorios with their horse-breeding and training. She was spending so much time there anyway, Magistrate Sorio reckoned she should benefit. So he spoke to Demetrios and me, and the upshot was we agreed she could make herself useful there in her spare time. Morcant says she seems to have grand plans about setting up a stud farm here at Bo Gwelt.'

'Oh.' Julia was momentarily distracted. Britta riding and liking it; ghosts driving away the estate's hired hands; Aurelia planning Bo Gwelt's future and wanting to spend

THE CARNELIAN PHOENIX

time with Drusus, who had been worshipping her fruitlessly for years — it was all a bit much.

But more urgent matters needed her attention immediately. Whatever the truth behind the 'ghost' stories Marcellus had reported, the death of Claudia and the unhappiness of Julia's estate workers needed to be tackled straight away.

Soon she was riding west along the Polden ridge with Marcellus and Britta. Britta was mounted on the same placid elderly mare Tiro had taught her to ride on, and seemed quite comfortable. Julia wondered what other changes she would find back at home.

She also wondered when, and how, to tell of her own changes.

***

Bawdrip villa was a few miles west of Bo Gwelt, facing south down the slight ridge of the Polden hills. The Sorio estate was comparable in extent and wealth to Julia's, but where Bo Gwelt was old, cosy and well-anchored into the rich soil, Bawdrip was flash, overbearing and — well, rather loud. They rode along a wide avenue of young beeches and passed a long mirror pool and large formal gardens in front of the almost painfully gaudy main range of the villa, before taking the horses round to the stables at the back. 'Stables' wasn't really the term to apply: the Sorios took their horses very seriously, and had built a special wing almost as palatial for the valuable creatures.

Aurelia and Drusus were there, of course.

'Julia! You're back!' Aurelia shrieked, rushing to embrace her mother.

'So I am,' Julia replied, hugging her slight, dark-haired daughter hard. 'And good day to you too, Drusus.'

The young heir to Bawdrip, only a couple of years older than Aurelia but much taller, even since the spring,

looked shy as he bobbed his head in greeting. A heavy lock of fair hair flopped down over his forehead. A gangling dog with a wiry coat, much larger than Julia remembered, romped in to see what all the fuss was about. He launched himself at Julia, one piebald ear folded while the other white one stood upright. His pink tongue lolled out. Julia was not alarmed, knowing all these to be signs of affection from Aurelia's young dog.
'Cerberus has not forgotten me, I see.'

'None of us have, Mother.' Aurelia was still clutching her mother, seeming unwilling to let her go. Julia tightened her hug and kissed her daughter on the top of her glossy dark head, enjoying the glow of affection. It was wonderful to be home.

***

'Lady Julia! So good to see you safe and sound!' The owner of Bawdrip estate and villa, dressed as always in a slightly too-tight toga and blowsy gilded cloak, came into the stable.

'Agrippa, my dear!' Julia took the hands the older man held out to her, smiling to see her neighbour. She was swept away into a large villa overflowing with smartly dressed scuttling slaves. She winced as always at the bright colours and overblown murals of the villa's reception rooms. Marcellus Crispus had already been ushered in by Agrippa's officious steward.

'Do sit, Julia,' said Agrippa, waving the two women to a luxurious couch as his housekeeper, who Julia knew for a fact also served as bedmate to the easygoing widower, bustled in with a tray of warm, spiced wine and honey cakes. Agrippa patted his concubine on her generous bottom as she left, then turned to Julia with a more serious expression.

THE CARNELIAN PHOENIX

'To business, my dear. Marcellus and I had arranged to meet with your people, to discuss between us how to deal with the hauntings at Bo Gwelt.' He paused, looking kindly at his neighbour. 'It seems it must be the shade of your dear departed brother Marcus, who cannot leave his home even in death. Do you know of any reason why he would linger around the living, Julia?'

Julia shook her head, holding a straight face. She understood that many people thought ghosts would haunt their nearest and dearest out of restlessness, engendered by unhappiness at some aspect of their deaths or an inadequate funeral. As a trained Wise Woman and well-educated Roman, she did not share these beliefs.

'Well, Marcus was honoured with a full funeral on our own property, and is regularly visited at his mausoleum by Aurelia, the servants and me, when I'm at Bo Gwelt. I can think of no reason why my brother's ghost would be unhappy.'

She turned to Marcellus, hoping to rely on his common sense. 'Centurion, could there be another explanation?'

The young officer did not disappoint. 'Yes, Lady Julia. I believe we may be dealing with a masquerader. Someone wishing to drive away the servants and farmworkers from Bo Gwelt, for reasons more to do with the living than the dead.' He spoke firmly, to Julia's delight. Here was the ally she needed.

She explained to both men that she had found and rescued Lucius Claudius at Burdigala, and told them what he had said about the actress-turned-plotter Fulminata.

'Good grief, Julia! Do you mean to say you have brought that dangerous young criminal back with you?'

Julia tried not to stiffen at Agrippa's tone of outrage; he did not have the benefit of either her medical training or her many years of education from Demetrios, the Greek tutor still employed at Bo Gwelt. She had had plenty of time to decide how to tackle the problem of Lucius and the present fevered atmosphere at her home, and she thought she knew how to deal with both. Indeed, her worldly-wise friend Fulvia had whole-heartedly approved her plans; they had discussed details at length while on the voyage to Britannia.

Knowing that both Aurelia and Drusus were listening with pricked ears, she outlined her thoughts. As she explained, Marcellus nodded approvingly. Agrippa listened and palpably calmed down, although his brow was still knotted. The two youngsters were frankly excited and impatient to get into immediate action. Cerberus began to bark loudly in his enthusiasm, and had to be dragged out by a slave and tied up in the kitchen courtyard, where he threatened the domestic fowls and tripped up a harassed laundry slave.

'We should all be in place tomorrow night, just before cockcrow. Can your men be ready by then, Marcellus?'

The Centurion nodded and got to his feet, bidding them a polite farewell. He saluted and left to ride back to Aquae Sulis.

***

By the time they got home to Bo Gwelt, Julia was very tired. Drusus had insisted on accompanying the three ladies, and Julia was glad of his escort. Through the cloud of her fatigue, she could see that her daughter had become closer to the fair-haired lad over the past months. Drusus had always worshipped Aurelia, and Julia acknowledged to herself that there was much to recommend an alliance with the Sorios — eventually. She still thought her quicksilver daughter was too young and flighty for marriage yet, though. Anyway, until matters were finally resolved with Quintus one way or another, she told herself, she had no intention of making any big decisions about Aurelia's future. And then her exhausted mind slid off into daydreams of how things might come to be resolved with her distant and difficult lover, until Aurelia demanded to know what she had done with "that disgusting Claudius boy".

'Lucius? Well, Aurelia, he is not wholly to be blamed, you know.' Two astonished young faces turned to hers.

'But, Julia — Mother — what about my father, Marcus I mean? Lucius killed him during the house fire, didn't he?'

Aurelia's face had gone white, except for the tip of her nose, which was blotchy red. She had felt the loss of her beloved adoptive father keenly, and was still distraught by the sudden death of the kindly Marcus.

Julia sighed. 'Yes, he did. And that can never be forgiven. He is paying the price though, and will always do so. Lucius is a very ill young man.'

More astonishment from Aurelia and Drusus; they waited in silence while Julia explained her conclusions after weeks of observing the disturbed young man during the long voyage to Britannia. 'I fear he may never fully recover from the blight on his mind. But he is sick, not evil. So, as his aunt Claudia is… is no longer able to make decisions for him, I have sent him to the hospital, to Anicius Piso, until longer term arrangements can be made for his care.'

In fact, Julia had realised it would not be safe to bring Lucius back with her to Bo Gwelt. She had asked Marcellus to arrange an immediate escort to take the ailing youngster under guard to her colleague, the head surgeon at the small hospital at Aquae Sulis. Being part of the great spa and temple complex there, Anicius had experience in the care of patients suffering from disturbed minds, brought by relatives from all over to seek healing from the goddess Sulis Minerva. She trusted Anicius absolutely, and could leave Lucius there with a quiet mind until she had sorted affairs at Bo Gwelt.

Including this so-called ghost.

***

In the small hours of the following night, a fair-sized party gathered in hiding around the burnt and abandoned west wing of the old villa. Taking position in plain view of any apparition that did turn up, Julia had as support the learned and sceptical Demetrios, and his extensive readings of Pliny the Elder and the plays of Plautus. The learned Greek had no doubt that Julia was on the right track, and had calmly discussed with her how to combat the panicked reports that had driven away fully half of the servants at Bo Gwelt. The rumours had made the tenants and farmworkers on their estate so uneasy it was affecting the farm's productivity.

In support, but hidden, was Morcant, Britta's brother. He was Julia's estate manager, a solid reliable man, as dark as Britta was russet.

'I don't hold with no ghosts, Lady Julia, and I tell you that straight,' he reassured Julia. 'There's summat else afoot here. Business is business, after all. I wonder if word of the missing silver has mayhap got around our parts.'

It was a shrewd guess, and Julia thought he was nearing the truth. She herself had no doubt who the ghost was, and how best to flush it out into bright daylight. Here again she had benefited from the weeks at sea discussing matters with clever Fulvia and the down-to-earth Artemidorus.

Julia had allowed Aurelia and Drusus to be present, too, under strict instructions on how to play their part. It would have been impossible to keep her headstrong daughter away in any event, and Aurelia had a secret weapon they could deploy to good effect, Julia hoped. Drusus too could be useful. He now had a tutor in the manly arts, and being newly emboldened by his lessons in swordplay, begged not to be left behind. The remainder of the party was also in hiding, being made up of the little troop of three that Marcellus had supplied from his fort. Julia had wanted army backup, and she was delighted when Marcellus himself joined them, cantering into the courtyard behind his men.

'It's my duty, ma'am,' he assured her. 'Quintus Valerius would want me to be here as his deputy.'

She wasn't going to argue with that.

***

It was a dark night, with the barest sliver of a new moon already sinking behind the hills when they all took up position. Waning summer it might have been, but Julia shivered in the cool night air and hoped the ghost would be prompt. A bare moment later, as the most conscientious of the kitchen yard cockerels rent the air with a premature alarm, a figure with long flowing robes suddenly appeared on the partially-collapsed portico of the west wing. It began to moan, its unhappy noises being dulled by the clanking of fetters round its feet. It bore a lantern containing a weak flame, barely enough to reveal that this particular ghost wore a deep hood obscuring its phantom face. Julia, looking keenly in the poor light for distinguishing features, was disappointed at first. But she held up her own lantern and began her part in their little drama.

'Marcus, dearest brother, what ails you? Why do you return to beset the living, driving away our servants and upsetting the workings of the estate?'

There was no answer from the apparition, which did not especially surprise or disappoint Julia. The figure was a little on the small side, she judged. Marcus had evidently shrunk and lost weight on the other side. Julia remained where she was as Demetrios joined her, a wax tablet in one hand and a stylus raised in showy anticipation in the other. Stifling a smile, Julia tried again. 'Marcus, speak!' Demetrios clearly readied himself to note everything the ghost said.

The ghost made no reply, but took a step back. Julia knew Morcant was concealed nearby behind a collapsed window frame, ready to catch the ghost if it tried to flee. And indeed, the phantom seemed uneasy, turning its hooded head from side to side, and forgetting to shake its curiously light fetters. But then, as so often happened when Aurelia was involved, things stopped going according to plan.

An unruly animal burst into the courtyard. The patrolling rooster immediately took exception to Cerberus entering its territory in the dark. Cerberus barked at the ghostly figure, the cockerel called an alarm, his brethren joined in and all four birds attacked the dog. The ghost turned in surprise, its hood falling away so that Julia at last caught sight of a beautiful white face, long red hair and the disfiguring scar raised on the ghost's cheek.

'Morcant, now!' she yelled. He lunged forward, and then true mayhem ensued. Aurelia had dashed out to save her dog, and the ghost, seeing its chance, dropped the lantern and leapt athletically off the veranda, catching the girl round the waist and tipping her backwards, almost off her feet. The ghost produced a thin knife with a long blade from under its robes, and held the blade glinting at

THE CARNELIAN PHOENIX

Aurelia's diaphragm, strategically under the sternum and aimed at her heart in a horribly practised posture.

'I'll kill her, Julia,' said the ghost. And Julia, who recognised the knife, knew Fulminata was wholly capable of carrying out that threat.

Chapter Twenty-three

Rome, the Flavian amphitheatre

Cassius cleared his throat, but it was Vibia who spoke.

'Brother, don't be too hard on Cassius. He was trying to protect me, weren't you, my dearest one?'

She gave Quintus a pleading look. 'Cassius has told me all: about the battle at Corinium, where he fought you and was captured after Antoninus died; how he was freed in the ambush of the prison escort party in Gaul by Marcus and his Praetorian allies; how his friend Gaius Trebonius — your old friend too, Quintus, I believe? — was murdered by a British woman who had followed them; and then how Cassius was brought back to Rome. None of that was his doing, and he has told me often how much he regrets his part in the uprising and murders. He told Marcus who I was, thinking my status as the daughter of a senator would protect me.'

Quintus was silent and grim-faced, thinking. Ever since Vibia had confessed her love, he had wondered what to do about Cassius Labienus. The man was undoubtedly a traitor and an insurrectionist, one who had probably caused the death of many people, whatever Vibia believed. By rights Quintus should run him through, here and now.

And yet, the anger he would need to fuel that execution had fled, and not just due to Vibia's pleading. The young

THE CARNELIAN PHOENIX

Cassius had always been a likeable lad, different from his haughtier brother Antoninus. As a boy playing in the streets, Quintus had seen him being kind to his foster brother and loyal to his elder brother. Both were good qualities. Quintus realised he was changing his mind about Cassius Labienus. He rubbed his scarred leg ruefully. He needed allies where he could find them, and this man, bound to Quintus by his love for Vibia, could be a valuable one.

Tiro ran both hands through his sweat-streaked fair hair.

'But I still don't understand why Whatever-his-name Epegathus would burn the granaries. How does that help him?'

Cassius frowned.

'Because as soon as word spreads that the Portus granaries have been burned down, the streets will be full of frightened, angry people. In Rome, we are only ever two days away from food deprivation for the masses. We're totally reliant on keeping the people fed with the daily dole of bread. The Prefect of the Annona, in charge of the Egyptian grain fleets, controls the food supply and so also controls the whole city. No number of watchmen will be able to keep the peace for long once the people hear rumours. Even the Praetorians will be helpless when a million panicking Romans take to the streets. This could spell doom for the Emperor and his mother. And it would leave Marcus pulling all the strings of power.'

Quintus looked at Cassius. 'Was this the plan all along? To end the dynasty, to replace the young boy on the throne with someone like Gaius Trebonius, or with Epegathus himself?'

Cassius shook his head. 'I'm not sure. When my brother Antoninus persuaded me to join him in raising insurrection in Britannia, he said we needed to return the empire to the old gods, to the trusted ways. He agreed with Marcus in rejecting the mystery religions, the worship of Mithras, Christos, Isis. And he was convinced by Trebonius that having such a vast empire in the hands of an untried boy and his power-hungry mother was madness. I…' he sighed, 'I believed my brother, and trusted his vision of a better, stronger empire, even if we had to be ruthless to do it. I too thought we should return to the days of the good soldier-emperors, selected to be Emperor as grown men who had proven themselves effective leaders. Ever since the days of Commodus, and especially since Caracalla took over the purple from his father, we have seen what a disaster the heredity principle can be. But I never believed my foster brother was Emperor material. Having the will to kill your rivals to gain power is one thing; it's not the same as developing the strength and vision to protect the people of Rome. And setting fire to the Egyptian grain stores to cause chaos and death in the streets — like you, Tiro, I just don't understand why Marcus would do that.'

'I do, though.' Quintus unsheathed his *gladius,* and raised it to point west, to where the pall of brown smoke was stretching upriver from the coast. 'If you want regime change, no better way than turning the people out onto the streets in uncontrollable numbers. In all that mayhem you can carry out whatever crimes you like, and you'll be unstoppable. And to make that million people act at once? You create a massive signal by burning the grain when the wind is in the right direction.' He lowered his blade, tapping the dry soil and raising little puffs of dirt. 'But I'm not sure Emperor Alexander, or even the Augusta, is the real target of this malice.'

Tiro looked distracted. 'What do you mean, boss?'

THE CARNELIAN PHOENIX

'Think: who really runs the empire, Tiro? Who is shaping the law, influencing policy, trying to curb the excesses of the army, teaching young Alexander to be a better, brighter, more compassionate Emperor than Rome has known for generations?'

Cassius and Tiro answered together. 'Ulpian!'

'Right. He's our enemy's target. So there's our mission. To stop Epegathus, we need to secure Ulpian and keep him safe. It's the same mission we've always had, but the stakes just got raised to Olympian heights.'

Martinus had apparently been following along, keeping quiet as if processing what he was hearing. He raised his hand in a wavering signal.

'Just a moment…'

The others all looked at him, waiting. The bulky young man screwed up his mobile face, an agonised expression spreading over it. Eventually, he sighed and his face cleared.

'Remembering something?' prompted Tiro.

'Yes…I think so. Tiro, what was the last thing I said to you before I collapsed?'

Tiro scratched his stubbly chin. 'Umm, that you were going to check with your contacts in the military, as your usual street informers had all disappeared. When you came back from that meeting, you told us you had news. Then you fainted.'

Martinus signalled to Tiro to stop talking. He stood almost in a daze, and Quintus could swear he heard cogs going round inside the young man's broad skull, like a watermill creaking. It would have been funny if they hadn't needed his information so desperately.

Suddenly Martinus burst out, 'Wedding! That's it! The wedding! I didn't find my soldier sources, but young Appius found me instead. He has a friend who sweeps the street where Hortensia Martial's house is, one of his paid street-rats. Quintus, he told me he'd seen your mother in a bridal veil. Out of curiosity he lingered till her new husband came to collect her, expecting to get the usual tip for sweeping the way clear for them. Well, what he told me was this: he thought he recognised the man who came to fetch her from home, the bridegroom as he thought; but he never got his coins after all.'

'What?' Quintus was distracted. The shock and curtailed grief at his mother's sudden death had driven the circumstances of his last meeting with her out of his mind, but now he began to see what Martinus might be driving at. It was customary for a wedding to be witnessed by the public seeing a new bride leaving her own home for good, to enter her husband's home. Only then was the marriage complete. It was also the custom for bystanders to clap and cheer wedding processions, and to be rewarded by coins, flowers and favours thrown by the bridal entourage. What did it mean that Hortensia had not in fact left her own house after her wedding, and never would, except to be carried beyond the city limits to her grave?

While he was trying to make sense of this, the ever-practical Tiro asked, 'Sir? What is this about?'

Quintus saw them all staring at him, and realised he had not yet told of his final meeting with his mother. He gave the story briefly, not looking at any of them, not wanting to see the shock and sadness on their faces.

Vibia was the first to speak; being a woman who had hoped to marry, the implications hit her soonest.

'So Hortensia was never truly married, given she died between the agreement to marry and actually leaving her home with her new husband. How odd she died then!'

THE CARNELIAN PHOENIX

'It's certainly strange,' mused Quintus. 'If Julia was here, she might be able to tell us, but to my mind the death was not of natural causes. I believe my mother was poisoned. But if so, by whom? And who is this "Julius" she thought she had married?'

He tried to recall his final conversation with Hortensia…that she and Julius had been youthful lovers, and that her intended had complimented her.

'He called her "a model of propriety",' he muttered, not knowing he spoke aloud.

'That's Livy, isn't it? Well, he too was a native of Patavium, after all,' said Cassius. 'You know how they call the people of Patavium moral and conservative.'

'What did you say, Cassius?'

Quintus spoke so sharply, his sister twitched in surprise.

'He didn't mean anything derogatory, dearest brother. I am sorry for your loss, of course, we all are, despite…well, despite everything. But it was well known that your mother was proud of her Patavian heritage. You had only to hear her voice to know it.'

'Exactly! Her voice…' he sank down on a bench, head in his hands, casting his mind back. Patavian voice — accent of Patavium — his mother in her youth…

He looked up to find four pairs of eyes fixed on him; in alarm, concern, and, in Tiro's case, alert interest.

'You're right, Vibia. I know who my mother was intending to marry. But now I wonder about the timing.'

He swept his gaze round his fellow conspirators, stopping when he reached Cassius.

'Cassius, you have been frank about your two brothers and their roles in plotting regime change, their plan to cast down the Severan dynasty. You said Epegathus may not have been doing this to raise himself to the purple, but rather to ensure a return to what he thought would be better for Rome. Think! If it wasn't to be Marcus himself as Emperor, and clearly not Gaius Trebonius, who was to be the new ruler? Do you have any clues at all?'

Cassius looked pale and solemn. He stared down, rubbing a sandal across the gritty ground by the deserted stalls before answering.

'I still believe that neither Antoninus nor Marcus intended to take the throne for themselves; their intentions were rather to permanently change the way the empire is governed. Their plan was to gain power over the boy Emperor. There was another, someone I never met, whose full name was not mentioned. But Antoninus once let drop that Gaius Trebonius was merely a means to an end. If Trebonius had prevailed in staging a coup in Britannia, he would still have been in thrall to the hidden plotters in Rome. His three British legions were to be marched on Rome, collecting support along the way in Gaul, and were to invade the city to replace the Praetorians and seize the palace. The aim was to remove the Augusta and her advisers from power, and stack the imperial council with men who believed in returning Rome to the old ways.'

'So,' Quintus also stood, unable to sit still any longer, 'Marcus Aurelius Epegathus was himself to be a tool in overthrowing the dynasty, along with your brother and you, Cassius. Someone else planned to be the power behind the throne, to direct the future of the empire. That man would hold all the strings, still will unless we stop him. Do you have anything, anything at all, to help us reveal this shadowy person?'

Even as he said this, Quintus had the fleeting sensation he himself had seen the prime plotter. He opened his mouth, just as Cassius replied, 'Well, I know it wasn't his

THE CARNELIAN PHOENIX

real name, but I did hear Marcus refer a couple of times to a Julius.'

Quintus paused in thought, mentally ticking items off: a ram on a ring, the symbol of the city of Patavium; the longtime lover and promised bridegroom to his dead mother from before her first marriage; an important learned man, with affairs of state; a grey man, with a warm smile, who had literally stepped out from behind the throne; a tall man, whose mild features had flashed warning when Ulpian called him "very able".

A man who emerged and disappeared into shadows, a clever man who would make it his business to find out how long a poison would take to kill.

But what if that clever man had got the timing wrong?

Chapter Twenty-four

Rome, the Flavian amphitheatre

Quintus turned to Labineus urgently.

'Cassius, get my sister away from Rome. Right now. Don't wait to pack. You are both in great danger here.'

Vibia stiffened, and her lover, instantly alert, nodded.

Quintus went on, 'You can send messages to me at the Castra Peregrina, but don't do that until you are safe and far away.' He held his hand out to the tall elegant man, adding softly, 'Look after her, please. She deserves so much better a life than she has had.'

Cassius gripped his hand hard in answer, but Vibia lifted her face to kiss Quintus.

'Do not be afraid for us, dear brother. I know a safe and happy place we can go. I will send you word when we arrive.'

He had to be content with that, frustrated at how little he could do for this sister who had become so dear to him. He knew he had to trust that Cassius would have the resources and determination to save them both.

He watched till they had disappeared into the crowd, turning back to find both Tiro and Martinus with eyes fixed on him.

'Sir? What next?'

Quintus knew Tiro was at his best when action was called for. He thought quickly. On the one hand, someone

THE CARNELIAN PHOENIX

— a fast-moving body of troops — needed to go urgently to Portus, to help limit whatever damage the set fires might do to the grain supply. If they could foil that arson, Epegathus's ploy would be in vain. The Praetorians, mixed bag though they were, would still be on patrol at the palace protecting the Emperor and his advisor Ulpian; there would be no risk of trouble in the streets; the plot would fail, or at least be delayed.

That would be only a temporary cessation of peril for the regime. If Quintus was right, as soon as Epegathus knew the threat of destruction of the food supply had been ended, he would simply bide his time and try again. The only way to completely stymie this attempt to overthrow the imperial government was to uncover the full plot, to pull out the shadow from behind the throne. But Quintus still needed proof. The ramblings of a dying woman to her son would not convince anyone, least of all the Augusta and a court of law. He had to expose the man at the top to the full glare of Roman justice.

He sheathed his sword.

'Right, you two. Go back to the Castra Peregrina, don't stop for anyone or anything. Tell Licinius Pomponius we believe the granaries at Portus are being fired, if he doesn't already know. And, Tiro — make sure Licinius understands that this is no random act of arson. This is nothing less than an attempt to subvert the government, and the Praetorians may well be in league. Do you understand? Licinius must get a troop from the Castra to Portus, as fast as possible.'

The two soldiers looked suitably alarmed. But Tiro persisted.

'And you, sir? Where are you going?'

'Where I should have gone earlier. To the Curia, to find the one person who knows the whole story.'

Martinus and Tiro threw hasty salutes, and left in the direction of the Caelian, jogging and swerving as quickly as they could through the growing crowds.

***

Quintus too began to run, dodging the worried spectators who were pouring out of the Flavian amphitheatre, pointing at the thickening smoke clouding the western sky and shouting to each other. It was a short straight line from the colossal stadium through the imperial forum to the senate house, the Curia, but it took him much longer than it should. At every step he was blocked by knots of anxious people pausing to gawk, or asking each other the news in worried voices. At one point, he was stopped by a watch patrol telling him to leave the city centre. He scowled at the officer in charge, showing the miniature *hasta*, the badge of high military office he wore pinned on his baldric.

'Out of my way, fool.'

The man saluted and fell back quickly.

***

The narrow Curia building was a scene of controlled panic. Many of the senators had emerged and were milling around in front, pouring into the open space of the forum. There was more delay before Quintus spotted his father's elderly little friend, Senator Proculus Caecilius, in company with two colleagues. He bade them a courteous farewell as soon as he saw Quintus approaching.

'My son, you look worried. What is happening, do you know? People are saying there is a fire at the granaries in Portus.'

Quintus took a deep breath, stilling his nerves and forcing himself to breathe more evenly before replying.

THE CARNELIAN PHOENIX

'Actually, Proculus, I was hoping you could tell me the news.'

The senator looked puzzled and alarmed. 'I've been in session in the Senate all morning. We just had word there were reports of fires at the docks. Naturally we are worried about the grain warehouses, and have just sent couriers to check.'

Quintus looked at his father's old friend, watching his expression closely.

'Tell me, Proculus, that day you came to warn my father that he was on Emperor Caracalla's proscriptions list — how did you know?'

'How did I know?' The little man seemed nonplussed. 'I, err, let me see…'

But Quintus couldn't wait any more. He glanced around; the immediate area around them was emptying, with the senators and civil servants streaming away from the Curia to get to their homes. He pulled out his *pugio,* setting the deadly point of the leaf-shaped blade against the bobbing Adam's apple in Proculus's wrinkled throat.

'No need to think, Proculus, or grasp for a story that I will swallow. Although, I have swallowed a lot from you. As did my father too, didn't he? That's why he died that day, Proculus, while I was lame in hospital and my brother was dead and buried in a bog in Caledonia. Bassianus died because of your story, didn't he? Didn't he?' Quintus pressed the knife tip harder into the scrawny chicken neck of the old man, through the folds of dry skin. He watched a drop of dark red blood emerge and make its slow path down into the white folds of toga below. Proculus stopped wriggling. He made no movement other than to draw ragged breaths.

Quintus wasn't finished.

'Tell me, Proculus, old friend, old ally, when did you decide to betray me? To finish the work you began that day? When did you start telling your tales to someone high above even a senator, someone who was close — very close — to the throne, and wanted only the final details to emerge triumphant into the glare of fame? When did you begin the treachery?' He pushed the knife again and the first droplet was soon joined by more, until a slow trickle of blood ran down the papery skin. 'Was it when you knew I was travelling to Rome, to tell all about the British conspiracy at the trial of Gaius Trebonius?'

Proculus tried to swallow; the knife at his throat prevented that, and for all Quintus knew or cared, stopped him from speaking too.

'Or was it when your master heard I had escaped the ambush in Lugdunum? Or perhaps later, when I foolishly spilled all the beans to you at the Mithraeum and, like a gullible idiot, asked you to gain me an audience with the Emperor?' Quintus laughed bitterly and, for a moment, lessened his pressure on the knife. Proculus stood as if stone, but he turned his eyes to look directly into Quintus's face. What Quintus saw there made him pause. His bitterness at the treachery surrounding him faded, enough to leave a tiny doubt.

Proculus lifted a fold of his toga to his throat and dabbed at the small cut, smearing blood. He remained calm.

'Quintus, I have known you all my life, since you were a babe in your mother's arms. Your father Bassianus was my lifelong friend — indeed, we were as close as brothers. Yes, I knew many of your family secrets. I knew how unhappy your parents were, how their marriage died early of your mother's despair and your father's dislike. How Bassianus later fell in love with a wonderful woman

THE CARNELIAN PHOENIX

he could never have, and how at his death he tried to protect the little daughter he would never see grow up. I knew his despair when Flavius died in the Caledonian campaign, and his fears of losing you as well.'

Proculus paused, keeping his gaze on Quintus despite the pain of his wound. 'I am an old man, Quintus. I have no living children; my wife died long ago, and I never cared to replace her. I have nothing to lose, and nothing to live for. Except you, my dear boy. I have never betrayed you; only sought to do what little I could to help. That is why I offered to be your go-between, to help you warn Ulpian and the Augusta. Alas, my efforts were all in vain. Then I asked Commandant Licinius Pomponius to do whatever he can to support you, despite the considerable political risk he runs in setting himself against the Praetorian cohorts.

'But you're right about one thing, Quintus. I did betray you in the effort to maintain what little was left of your family. I knew Hortensia was in recent times seeing someone from her youth, and I chose not to tell you.

But I did worse than that, Quintus. Maybe I deserve to die for this. I began to suspect — only suspect, I had no proof — that someone else close to you was being put under intolerable pressure to feed information about your whereabouts and doings. I spent many sleepless nights agonising over what to say or do about this suspicion, and I did nothing. And when that person removed himself from Rome, I thought it best after all to remain silent. I'm so sorry, Quintus. I have at the least let you down, if not betrayed you intentionally. Do what you will with me.'

The point of the knife quivered. Quintus let it fall; he sheathed it without noticing. He sat down heavily on a bench and dropped his head into his hands. It was all so clear to him now.

Dear Lord Mithras, strike me down, I beg you. I do not deserve to remain alive. So many far better than I have died: Bassianus my father, Flavius my brother, even my sad, damaged mother Hortensia. Now, I have threatened the man who was my father's best and most faithful friend. I failed Justin, too. I am so ashamed. I have driven off the woman I adore; missed the childhood of my only daughter; caused my sisters, both of them, distress and uncertainty, and lost my way in my mission, a mission I swore on oath to my governor I would carry out. I am worthless.

He waited, head still bowed. But it seemed Lord Mithras, the god of light and love, would not deign to remove Quintus from this world, yet. Quintus sensed movement and a change in the balance of weight on the wooden bench. Proculus settled his creaking old hips as he sat. There was a long wait until Quintus could bear to look up. He saw a kindly, forgiving face.

'There is still one final secret to tell you, Quintus. Your father and sister, Vibia, were not the only Christians close to you. When Bassianus went to the secret communions where he met the lovely Fabiola, I went with him. I worshipped with him. I too am a follower of Christos, although, I knew our faith was the reason why Bassianus was forced into suicide. My god is a god of love, Quintus, as I know yours is too. We must forgive each other, accept what has come about, and know we did our best. And you must forgive Justin, the one who has perhaps betrayed you more than I. He did it to save the ones he loves even more than he loves you.'

Quintus found he couldn't see: his eyes had blurred, and there was a heavy stone in his gut. He sat in silence, appreciating the presence of the little man by his side.

THE CARNELIAN PHOENIX

When he did eventually look round, blinking to clear his vision, Proculus had gone.

***

Noise was growing behind him, though: the noise of a gathering crowd, venting anger at a speaker. Quintus could hear someone talking, calling in an authoritative voice for calm and order. He knew that voice. With a thudding heart, he got up, checked his *pugio* and *gladius* were both sheathed in place, and pushed his way quickly towards the Temple of the Divine Julius.

Opposite that venerable temple, and right next to the arch of Septimius Severus under which he and Tiro had walked all those weeks ago, was the famous Rostra. It faced into the open space of the forum. The bronze naval rams of ancient enemies of Rome still embellished its wall. This raised platform was where prominent people, politicians, lawyers, magistrates, stood to address the assembled populace on matters of public importance. Seldom had the speaker been more prominent, or the issue more dire than today.

Ulpian was pacing along the speaker's platform, his face animated, his toga swishing round his ankles as he walked to and fro. Quintus saw to his distress that the chief minister was alone, unaccompanied by any guard. *Where are his lictors? The Praetorians? This is madness!*

But Ulpian seemed not to notice. He spoke out confidently.

'People of Rome, dear fellow citizens! Listen to me! There is no need to gather in fear, no need to fill the streets in your anxiety. Your Emperor Alexander Severus, your beloved *princeps,* is aware of the rumours of fire at Portus and has sent his Praetorian Guard to secure the granaries. You must clear the streets. I call upon you to act in a lawful fashion. Return to your homes, dear Romans! These are idle rumours; there are no fires!'

Ulpian moved to the edge of the Rostra and held out his arms to the restless crowd, as a father might appeal to his unruly sons. Quintus shook his head in trepidation; he judged this crowd to be right on the edge of getting ugly. He began to work his way to where the press of people was thinner, angling to reach the steps at the back of the Rostra, to try to get Ulpian away safely before matters deteriorated.

'No fires?' a belligerent voice called from near the back. 'What in Hades do you call that, then?' The man, a labourer or small tradesman by the look of his short tunic and grubby face, pointed to the lowering western sky. The afternoon was wearing on, and the sunlight of the hot day was diffused by a thick veil of brown drifting ever closer, carried on the sea breeze. Quintus looked around, seeing more and more people pouring into the Forum, and his heart sank. He thought he caught glints of raised metal from the end of the *via sacra*. His face set, and he began to push ruthlessly, using his elbows, knees and the pommel of his gladius against the throng to force a faster path to the back of the Rostra.

A woman screamed, and he heard shouts of 'Fire! Fire at Portus! The grain dole is burning!' The crowd, ever a dangerous headless monster when aroused, became agitated. People began to push randomly, some trying to get away, clogging the routes out of the Forum in their panic; others were rushing the Rostra, preparing to commit whatever insanity occurred to them in their anger and alarm. Quintus drew his large dagger and held both his weapons point up, not caring if he had to cut his way through this mass of heat, sweat and foul breath. A madness had swept across the crowd; there would be no more reasoning. These were no longer individual Romans who could be bargained with, but a single many-headed hydra of menace and destruction.

Quintus went into trained mode: swiping, stabbing, tripping — anything to cut his way through to Ulpian. As he neared the wide steps running up the back of the Rostra, he was hit slantwise on the shoulder by a large stone. Fortunately the trajectory made it a glancing shot which stung more than it damaged, but he saw that a group of workmen had taken possession of a heap of building stones and bricks, and were heaving them recklessly towards the podium. They fell short amongst a knot of loud-mouthed younger men surging to the front, who were apparently enjoying egging on the violence. This group immediately retaliated, picking up the missiles and hurling them back, reckless as to where they landed. People began to scream, and Quintus saw a pregnant woman stagger, clutching her head. Blood rushed down from a cut above her eyebrow. She was dragging a child along by the hand. The little girl struggled to keep up; stumbled and fell over.

Quintus cursed, sheathing his sword and swerving back to pick up the child and set her on her feet. Her mother, a young woman in the common dress of the class to whom the bread dole meant life or death, looked dazed. Quintus cursed again. He cast a quick glance at the speaker's platform, where he saw Ulpian was waving his arms, still trying to calm the disorder. Quintus grabbed the young mother's hand, shouting at her, 'Hold on to me!' He forced a channel through the turmoil, waited to see the pair safely out of the Forum, then turned back to check the Rostra.

Deodamnatus! Ulpian had disappeared.

He spun round, checking in all directions. The glinting metal he had seen a few minutes earlier had hardened into an approaching line of soldiers, shields held up as they forced the riotous crowd back into the Forum. If he wasn't careful, he would himself become trapped and crushed. But at least he knew where Ulpian had gone: the plumed Attic helmets visible above the crowd were those worn by the Praetorians. Ulpian had been rescued, and would be safe in their escort.

Quintus could concentrate on saving himself, and working out how to rejoin his colleagues.

Chapter Twenty-five

Bo Gwelt, Britannia

'Call off your man. Where I can see him. Now.'

Julia saw her daughter palpably stiffen, and Morcant backed away. It was too dark to see the expression on Aurelia's narrow face, but Julia guessed she would be calculating the odds, shaping a strategy.

No, Aurelia, don't try anything! Julia begged silently. *This woman is ruthless, and without mercy. She has killed so many times: Velvinna, my dear friend in Aquae Sulis; Tertius, the brave little Syrian mines manager from Vebriacum; Gaius Trebonius, dying in a swelter of his own blood at Lugdunum. Probably others that have never come to light. Lady Minerva,* Julia prayed, *protect my daughter, and prevent her from doing something stupid.*

The prayer worked. It wasn't Aurelia who did something stupid.

It was Drusus.

Just as Julia was wondering how to negotiate with the red-haired assassin holding her daughter at knife-point, Drusus called out fiercely, 'Cerberus! Attack!' The young dog immediately bounded towards the portico, his muscled white body stiffening to leap over the veranda balcony. He took Fulminata by surprise, knocking her sideways onto the rotting floor. That could have been the end for Aurelia, who got dragged sideways onto her knees while the sharp end of the thin knife flickered around and settled, still pressing under her ribs. Cerberus growled at Fulminata, who wrestled with her ghostly raiment to maintain her balance, but never let her clutch of Aurelia waver. Being a trained actress and acrobat along with other more dubious talents, she was strong, lithe and quick. Julia guessed she would never let go of an enemy, or an opportunity. Cerberus seemed to realise he couldn't bite Fulminata without endangering his young mistress, and jumped back down to Drusus, while still growling at the ghost.

There was a quick tap on Julia's shoulder, and Marcellus breathed into her ear, 'My men have moved into place. If we can distract that woman, they'll do the rest.'

Julia let go of the tempting fantasy wherein she rushed in to rescue her daughter and kicked Fulminata to death, stamping down on her scarred cheek to crush her skull. Instead she remained where she was, wrapping her arms protectively over her belly and feeling useless. She would have to let Marcellus do this, while wishing beyond words that Quintus was there to come to the rescue.

She called out, 'What do you want, Fulminata?', desperately hoping that engaging the woman in conversation would mask any noise from the soldiers. Fortunately, Cerberus kept up a *sotto voce* growl which helped until Fulminata replied, her voice tight and menacing, 'Shut that damned dog up, Sorio boy, or the girl will suffer.' Drusus put his hand round the jaw of the dog, who reluctantly subsided onto his haunches.

'You know very well, Julia,' Fulminata went on. 'I want the silver.'

Julia risked a small gamble to stretch out time.

'What silver?'

THE CARNELIAN PHOENIX

That was a mistake. Aurelia yelped as the knife flicked up and slid along the side of her face, cutting her.

'Want me to damage her like you scarred me, Julia?' The voice was that of a serpent, cold, emotionless and sibilant. 'You know where the silver is. Send the Sorio boy, with a torch so I can see him, into the estate office, and get it brought back to me. Right now, or I cut her again, worse. And take great care, boy, I have excellent sight and hearing. A foot wrong, and I'll carve your little girlfriend to pieces.'

Aurelia was keeping very still, but Julia heard a muffled intake of wobbly breath, and knew in her enraged soul that the bitch had hurt Aurelia. Her precious daughter was in pain and bleeding. The invisible hand on her shoulder tightened. She knew she had to do as Marcellus directed, but this was so hard. All her instincts were screaming at her to act savagely, and Julia rarely ignored her instincts. Only the slight fluttering in her belly under her hands reminded her what was at stake. She gripped the hand on her shoulder back hard in acknowledgement, and nodded to Drusus. He had been passed a torch by Demetrios, and was looking at her, still holding back the dog. He rose slowly, releasing Cerberus, and made his way towards the broken and blackened steps leading up into the west wing.

This wing contained the estate office where the fire had been set by Fulminata's accomplice, Lucius, back in the spring. It was where Julia's brother Marcus had died. Lucius had been disturbed by Marcus while pillaging the silver he'd stolen from the nearby Vebriacum mines. He'd taken enough to fund the failed British uprising, all the same. But as Julia had heard from Lucius at Burdigala, Fulminata had later extracted from the increasingly deranged young man the confession that he had left enough silver still hidden at Bo Gwelt to finance a luxurious love nest for them both.

Julia had no great faith in Drusus's quick-thinking, knowing how often Aurelia had persuaded him into trouble. In fact, she was bitterly regretting allowing him to come along on this increasingly dangerous jaunt, and wondered how she would explain to the indulgent Agrippa the wounding or death of his only son.

Then Drusus surprised her, again.

It was obvious when she thought about it later: Drusus was so proud of his newly-acquired swordsmanship, and yet she hadn't noticed when they were preparing for the encounter with the ghost that his shiny new sword was not on display. Neither was she aware of the extra time he'd spent with Aurelia training Cerberus. So when, instead of mounting the veranda steps as she expected, he suddenly vaulted over the tumbledown railing out of the lamplight into the pitch-black beyond, simultaneously whistling a piercing distinctive three-note signal, and then back-flipped his way upright with sword in hand, she was very surprised indeed. The dog rushed the portico and took Fulminata off-balance. Her knife was knocked clear out of her hand, and off the veranda. Aurelia pulled away from her as the heavyset dog barrelled into the woman from the other side. The merest instant later, Fulminata found the Sorio sword at her throat, the fine point already pricking in. She swayed, and Drusus kicked her, hard. Cerberus closed his strong muzzle round her lower arm.

Drusus spoke. 'One move from you, and the dog gets an early dinner. He has sharp teeth and a very strong jaw, so keep still.'

Julia was further surprised. This was not the quavering voice of an untried stripling. This sounded like a man, young admittedly, but full of force and determination. He stood with his sword very steady while Aurelia made her escape. Cerberus, mumbling a constant threat round Fulminata's wrist, remained at full attention.

Julia suddenly felt faint, and had to sit down on a step in a hurry as three troopers from Aquae Sulis stepped up to arrest Fulminata. Marcellus briefly put his arm around her in support.

'I'm fine, just a bit of a shock,' Julia said, ashamed. Marcellus gave her shoulder a final squeeze, and hurried across the courtyard to take the furious ghost into custody.

He made the arrest formal. 'Fulminata of Londinium, I arrest you for the murder of Claudia, widow of Magistrate Marcus Aurelianus. Further, for attempted theft of silver bullion belonging to our gracious Emperor Alexander Severus.'

Fulminata spat in the general direction of Julia, her voice full of cold contempt.

'It was that mad boy, Lucius Claudius. He killed his aunt in a fit of lunatic rage, and told me to collect the money. He said it was his, hidden after his father died, to keep it safe from that woman Julia and her illegitimate daughter.'

Julia controlled her rage, pulling herself together to bat back the accusation.

'A court will no doubt be convened in due course to try the prisoner, but I bear witness here and now that Lucius Claudius was still aboard ship with me and not even in Britannia when Claudia was murdered. I leave it to you, Centurion Marcellus Crispus, to arrange the trial of this prisoner, and to call on me for further evidence if you have need.' Fulminata spat again, but it was a hopeless last effort as the soldiers removed her.

By then Aurelia had rushed over to her mother, flinging her arms around her and sobbing in a most uncharacteristic way. Thus Julia was spared the darkling looks and curse-casting motions Fulminata made, as she was shackled and dragged away. Drusus joined them, and Aurelia turned a blinding smile on the young man.

'You saved me, Drusus. Just like Quintus would have!'

Drusus blushed, and Julia left them to it.

***

Some days later, when she had rested and caught up with estate affairs at Bo Gwelt, Julia travelled to Aquae Sulis. Not on horseback this time: Britta's counsels had prevailed, and Julia still felt fatigued and a little out of sorts.

'Not quite yourself, Mistress?' Britta enquired. They were seated across from each other in Marcus's comfortable but slow mule carriage. Julia sighed, and curled her feet up onto the cushions to rest them.

'I'm fine really, considering.'

'Considering you're how many weeks pregnant?'

Britta could be ruthless in her frankness, Julia had discovered many years ago. She'd already had a confrontation with Aurelia, who demanded to know whether her father knew about the baby.

'What?' Julia had been momentarily confused, as never before had Aurelia called Quintus her father.

'I'm not stupid, Julia. I know this is Quintus's child.'

'If you know, then you don't need to ask,' Julia snapped back. 'And I'll thank you to be more respectful and courteous when you speak to me. I'm still your mother!'

They glared at each other, and then Aurelia hitched a bony shoulder and left the room. Later, she brought Julia some hot milk, and asked if she would like her feet rubbing. They had made up, but Julia was beginning to realise how much had changed while she'd been away. Really, it was all so tiresome. She thought indignantly of Quintus, whose fault all of this was.

'Well, Britta, I think the baby will be born in late winter. Plenty of time yet.'

Thinking of Quintus reminded Julia of something else tiresome that needed sorting. Britta looked up.

'Time for what?'

'Oh, things. You know — the future.'

'Isn't that in the hands of our Lady Minerva?'

Julia lifted an eyebrow, irritated. 'I think you know what I mean, Britta. Anyway, our Lady expects us to use our own wisdom and follow her guidance when she gives it.'

'So what is her guidance?'

'What?' Julia asked again, but Britta was not to be put off. She shifted seats, taking Julia's hand and stroking it in silence.

Then she said, 'Come Julia, we've been friends a very long time. Mayn't I ask what is in your heart?'

Yet again, Julia was taken by surprise. She felt a great tearing sensation, a huge wave of painful hope rising from her gut. It surged through her, tossing the tiny kernel in her belly around, then burst out of her mouth in the sort of gulping wail she hadn't let rip for a long time. She shook as the noise and hurt poured out of her, and fat, hot tears poured down her face. Britta sat there and hugged her in silence.

Later, face cleaned and patted dry, and hair put back in shape by Britta's clever hands, Julia remembered something she'd been meaning to say.

'Umm, Britta, Tiro told me he'd asked you to marry him.'

'Did he now?' It wasn't an encouraging response.

'And? Don't you want to marry?'

'Was that what he told you I said?'

'Well, he seemed upset that you weren't as keen as he was.'

'That's right.'

'He would make a good husband.'

'I'm sure he would, for them as wants a husband.'

Julia pondered on this. 'Is it Tiro you object to, or husbands in general?'

'What do I want with a husband, when I have you, and Miss Aurelia, and that difficult man of yours, and the whole of Bo Gwelt to occupy my time?'

Julia asked quietly, 'You don't want children of your own, Britta?'

'No. Anyway, we'll soon have a little Flavius or a little Albania to keep me on my toes, won't we?'

It was said firmly, and Julia decided to let the subject drop. She was disappointed for Tiro, but pleased for Bo Gwelt. Once Britta had decided something, nothing would shift her.

Anicius Piso, the military surgeon in charge at the little Aquae Sulis hospital, bustled out
immediately after they were announced, delighted to welcome Julia.

'My lady, such a pleasure to see you back, safe and sound.' The rotund little man looked the same as always, as busy and interested in everything as a robin redbreast, and as bright in neck and face.

Julia smiled, and grasped his outstretched hands. 'Wonderful to see you too, dear Anicius. I hope you haven't killed off too many of my patients?'

He grinned, delighted at the sally. He knew himself to be a competent surgeon, whilst always happy to

THE CARNELIAN PHOENIX

acknowledge his unconventional colleague's skill with diagnosis and herbal treatments.

'The new boy you sent for admission last week — I've had an idea,' he said, leading Julia and Britta into a side ward to see Lucius Claudius. 'I agree with you that this patient is sick of the mind rather than the body. I judge that a quiet settled regimen of peace, good food, warm baths and careful nursing could benefit him.'

'That seems to be what Galen would recommend,' said Julia. 'Do you have somewhere in mind? You're not really geared up here for long-term treatment of such delicate cases, are you?'

'No, this busy clinic and my other cases, even with our Wise Women apprentices helping, keep me too busy. If you approve, I have decided to send Lucius Claudius under careful escort to my colleagues at the Temple of Nodens, south of Glevum. They have some skill there with dream interpretation, they tell me. I understand there is a property in Iscalis, which belonged to his aunt and was being held in escrow by the authorities while her murderer was sought. The priests and doctors at the shrine would no doubt find the proceeds from that property acceptable as an endowment to care for Lucius, for as long as he needs. Ah, here he is.'

Lucius was sitting on a bench in a pool of sunshine in the courtyard, playing a game of counters with an orderly. He started a little at their approach, but smiled shyly as he recognised Julia and settled again. Julia sat with him. The unhappy, emaciated youngster she had rescued at Burdigala seemed to have filled out, and looked calmer than Julia had seen him before.

'Do you remember me, Lucius? Julia, from the sea voyage on the *Athena*?' Lucius nodded, and Julia was pleased he was able to keep eye contact with her while they spoke. She patted his hand, saying, 'My friend Anicius here has found a lovely place for you to stay while you carry on getting better. It's called the Temple of Nodens, near the great river Sabrina. You'd get plenty of fresh water, good food and warm sunshine, in a lovely hilltop setting. Nodens will, we hope, bless you with better health. And I will bring Aurelia to see you when you're settled there.'

Lucius nodded absently, his attention straying back to the board game. She left him, content with his progress and with Anicius's plans.

***

Anicius was ready for a break between his ward rounds, and accompanied Julia on the short riverside walk to see Centurion Crispus at the small Aquae Sulis fort. They dropped Britta off on the way at Julia's townhouse, no doubt to enjoy a comfortable gossip with Senovara, Julia's cook.

Marcellus, forewarned, met them at the gateway. He was bursting with news, judging from his eager stance, but waited politely till they were seated and had been served beakers of well-watered wine in his tiny *Principia* office. He turned to Julia.

'Well, my lady, I was visited by the Elder Sister of the Aquae Sulis Sisterhood this morning.'

'About Fulminata?'

'Yes. It seems Fulminata broke the terms of her banishment by returning to Britannia. She has taken herself beyond the bounds of the Sisterhood's mercy. They asked me to bring her to their temple, which I did a few days ago.' Marcellus shifted uneasily in his commandant's field chair, clasped his freckled hands together and swallowed before continuing. But Julia already knew what was coming. By breaching the terms

THE CARNELIAN PHOENIX

of her banishment for murder of a Sister — Julia's dear friend and former teacher, Velvinna — Fulminata had put herself into deadly territory. And that was without consideration of the subsequent murders she had committed, including Gaius Trebonius and Claudia Claudius. Her fate was sealed.

'What did they do with her, Marcellus?'

The young man sighed, and shook his head. 'I don't know, Julia. They didn't give any details, and it wasn't my place to ask. The Elder Sister came to tell me that sentence had been carried out on the recidivist murderer Fulminata, who had forfeited her right to life. It seems she never came back out of the temple, and will not be seen again by the living.' Marcellus, well-trained Roman officer that he was, shuddered as if a real ghost had walked over his grave.

For her part, Julia tried to resist the temptation to rejoice. Fulminata had murdered good friends of hers, and for that alone Julia would willingly have torn the actress's eyes out long ago.

Marcellus recovered, and held out a wax tablet to Julia. 'But here is better news for you. This has just arrived by imperial courier. The governor notifies me that he is coming on his annual tour of district assizes at Corinium, Lindinis and Aquae Sulis. His wife accompanies him, of course, and Servilia Vitalis would like to renew her acquaintance with you. She asks if they might be your guests at Bo Gwelt.'

Julia took the wax tablet, smiling in genuine pleasure. Of all the people she would most welcome at this moment, Servilia was high up the list.

'Drink up your wine, Julia,' said Anicius, who also looked pleased. 'You and Britta have something nice to prepare for, it seems.'

Chapter Twenty-six

Rome, the Trigemina Gate

'Oi, Tiro! This is useless!' Tiro turned in his saddle to look at Martinus, whose ruddy hair was darkened with sweat and smudged with floating smuts swept along by the hot breeze.

Commandant Licinius Pomponius had swiftly agreed to Quintus's request to send Tiro with a troop in haste to Portus, to check the safety of the granaries; he'd even joined the mounted party himself. He insisted Tiro take the lead as Quintus's deputy, with the full-size *hasta* hoisted in front of him. Licinius himself brought up the rear, which he knew in a riot situation would be the most vulnerable place. The troop had gradually become more strung out along the Via Ostiensis as they approached the Trigemina gate to leave the city. The men were well-mounted and well-armed, but the slight delay while they got ready meant they struggled against a constantly increasing press of people, carts and animals in disarray, streaming out of the city. At the gateway was a roiling mob of shouting people, all fighting each other to get through the bottleneck. The gate guards had given up trying to control entry and exit, and had locked themselves into their guardrooms. They waved dismissively as the Castra troops tried to knock them up. Beyond the arch, the Via Ostiensis was blocked westwards towards the coast. Worse, Tiro could see and smell smoke behind them. They were riding towards fire, with fires also raised behind them as riots spread inside the city.

It was all of thirty miles to Portus. Tiro reluctantly drew his horse to a halt, signalling to Martinus to hold the head of their little column steady. He pulled on one rein, clapping his booted heels into the sides of his well-trained amount. The chestnut dutifully turned, moving into a canter.

Licinius had paused at the rear, and was peering back behind them. As Tiro pulled up, he shook his helmeted head at the British *optio*.

'Whatever is happening at Portus, I think matters are also getting out of hand in the city, Tiro. I'm afraid we'll have to go back and do what we can to restore order.' As he said this, a tired despatch rider in the dust-stained uniform of an imperial messenger hurtled towards them, seeking entrance to the city. Licinius calmly halted the frightened man, who drew rein at the sight of the senior officer.

'Report! What's happening at Portus?'

The messenger gasped, and Licinius passed him a leather water bottle. The man gratefully gulped water down, wiped his soot-smeared face, and saluted briefly.

'Fire at the docks, sir. Not yet all the warehouses, but it's spreading. It's strange — someone seems to have stored timber against one end of the grain warehouses, and in all this heat the wood must have caught fire. The firefighters are there and doing their best to put out the flames, but we're going to lose at least some of the wheat cargo from Egypt, if I'm any judge. You'd think they'd be more careful where they store lumber.'

'Wouldn't you just?' said Licinius drily. 'Who do you report to in Rome?'

'Prefect of the Annona, sir.'

'Of course. Well, off you go. Oh — one thing. What time were you sent to Portus?'

'First thing this morning, sir. It was a routine job. Although, funny, the officer I was to report to wasn't there when I arrived. He was on leave, gone to his mother's in Cannae a week ago.'

'Really?'

Tiro caught this exchange, thinking you could dry out a team of river-swimming Batavians with the commandant's desiccated voice.

'On your way then, son. Be careful!'

Once the courier had urged his lagging horse away, Licinius turned to Tiro.

'Well?'

'Don't like it one little bit, sir.'

'Neither do I. If this fire is intended to deflect from the real source of trouble, it's certainly worked well. Pray to Mars your boss is better placed than us, Tiro, and still in one piece. I very much fear we've been caught sitting on our hands.'

'Yes, sir, I am praying. A clever deflection, from a clever man.'

The commandant quirked an interrogatory eyebrow.

Tiro went on, 'It's causing a massive riot in the process. And anything can happen in a riot in Rome, I'm told.'

Licinius Pomponius ran his hand through his short grey hair, clamped his sweat-stained helmet back on his head, and whistled sharply. The whole line of his officers at once turned their horses neatly. They passed back under the gateway arch in single file, then quickened their pace as urgently as they could against the flow of the anxious straggling crowd.

***

At the foot of the Caelian, Tiro spotted a very young man, leaning dangerously far out of a first-floor window and waving frantically to attract his attention. He wheeled away from the line of troops, recognising Appius as the boy clattered out of the building.

'Tiro! Thank the gods! I've been waiting here to catch you ever since I heard.' The boy looked upset.

'Heard what?'

' Two things. Some of my lads were in the forum crowd watching the fun, when Chief Minister Ulpian got up on the Rostra and tried to persuade the crowds to go home. They started throwing stuff, bricks and such. My lads saw your boss fighting the crowd to get to him. Ulpian got down all right in the end, but not with your boss. He must have seen someone else coming, and just ran away.'

'Ran towards someone else?'

'No, he turned and ran, looking well-scared. My lad shouted that *Beneficiarius* Valerius was trying to reach him, but he didn't seem to hear. He just got down off the platform, all on his own, no escort nor nothing, and ran away towards the Palatine. The soldiers saw, and went after him. But he's an old bloke, and they're fit — they'll soon catch him up all right.'

'What soldiers?' An iron hand of dread gripped Tiro's guts. 'What soldiers?' *Please, Jupiter Best and Greatest, let them be from the Castra Peregrina.. Or even a bunch of urban cohorts.'*

'Why, the Praetorians, of course. Who else would go after Ulpian?'

Tiro groaned. This was just about the worst news he could have heard right now.

'So what's the second thing?'

Appius hung his head. 'I'm sorry, Tiro, I did try. It was me what saw your lady, that Vibia, with her tall fella, and they were all cloaked up and on foot, trying to get out through the city gate heading east. I think they were planning to get away on a boat to Greece, 'cos they were making for the Appian Way. There were some soldiers following them, and the soldiers sang out and told them to halt. And your lady, the lovely pale little lady —' Appius paused, looking at Tiro. Tiro managed a nod for him to continue, though he had lost command of his voice and suddenly couldn't see very well either. Appius went on, 'Well, Vibia and her bloke turned round, backing away from the gate. The lady saw me, and smiled. I asked where they were going. The man looked sad, but she smiled again at me — so happy — said they had a safe and loving harbour where no one could hurt them. She gave me a note for you, sir.' Appius reached a shaky hand into his filthy tunic, and from somewhere he pulled out a scrap of papyrus. It was a bill of housekeeping, crossed out on one side. On the other, in small fine letters, Tiro made out:

Don't be sad for me, Tiro. I am with my darling man, and we will be truly happy for ever in the loving arms of my Lord God, where none can do us harm. I wish you well, and safe homecoming, dearest Tiro.
Your Vibia.

'Which way?' It was a croak, all Tiro could manage. Afraid Appius had not heard him, he grabbed the boy's arm too hard, leaving red finger-marks on it. 'Which way did they go, Vibia and Cassius?'

THE CARNELIAN PHOENIX

Appius swallowed, and looked away. 'I saw that fancy green cloak a few moments later. They went to the Capitol.'

Tiro was a talented rider, and very fond of horses. Despite that, he did something he never thought he would do: he gouged his poor horse with the full force of his iron spurs. The surprised creature leapt into action, carrying Tiro at breakneck speed away from the cavalry line. As he passed Martinus, he called out, ' Tell the commandant I'm sorry — I've gone after my boss's sister. I've got to stop them!'

***

Afterwards, Tiro had no idea how his friend got there, just that Martinus too broke ranks from the special service troops, and was pelting his horse along behind, trying and failing to avoid pedestrians and screaming at Tiro to slow down. As they approached the ancient citadel of the city on the Capitoline Hill, the crowds thinned out, unsurprisingly given that fewer people lived on this sacred hill. Still, Tiro kept up his breakneck speed, tearing past the magnificent temple to Jupiter Capitoline that was the spiritual centre of the city. At the top of the hill, facing south, Tiro eventually reined in his distressed chestnut. He leapt off the horse, and ran full tilt to the lip of a steep cliff. He could hear Martinus from behind roaring, 'Stop! Tiro, stop!' and then he did so, knowing he could go no further. Instead, he flung himself face-down into the dust at the edge of the sheer cliff, and inched himself over as far as he could without actually falling. Martinus reached him, panting and exclaiming.

'You madman, what in the names of all the gods are you doing?'

Tiro just pointed, all the way down the sheer rock face to the bottom, where so many criminals and political prisoners had met their end. Martinus got down on all fours to crawl cautiously to the edge, and looked over. There in the glimmer of approaching sunset, with the sun lying like a gently gleaming blanket over their bodies, lay two bodies. A tall man, with a green cloak mercifully sprawled over his head. And a tiny young woman at peace, lying with her hand in his, staring at the sky.

Tiro groaned very softly, and banged his forehead against the ground. Martinus intervened before he could knock himself out, saying gently, 'This is not what she would want of you, my friend. We must go down to them, and give them what dignity we can. Come, she is waiting.'

In the diminishing twilight, Tiro forced himself to clamber back downhill on quivering legs to the craggy foot of the Tarpeian Rock. Martinus was right: she was lying with dead eyes open, her face serene. This was no longer Vibia, just the husk of the body that had carried her beautiful spirit for sixteen years. All the same, Tiro cradled her little head against his shoulder, hugging her fiercely and sobbing in ugly gasps. At last, Martinus prised her away from Tiro, and laid her on the ground, gently smoothing out the twisted silver fish pendant around her white throat. Then Martinus wrapped up the smashed thing that had been Cassius Labineus in the fine green cloak.

Tiro released Vibia from her handclasp with her lover, discovering that her other hand was wrapped into a tight fist. He gently unfolded the slender fingers to find she had been clutching the carnelian intaglio ring. He wept more, silently and softly this time, wrapping the ring carefully in a piece of cloth to stow away in his pouch for Quintus. Then he rubbed his hand roughly across his eyes, and went with Martinus to retrieve the horses. They moved the shattered bodies to lie together under the shelter of a rock face.

Time enough later to arrange their lasting resting place, together.

***

As they made their sombre way back down the Capitoline hill, Tiro gazed out over the Eternal City. The initial panicked rush of people into the streets had hardened into full-scale riots. Running street battles between plebs and soldiers were taking place below the stink of low smoke hanging over alleys and squares. Everywhere he looked, buildings were being fired and looted. He saw men, young boys, and even women hurling stones, bricks and lumps of wood from upper floors at the Praetorians, as the soldiers filed along the narrow streets. The troops seemed not to care about restoring order, and were taking casual revenge and settling scores all round. There was no control, no discipline, just blood lust and horror. As Tiro watched, numb, he saw a group of Praetorians swing a lantern high to set fire to a wooden balcony, forcing a couple of youths who had been launching stones to leap for the next building. One boy missed the jump, slid, screamed and hit the cobbled filthy street below, smashing into a bloody tangle of limbs.

Tiro knew whatever happened to him, he would never come back to Rome. This city was not the greater version of his beloved Londinium he had always imagined it to be. It was a deranged, monstrous urban sprawl of filth, hate and death. The merciful numbness lifted, and he suddenly felt overwhelmed with homesickness for Britannia.

Martinus turned to look at him, slumped in his saddle as their horses plodded side by side, soot-blackened, exhausted, raging with thirst. Tiro nodded, straightened his shoulders, and looked ahead.

There was still a job to do and his boss to find. And then, and only when the Governor's Man said the job was over, he would go home.

Chapter Twenty-seven

Rome, the Forum

Quintus took a moment to think. Ulpian was out of danger. The Praetorians were hard men, well-armed and wouldn't hesitate to use force. They would escort their Praetorian Prefect to the safest place they had. But would that be the Castra Praetoria, their own vast fort built beyond the old city?

No, he judged, that would be too far in all this turmoil. They would be more likely to take him to the Palatine, into the protection of the Emperor with his full-time guard, the Praetorians who would already be on duty at the imperial palace. Yes, of course, the Praetorians would do the obvious thing and unite their forces at the palace.

And thank Mithras, he needn't worry any longer about Vibia. By now she and Cassius would be well on their way out of the city. What about Tiro, Martinus and the special services men? Should he try to join them? But they could be anywhere on the road to Portus, and be easily missed. He decided reluctantly that he would be most useful at the palace. But first he looked about for a drinking fountain. *Hades,* he was so thirsty!

Thanks to Roma Dea and the fathers of the old city, there were abundant supplies of fresh water piped continuously into Rome, and these had not been affected by the riots. But there were many citizens ahead of him, collecting water to fight the fires springing up throughout, or just damned thirsty like he was. By the time he had reached a fountain and slaked his dreadful thirst, the sun was dropping, and despite the heat still choking Rome, the terrible day was coming to an end.

The quickest route to the palace from the senate house was also the widest one, directly uphill from the forum. Most of the crowd had dissipated, he supposed driven off the streets by armed soldiers, or anxious to save their homes from the ruthless arson he had witnessed. In fact he was gradually catching up to a group of Praetorians, strung across the street as they swept the way clear ahead.

There was still the crackle of fire and occasional falling masonry, which in the growing dusk was a significant hazard. Thus he kept to the centre of the street as much as he could, and did not immediately recognise the man some way ahead, running as if all the Furies were in pursuit. Quintus paused for a moment, automatically drawing his *gladius* as his well-honed hackles rose.

The running man was staggering, as if at the end of his tether. The full-length toga he wore was hampering his efforts, and the soldiers behind were trying to catch the runner… and getting closer. The running man turned at bay, under the flaring light of a wall-mounted torch and began to speak to the pursuing soldiers. His words were swept away by the fitful breeze, but Quintus had caught up. He no longer cared whether he was seen. The runner was all too familiar.

'I am your commander,' the bearded, panting figure was saying, between gasps. The leading soldier stepped forward, holding out his sword menacingly.

'Not any more. We have orders for your immediate execution.'

THE CARNELIAN PHOENIX

Quintus, *gladius* in hand, moved silently up behind the row of armed men; they were all intent on their unarmed civilian prey. Quintus quickly stabbed the man in the middle of the row, turning his sword in threat as the soldiers swung around to confront him.

'Run, Ulpian,' he bellowed at the top of his voice. 'Run to the palace. Run for your life. I'll hold your rear.'

He stopped watching the wretched old man, hoping he had heard him and would get away. All his attention had moved to the shifting line of Praetorians, as they curved into formation to surround him. In the dark, beyond the flickering single torch, he struggled to see how many faced him.

But what did it matter? His sole job was to hold as many of them at bay here as he could, to give the Emperor's father-figure, his own governor's much-loved cousin Ulpian, the chance to escape to live another day. This was the moment he'd waited for all his life, the chance to be worthwhile. He felt the shades of his brother Flavius and his father Bassianus watching approvingly.

Quintus gritted his teeth, flexed his knees into position, set his sword in balance, and waited.

***

'There they are!'

Tiro peered at where Martinus pointed. They were back inside the city walls, and the centurion was shouting to be heard above the din of yells and screams and collapsing buildings, overlaid with the constant spit of flames. Tiro's eyes watered continuously with the dirty smoke. He could just make out a line of horsemen forcing its way into the forum.

'The commandant is in the lead, he must be trying to get the men back to the Castra Peregrina.'

Tiro found he didn't really care much. He felt wooden, punch-drunk and fatigued beyond anything he had ever known. Vibia had gone for good, his boss was gods knew where, and the whole city seemed to be collapsing about them. He hoped Julia at least would get back safely, to Bo Gwelt, to Aurelia and Britta… But he couldn't bring himself to think even about Britta. That hurt had vanished, too. It was all so distant, his own country, and he couldn't see how he would ever get back home.

Martinus smacked him hard on the arm, nearly knocking him off his exhausted horse.

'No,' he yelled, 'look. Commandant Pomponius is turning up to the Palatine. He must have heard some news.'

Tiro sat up, squinting into the encroaching gloom of the broad street. He saw two things. The first was Appius, the most reliable little urchin he had ever come across, even more than he had been himself as a Londinium guttersnipe. The skinny boy, dirty tunic flapping, was running alongside the special service troops and shrieking, 'Get to the palace! Get to the palace! The soldiers are chasing Ulpian! He's trying to reach the gates!'

Martinus slammed his heels into his horse, and raced away to catch up with Commander Pomponius. Tiro snatched up his reins to follow, and then saw the second thing. It was an old-fashioned but well-loved sword, its ivory pommel carved into a sun god's head with outstretched rays. He knew this sword; well, why wouldn't he? He'd spent enough time over the months polishing the yellowing handle and honing the steel sword's edges to murderous sharpness. An excellent sword, despite its age, and normally either in the scabbard or the hand of an excellent officer.

THE CARNELIAN PHOENIX

Tiro dismounted in a hurry, searching the ground.

Beyond the reach of the only torch in sight lay a bundle, a motionless body. Could have been any old beggar, dead in the gutter. But Tiro knew who it was. His mouth went foul and dry, and although he had thought earlier he was at rock bottom, he discovered there had been some way still to plummet.

He crouched down by the body, reaching out a quivering hand. There was a small puddle of blood under the shoulder, but not enough to bleed the man dry, surely? He hesitated. He really didn't want to touch this corpse, he couldn't do it, it was too much to ask. He'd just get up and walk away, not look back. Maybe he'd go back up that hill, to the cliff, jump off the Tarpeian Rock himself...

'Tiro,' said a faint familiar voice, 'if you don't stop fucking around and get me on my feet, I'll have you cashiered. The moment we get back to Britannia, so help me Lord Mithras.'

Tiro found he was suddenly galvanised, his senses ricocheting and his heart beating a faster tattoo than the thud of a racing horse on hard ground. He settled his arm under Quintus, and slowly raised him to sit. Quintus's tunic was ripped along the shoulder as if by the tip of a sword, but the bleeding had puddled on the cobbles from nothing more than a cut. Doubtless a bad bruise was forming under it. But there was something crooked there too, something out of alignment about the left shoulder. Dislocated, or maybe a broken collar bone. Still, the boss was alive and complaining, quite a result.

'Oh Jupiter Best and Greatest, I really will do something special for you. I'll sacrifice an ox. A whole ox! Can't say better than that, hey Jupiter?'

'Never mind bloody Jupiter, just give me your arm while I come round. We have to get to the palace.' Quintus got to his feet, let go, and began to stagger. He stopped, lifted his right arm across his body to clutch at his left shoulder and dropped it again, obviously in pain.

'Where's my *gladius*? Give it here!'

And without a word of thanks, Quintus lurched away, weaving his way up to the gate of the imperial palace. Tiro shook his head, following the Governor's Man at a trot.

He was relieved to see his boss straightening up somewhat by the time they got to the entrance. The gates had been smashed open and the gateway blockaded with broken planks and singed furniture. The guardroom was abandoned. There was no sign of Licinius Pomponius or his troop. He and Quintus broke their way in together and followed the same path to the audience chamber that Quintus had taken last time he was here. Tiro guessed things looked very different this time. It was disturbingly quiet and deserted. Tiro grimaced. He didn't like the Praetorians — had very little reason to after what they'd done to good old Felix at Lugdunum — but the absence of any patrolling imperial guards was alarming. He tucked his head down and lengthened his stride, wondering just what they were going to find in the throne room.

The eerie silence held till Quintus and Tiro turned out of a corridor and into the airy antechamber leading to the throne room where the Emperor and the Augusta held their morning audiences. They found a clutch of frightened imperial attendants huddled together, whispering. Still no guards. Quintus heard voices raised inside, and grabbed the nearest servant, the palace major domo, judging by his gilt-edged tunic.

THE CARNELIAN PHOENIX

'Who's in there? If you value your Emperor's life, tell me!' he hissed fiercely. The man looked frozen in shock, and Quintus shook him hard. He regretted that immediately, as jagged pain shot across his chest from his damaged shoulder. He blinked away the eye-watering pain, still grasping the steward. 'Is Ulpian there, the chief minister?'

The man managed a scared nod, and one of the others, a young serving maid, came over to whisper that the minister was indeed there, had burst in a moment ago to seek refuge with the Emperor.

'Any soldiers?'

'Yes, sir,' she said, her breath coming hard in fright. 'The imperial bodyguard, eight of them, along with Prefect Epegathus, chased Ulpian in, then closed the door. No one else.'

'Good girl,' said Quintus. He signalled to Tiro, who knocked over and extinguished all the lamps but one behind them. Quintus risked a quick look through the nearest of the open full-length windows leading out onto a surrounding balcony. He beckoned to the girl.

'Listen.'

The girl nodded as he spoke quickly. Quintus smiled when he'd finished, and she looked down at her feet, shyly. He knew she would do as he had asked. After that, all was in the lap of the gods. It was a wild-card chance, but the only one they had.

Quintus pulled Tiro in close, speaking softly. 'When we go in, I need you to be my left arm. I can't trust this left shoulder, can't move it.'

'Understood, sir.'

Quintus and Tiro took up position on either side of the closed throne room door before Quintus nodded back at the girl. The other servants had left the antechamber, and were already making crashing and banging noises, using whatever furniture and lamps they could find in the corridors to hammer on the walls. The girl acquitted herself magnificently for such a little thing, letting out a monstrous scream and yelling, 'Guards, guards, someone's breaking in! There are foreign soldiers!'

The door of the throne room burst open, and four Praetorians rushed out. Pretty much as Quintus had expected. The first two immediately fell and were kicked aside, skewered by Quintus's sword and Tiro's long dagger. The following pair paused in the open doorway. Quintus waited for them to approach, knowing he and Tiro couldn't fight side by side together in the same doorway. This was the critical moment; he strained to hear what was happening in the room beyond. But the next soldier was a wily older man, experienced and burly. He paused in a crouch to take in the threat, his *spatha* waving to and fro. Quintus stood his ground, his own shorter *gladius* held up, blocking the man's view into the badly-lit antechamber behind him.

Someone shouted in the throne room, and the soldier evidently felt impelled to act. He stepped out through the door. Tiro moved like an unseen snake from the right, and tackled the man's feet from under him. The attacking Praetorian fell to the floor on his belly like a lead weight, and Tiro sat heavily on the soldier's head, which judging by the hideous cracking sound probably killed him instantly. Quintus stabbed him between the shoulder blades just to make sure. The fourth man, looking uncertain, sidled forward.

'Oh, for the sake of Mars! Can't you take a hint?' Tiro had his *pugio* up, and leaping like a monkey to his feet and still straddling the dead soldier, slashed the blade across the unlucky fourth soldier's throat.

THE CARNELIAN PHOENIX

Heedless of the dead soldiers strewn about, Quintus and Tiro surged through the door together, and paused to take stock.

There were four more Praetorians in the audience chamber, just as the slave girl had said. Two of them moved to intercept. Two more were backing away to the throne where the boy Emperor Alexander was perched, white-faced. His mother sat in her ivory inlaid chair next to him, still as a stone, hands folded tight in her lap. In the middle of the room stood Ulpian, shaky, but on his feet. He was panting with exhaustion and fear, trying to block the way to the boy on the throne. It was his rich voice, raised in protest, that Quintus had heard.

'Listen to me, men, it is your sworn duty to protect your Emperor and his family. Stand down, drop your weapons, and I promise on my honour that any grievances you have will be urgently addressed.'

A curt laugh came from a short figure seated by a window. He moved into the brilliant light of a huge chandelier hanging from the centre of the high ceiling. Quintus recognised Aurelius Epegathus. The Prefect of the Annona nodded at one of the soldiers, a centurion judging by his red tunic, whose *spatha* was unsheathed. The centurion moved towards Ulpian, and to Quintus's horror, raised his sword and with a grunt of effort slowly pierced the old man's gut. Ulpian looked down with an astonished expression as the soldier pulled out his blade, releasing a gush of blood. Then the old man groaned and collapsed. Epegathus stared at the bleeding Ulpian.

'You were so certain of everything, weren't you, Ulpian? But it isn't the Emperor we want dead, not yet. It's you.' The curiously light voice that had been so pleasant at the party now sounded evil.

The boy Alexander leapt from his throne, shaking off his mother's restraining arm, and ran to gather the chief minister in his thin arms.

'Ulpian — Father, what have they done to you?'

Quintus finally caught the noise he'd been straining to hear — a single click and soft shuffling on the balcony outside. He glanced at Tiro and moved forward, trying to reach the boy and the old man. He was stopped abruptly by a pair of swords pointed at his chest and throat. His *gladius* was knocked out of his hand. As it skittered across the shiny marble floor, he felt a towering wave of anger crash over him, sweeping away the pain of his broken clavicle. His anger scooped up all caution and left him determined to end this. He stepped forward again a single pace, thrusting his good arm against the swords pinioning him, and getting a warning slash for his pains.

Desperate to buy time, he called out to Epegathus.

'Marcus — Little Dog! You don't need to do this! You are being manipulated. You won't be the victor here.'

Epegathus swung round to look at him. His piercing pale eyes were full of scorn.

'Quintus Valerius, last scion of the noble Valerius family! I remember you so well, from our days playing in the streets as boys. Who are you to threaten me? You, brother to a filthy Christian, son of a cowardly suicide, bested by my brother in Britannia.'

Quintus held his fury in check, awaiting his moment. Blood trickled down his right sleeve, but there was no pain. *Would they never come?* He played on for time.

'Little Dog, you speak of your brother Cassius, who loved you and trusted you. But I know he despairs, and has left Rome to escape your deeds.'

Tiro shook his head at Quintus, trying to warn him. There'd been no chance to tell Quintus about Vibia and

THE CARNELIAN PHOENIX

Cassius. Quintus saw the look of loss on Tiro's face, and fell silent as a horrid doubt assailed him.

'Are you so sure, Quintus? It seems Cassius did not have the courage of my brother Antoninus. And your little whore of a half-sister?' He shrugged his shoulders. 'No loss, either of them.'

How does he know these things? Quintus found time to wonder in his anger and grief, but worse was to come.

Epegathus turned his attention back to the chief minister lying curled on the blood-soaked marble floor, bleeding to death, his breath drawing shallow in his slow agony.

'No oath was sworn to protect you, Ulpian. Or this failed *beneficiarius* and his deluded, provincial *optio* who have come so far, so uselessly, to protect you.' He laughed again, and the sound was as cold as the north wind cutting across the grey waves of the German Sea. Epegathus drew a dagger from his pouch and stabbed Ulpian deep in the throat.

Quintus closed his eyes in a final moment of acceptance. It would be as the gods willed it; he could struggle no more.

Chapter Twenty-eight

Rome, the Imperial Palace

'Sir!' Tiro hissed. Quintus's eyes snapped open; everything had changed.

Licinius Pomponius and most of his troop of secret service officers had gathered silently along the balcony. They crashed in through the tall open windows, landing with weapons raised. In the confusion they quickly surrounded the Praetorians. The rest of the *peregrini* arrived more conventionally, shown the way by the helpful slave girl. They blocked and secured the doorway. Aurelius Epegathus swore and turned, but he was no warrior and his Praetorians had been nullified. The *peregrini* soon had him pinioned and handcuffed. He was dragged out of the throne room, red-faced and swearing.

The chief minister lay motionless with eyes closed. Blood had ceased to pump from the old man's terrible wounds. Alexander was weeping quietly over his body. Quintus glanced at the unmoving Empress, then went over to crouch down next to the boy.

'I'm so sorry, Caesar. I'm afraid nothing more can be done for Praetorian Prefect Ulpian. He died as he would have wished, defending you, sir.' Quintus raised Alexander and led him back to his mother's side. She was still seated, a model of calm authority. The Empress glanced once at the dead Ulpian, her face still and pale as

THE CARNELIAN PHOENIX

she gathered her sobbing son to her side. Quintus looked at the Augusta. He thought he detected a flicker of expression in her eyes. Was it regret, empathy, or shame?

'Summon new Chief Minister Julius Paulus,' she commanded. The shaken major

domo bowed and left the room. Quintus, amazed, threw caution to the winds. He approached her chair.

'Augusta Mamaea, I must warn you there is mounting evidence that Paul himself is the leader of the plot to murder Chief Minister Ulpian.'

Mamaea shrugged her elegant shoulders.

'What does it matter? Ulpian, Paul — my son is the Emperor, regardless of who advises him.' *Except me,* said her flinty eyes. *I'm the one in charge.*

Quintus stared at Mamaea. Her mouth was the one feature that defied the marble smoothness of her face. A mouth that was set hard, a trapdoor fit for the Flavian amphitheatre. In a last rise of rage and pride, he lost all sense of protocol and spoke unwisely.

'You will not listen to the evidence, madam?'

She spoke sternly.

'This empire, this city, and my son, need the right man to help in the heavy task of governance. It is my judgement that Paul, with his legal expertise and coaching from Ulpian, is that man. Remember your place, *Beneficiarius*!'

Quintus swallowed, reining in his anger. He must keep calm long enough to retrieve some remnant of justice from this appalling situation. He looked at the Emperor, young Alexander Severus, and his heart broke for the lad. Nevertheless…

'And Marcus Aurelius Epegathus, Augusta*?'*

'I will deal with him as I deem appropriate.'

Mamaea's voice was icy. Quintus abruptly became aware of the downcast eyes of the returning court officials and soldiers, and realised he had gone further than was healthy for his own future. But he kept his gaze firmly on the Empress. He was his father's son, and beyond caring at this moment.

The boy Emperor had been watching in silence as Ulpian was wrapped in a pall before the servants carried him out. Alexander seemed dazed. He brushed down his bloody tunic, ineffectually, and left his mother's side to step hesitantly to Quintus. He held out his hand, speaking in a light, tremulous voice.

'I am grateful to you, *Beneficiarius.* Your governor is a lucky man. I am sure your actions, and those of the Castra Peregrina commandant, have saved my mother and me today. We were much mistaken in Epegathus. I will not forget your loyalty. I just —' he choked a sob down. 'I just wish you had been able to save Ulpian. He was a father to me. I never really wanted to be Emperor, you know. I just wanted to be like him.' The last few words were spoken so softly, Quintus was sure the Augusta couldn't have heard them.

He bowed deeply to Alexander, and turned to salute the Empress too. She gave him a final look, but her face never softened.

'Farewell, and may the gods speed your journey home to Britannia, Quintus Valerius. I, too, thank you for your service.'

The Augusta's arm tightened around her son as she stood. The imperial pair, mother and son of the Severan dynasty, left the throne room together. The last Quintus saw of his Emperor was the young lad being embraced by his mother, her voice low and loving.

THE CARNELIAN PHOENIX

'Come on, sir.' Tiro held out his arm, and Quintus gratefully leaned on it. He was tired to the depths of his soul, his arm was bleeding and a fierce pain racked his left shoulder. They left the palace with the Castra troops, headed by their commandant Licinius Pomponius, heads held high. But Quintus knew he would regret this day of failure all his life.

***

The young man is standing, feet planted apart, thrusting his Roman sword at the cowering faces of his Caledonian enemies. The hill mists of northern Britannia swirl and part around him. He turns, smiling radiantly at his elder brother.

'You should be proud, Quintus,' Flavius says. 'I have never ceased to be proud of you. I have never ceased to love you. Remember me. Remember Father.'

The Caledonian mists cover him up for good; he is lost to view.

As Quintus wakes, a light sweat pooling on his chest in the humid Roman morning, he does remember.

***

'Right, you'll do,' said the Castra surgeon. 'I can sign you off. A simple break of the clavicle,.Should heal nicely provided you keep it in the sling for a month or so. The cuts are also fine. I've popped a couple of stitches into that slash on your arm. Just keep it clean, and get a military surgeon to check the shoulder is working freely when you get back to Britannia.'

'My wife is a trained healer, works at the Aquae Sulis military hospital,' Quintus responded absently, forgetting that he had no idea where Julia was. Tiro raised his eyebrows, and Martinus turned away, coughing to cover a grin.

Licinius Pomponius looked into the surgery. 'A word, Quintus?'

***

The commandant waved Quintus to a seat. Not the one in front of his desk, as Quintus recalled from the previous time he'd been summoned to this office. That summons had been about his mission to retrieve silver stolen from the imperial mines in Vebriacum, Britannia. Only last winter.

It seemed aeons ago.

This time, Licinius Pomponius indicated a comfortable, cushioned bench by the open window in his quarters, and settled himself into a chair angled beside. A slave placed a jar of cooled wine on the small table in front of them, and Licinius poured.

'Well, Quintus, how are you feeling?'

Quintus raised the glass to his lips, sipping the excellent sweet wine. How *did* he feel, he wondered? Empty, forlorn, abandoned? A failure?

He settled for, 'Fine, sir. A little sore.'

'That's not what I meant, and you know it.'

There was pause while they both drank. The commandant searched Quintus's face, apparently expecting an answer, and sighed. That sound at least was familiar, and brought a wry smile to Quintus.

'I seem destined to disappoint you, sir.'

'Licinius to you, after all we have been through together. As for disappointment — Quintus, I expect we will not have you and your man Tiro here as our guests much longer. There are your mother's affairs to sort out, and then you must go home to Britannia, to report to Governor Rufinus. But I want you to know that you will always have friends here in Rome. I would be honoured if you would count me among them. As I said to you once before, you are welcome to the cave of Mithras here, and to the Castra, anytime while I am in command. Although the cave will feel bereft without our Pater.'

The grey-muzzled soldier stood to embrace Quintus, careful to avoid his sling, and laying an arm across his good shoulder strolled with him into the courtyard where Tiro waited.

Despite Licinius' comforting words, Quintus knew his business here was not finished — not quite.

***

The next day he was summoned back to the palace. He had arranged for Tiro to go out on morning patrol with Martinus and his troop, carrying the *hasta*. It was a final chance for the Briton to spend time with his Pannonian colleague, and to reward Appius and the street rat gang. Once the patrol had clattered out through the Castra gateway, Quintus went on foot into the Forum and took the road up the opposite hill. It was a route he hoped not to take again.

Paul had already taken possession of Ulpian's rooms on the Palatine. After all, thought Quintus savagely, he'd taken everything else, so why not? A stooped steward with a creased frown led Quintus into the same room where Ulpian had held his party, the night he'd first met the man from Patavium.

'Welcome, Governor's Man.' Paul smiled warmly at Quintus, who felt his face growing rigid despite his best intentions to look calm. 'Without your British colleague today?'

Quintus made no reply. He was not offered a seat, or any refreshment. He remained standing to attention.

'Speaking of Britannia...' Paul clicked his fingers, and a prompt clerk hastened in, passing a scroll to Paul before scuttling away. 'Ah yes, here we are. Mmm, well, a small and dismal province of very little worth, isn't it?' Paul laughed, seeming to invite Quintus to join in. He handed the scroll over to Quintus.

'Britannia, home of Governor Aradius Rufinus, the caring cousin of our noble ex-Praetorian Prefect.'

Quintus closed his eyes briefly, feeling bile rising in his throat. He forced himself to look down at the scroll.

'It's all in order,' the cheerful voice of the new chief minister bore on. 'The Emperor has full confidence in his governor of Britannia Superior. So much confidence, in fact, he has extended the governor's stay in Londinium — indefinitely. And you, Beneficiarius, as the governor's right-hand man for security and policing in that chilly northern province — naturally you will stay there with him.'

Paul lowered his voice. His eyes, normally so charming, had taken on a reptilian aspect. Quintus suppressed a shudder.

'Yes, right by his side, come what may. Should you ever be found back inside the ancient *pomerium* of the city of Rome, or in any way make yourself a nuisance to the Emperor or his wise senatorial advisors…' He let a long silence draw out. 'Well, let's just say we'll be keeping a close eye on your living sister and her malleable husband in Etruria; we wouldn't want anything unfortunate to happen to your remaining family.'

This open threat restored some agency to Quintus. He looked at Paul with hatred, no longer troubling to hide his feelings.

'Sir,' he said, 'I heard a strange rumour, a few days ago. I heard you had married Hortensia Martial, just before her untimely death.'

Paul's face remained pleasantly interested; not a flicker of expression revealed any emotion.

THE CARNELIAN PHOENIX

'Dearest Hortensia. That is indeed a sad case,' he nodded. 'And such a shame that our nuptials were never formalised. But then, Quintus, it might have been a little… awkward, shall we say…? If you had become my stepson? And of course, when Hortensia happened to mention that you were following nose-down on my trail to power — well, I couldn't let her accidentally drop any stray words that might warn you. A pity, really.'

The words hung in the air, heavy between them.

Quintus had left his *gladius* at the Castra, knowing it would have been forcibly removed the moment he stepped into Paul's chambers. He wondered idly how long it would take to strangle the destructive monster before him, then remembered he was hampered by a useless arm. Paul saw the look, and laughed.

'Never mind, *Beneficiarius*. We can't always have what we want in life. Not all of us, anyway. I learned that many years ago, when your snobbish grandparents refused my offer of honourable marriage to Hortensia.'

A sneer crept into his voice, and his face was ugly with resentment. 'They insisted on her marrying into the Roman aristocracy. A senatorial family was their aim. My honest equestrian family in Patavium wasn't good enough, it seemed. But look what happened, hmm? It took a while, but I turned the tables on your family. Your grandparents lost their noble son-in-law when I persuaded the Emperor Caracalla that Senator Bassianus Valerius had betrayed him, favouring his hated brother Geta.'

Paul laughed, but his face was twisted in derision.

'But that was just the beginning, Quintus Valerius. Even before that I had been watching your father, knowing he was making your poor mother so unhappy. I had him and his mistress followed. Oh, I knew about

Fabiola, right from the start. I knew about his weakness for that slaves' cult, Christianity. I knew about the sordid affair resulting in his illegitimate daughter, Vibia, your unfortunate sister. I felt your dear mother should know, and watched as she took matters into her own hands in the most delicious way.

'So, you see, I had my revenge. I watched you too, as your career faltered and sank into cowardice. It was my influence that saw your request to leave the Praetorian Guard granted, Quintus. How has that worked out for you? Defeat in battle, the sideways slink into Pomponius's paltry secret service — pah! And then the return to burrow into that dark muddy province at the end of the world. You've even managed to father your own illegitimate child. Like father, like son, it seems.'

Quintus stood rigidly still. All the discipline of his decades of army service, and the calm exterior he had carefully cultivated to cover his instinctive anger at injustice came to his rescue. He controlled his emotions as he had learned years ago, watching his breath in the mystic eastern way. And it was saving his life, he realised, when he saw four guards, swords out and raised, filing into the room. So he remained calm, looking Paul full in the face.

There was a long silence. He sensed that Paul was disappointed, had been relishing the opportunity to solicit a violent reaction from this bereft son of his rival. Paul had wanted Quintus to attack, so he could have him cut down. It would have been a neat ending.

An ending Quintus was not going to allow. As it happened, he did have that muddy province at the end of the world to go back to. He had a governor he trusted there. And people he loved unreservedly. He thought of the pale face and club foot of Aradius Rufinus. He

THE CARNELIAN PHOENIX

thought of Tiro, barely literate, drinking in British taverns and riding recklessly through icy mud. He thought of his daughter Aurelia, all torn tunics and headstrong manners. He thought of Julia, proud, determined, generous, loving.

He looked his enemy full in the face.

'I am grateful to the Emperor for sending me back to Britannia. It is my home, and I am proud to serve there. I will leave now, to carry out my Emperor's orders.'

Without awaiting response or permission, he turned smartly on his heel and marched out of the room.

He did not look back.

Chapter Twenty-nine

Rome, Quirinal Hill

The Briton looked round the little house one last time, shivering despite the sullen heat still cloaking the unhappy city.

Three days of riots had ended suddenly, with a heavy thunderstorm crashing in upon them during the final night. It was as if mighty Jupiter, hurler of thunderbolts, was telling the fractious, ungrateful people of Rome, 'Enough!' The sudden downpour had helped extinguish the last of the fires, and now the streets were empty except for miserable citizens hurrying out to buy what food was available, or looking for shelter with luckier relatives and friends. But though the rain was very welcome to Tiro, it seemed not to have washed this over-heated city any cleaner.

Quintus was in another room, giving final instructions to Silenus and the few servants left. They were packing up Hortensia's furniture and household possessions, to be taken by cart to Lucilla in Etruria. The funeral of Hortensia Martial had been a small and subdued affair, a sad ending to a long, but often unhappy, life. Tiro noticed that only Drusilla had openly wept for her betrayed mistress. Senator Proculus Caecilius had been one of the few old family friends who had attended, and Tiro was relieved to see his boss' face softening when Proculus sat

THE CARNELIAN PHOENIX

with him. Tiro didn't care to know all the ins and outs, but he did know that Quintus had pieced together how and why his father had died.

Once the house was emptied and locked up, Quintus bade farewell to the two old servants as they took their places in the carts, handing them a handsome donative, and hugging Drusilla. Silenus visibly swallowed hard, and Drusilla had red eyes. Quintus distracted her by asking about the sores on her arms; they'd healed well, apparently. He was able to cheer the pair more by talking about how much Lucilla would value their help, what with the new baby and all the bustle of the house and estate to manage. In the end, the old couple set off onto the northern road in better spirits, and Quintus was smiling with relief as he waved them farewell.

It was good to see the boss smile. Tiro hadn't asked what had passed between him and the new Praetorian Prefect in their final meeting; Quintus had come back tight-lipped, and told Tiro curtly to pack his saddlebags. Then, he accompanied Licinius to the service at the Temple of Mithras, seeming to need the comfort of the cult.

Tiro himself had gone out to enjoy a farewell meal with Martinus. He'd drunk rather more than he intended, because after all, that's what farewells were for. He sort of wished Martinus was coming with them to Britannia, but thought it would sound silly to suggest. So he said nothing, just got another two jars in. This time they didn't visit the brothel afterwards.

Martinus asked him a little wistfully if he was going back home to marry his British woman, but Tiro shook his head.

'She doesn't want me.'

'What! A well set-up bloke like you, good job, nice pay packet? What's wrong with her?'

Tiro felt a residual loyalty to Britta surface in him, and was annoyed. 'I think she just doesn't want to marry. Not yet. She's got a big job too.'

Martinus looked incredulous, and Tiro remembered he wasn't back in Britannia. He said defensively, ' She's a clever woman, can read and write, and you should see her add up a column of numbers, and haggle with the tradesmen and farmers on the estate.'

Martinus still had a doubtful expression, and Tiro gave up. He felt unhappy all the same. Martinus wasn't the only one who wanted a warm armful and a tasty meal waiting for him at the end of the working day. Tiro wondered gloomily if he would ever meet the right girl, one who would settle down with him. That made him think of Vibia, and then he got cross and told Martinus he couldn't drink like a Pannonian sot any more, not with a long journey the next day. They went back to the Castra in moody silence, but in the morning, when it came to farewells, Martinus slapped Tiro hard on the back with his wide grin.

'You never know, I might just ask for a transfer myself. Lots of adventure and action to be had in the western provinces, they say. Look out for me, Tiro!'

***

Commandant Pomponius had instructed his clerk to book the fastest passage home for Quintus and Tiro. This would take them across Mare Nostrum to Narbo, overland by river and fast carriage to Burdigala, and then on to Londinium by naval packet. Three weeks in all, if they were not unduly delayed by bad weather.

But what would they find back home? Tiro wondered. For a start, they couldn't know for sure they would find

THE CARNELIAN PHOENIX

Julia there, back safe. That one letter from Burdigala had been encouraging, but there were many hazards on the deep ocean, and even more, it seemed, to be dealt with at home in Britannia. Tiro shivered, remembering the redheaded witch Fulminata, and her nasty habits of murder and dangerous insurrection. Not to mention that lunatic boy, Lucius. How had Lady Julia ever been persuaded to take him with her on the long voyage to Britannia? It made no sense to Tiro, who not only couldn't swim, but had never sailed further than the mercifully calm trip across from Massilia to Portus.

There had been no more correspondence from Julia. One way or another, in a few weeks they would know the worst.

***

Bo Gwelt, Britannia

Servilia Vitalis tucked her arm into Julia's, her little head reaching just past the shoulder of her taller companion. She steered Julia towards a pretty wooden bench in the garden. They sat in the late summer sunshine, looking out over the flats of the level Summer Country marching into the misty distance of the Mendip Hills.

'This is such a delight, my dear. I'm so glad you invited Aradius and me to visit you at Bo Gwelt. It's the first time I've been to the west of the province since our posting to Britannia Superior, and it's just beautiful here. A shame we can't stay more than a day or two, but you know how it is. With the assizes to chair, Aradius has a lot on his plate, and we must complete the law courts tour before the autumn rains sweep in.'

The elegant little Roman paused in thought, then glanced at her fairer companion. She smiled to see Julia looking back at her. 'I was just remembering our last meeting in the spring, in Londinium. You were telling me about your trip to Rome, and your plans to meet Quintus's family. You've been on a long journey, my dear, in more ways than one.'

Servilia paused, a gentle look of enquiry on her face. Julia smoothed her fine woollen *stola* over her stomach, and Servilia nodded.

'Ah, I see. Has one door shut, or another one opened, Julia? Or perhaps both?'

Julia had avoided considering her future too much since arriving back home. She realised at this moment, under Servilia's sympathetic gaze, that she had indeed made her mind up--about everything.

Noisy movement cascaded from the old house, heralding the imminent arrival of Aurelia. The governor limped more sedately behind her, a broad smile on his face. Aurelia almost screamed at her mother.

'Julia! Julia! They're coming! Governor Rufinus's courier met them off the ferry in Londinium, and sent a fast messenger. Quintus and Tiro, both safe! They're almost here!'

And Aurelia, headstrong, mercurial Aurelia, did something Julia had never seen her do before, except with animals: she burst into tears.

Servilia and her husband discreetly left, going back into the old honey-coloured villa to rest until dinner-time.

***

As they turned off the road from Lindinis, and saw the golden-hued house ahead crouching in the late summer hay like a mother hen on a straw nest, Quintus drew rein momentarily. It was a beautiful mellow afternoon, with all the trees still green-leaved. The brambles along the verge of the straight road were heavy with juicy blackberries and wild rose hips.

THE CARNELIAN PHOENIX

'Well, Tiro? Are you glad to be home?'

Tiro fidgeted a little, making his horse flick its ears.

'To tell the truth, sir, I'm feeling a bit nervous.'

'Oh?'

'About Britta. We left things — well, not on the best of terms, her having turned me down flat. So I just don't know what to expect.'

Quintus suppressed a smile. 'You think your position is more awkward than my own, then?'

Tiro scratched his chin. Now he came to think about it, he had to feel sorry for the boss. There was going to be a lot of explaining to do between him and the Lady Julia.

***

In the end, it was Enica who greeted them first.

She was busy in the kitchen, putting the final touches to a veritable feast planned in honour of the governor's visit. The kitchen was bustling with her own assistants, and extra hands hired in for the occasion. All the food was prepared. Just as she was warming their own estate honey to add to the best Gallic wine for the first course, Morcant's little girl, Narina, came running in shouting that Tiro with the funny Londinium accent was back. Oh, and Miss Aurelia's father too, of course. They were bound to be tired and thirsty; could Enica have drinks ready?

Enica could, and she did, which was very welcome to the travellers. Quintus could not help noticing that Enica cast her eyes down when Tiro exclaimed his thanks and said how happy he was to see her.

'Pretty girl,' murmured Quintus.

'And a bloody good cook,' said Tiro, looking happy for the first time in weeks. Quintus smiled, as did Britta as she went past the kitchen and glanced in.

***

Quintus walked out into the Bo Gwelt garden. He'd already heard that Julia was safe and well; but how she might greet him after the heartbreak of their sudden parting at Massilia had him in a state of anxiety as bad as any he had known. For a moment, he wished he was still on the journey, that this dreaded and longed-for moment hadn't yet arrived. He schooled himself to stay calm. There were gardeners around, and who knew when his daughter would burst onto the scene? As she inevitably would.

Julia was sitting alone on a bench as he approached. She turned to look at him, and then got to her feet after a moment of what seemed like hesitation. He watched as the beautiful woman came towards him, the westering sun casting her figure into silhouette. His feet urged him to run towards her. But he paused, unsure.

Something about her was different. Something in her gait, her carriage, had changed. He stopped to shade his eyes with one hand in an effort to see her more clearly. She kept coming, her face in shadow, but she was holding her arms out to him as if she couldn't help herself. He moved instinctively, running towards her then, not noticing Tiro laugh behind him, not hearing Aurelia call out, unaware of the gardeners staring at him. He ran to her, he grabbed and lifted her up despite the residual ache in his shoulder. He held her, gazing at her until she said breathlessly, 'Put me down, Quintus, he doesn't like it!' Only then did he feel it hard up against him, the growing bump in Julia's belly.

***

There was so much to say, but it would have to wait till they had some privacy. He contented himself with opening his saddle bag and fetching out the carnelian ring.

THE CARNELIAN PHOENIX

'Ah! Your father's ring!' She took it, cradling the circle of gold in a trembling hand. She wiped the back of her other hand across her eyes. 'And Vibia's. I wish…'

He put a finger to her lips. 'So do I. There has been so much loss, Julia. But Vibia truly believed that she will have everlasting joy with Cassius, where she has gone to.'

Julia nodded, adding, 'Then we'll keep the ring for Flavius, perhaps?'

'Yes, for Flavius. If it is to be a boy?' She nodded again, confidently; he had no idea how women seemed to know these things, but was content to trust her.

'There's something else, Julia.' He reached for another packet: a flame-coloured veil, carefully folded. He held the fine fabric out to her. She watched him closely.

'Is this another proposal of marriage, Quintus?'

'Well, the last proposal didn't work so well, did it? I thought actions might speak louder than words this time.' He continued to hold it out, and now it was his hand that trembled.

She smiled, her generous mouth lighting up her oval face. He took hold of her again, gently, and found there really was no need for words.

At last Julia answered.

'Well, we should have a proper wedding, British-style as well as Roman. Hand-fasting, of course; maybe hold the ceremony by the well in the courtyard; but I'm not sure whether I'm still limber enough to jump over a fire.'

'No, indeed,' said Quintus quickly. 'Anyway, I've had enough of fires to last me till winter.'

***

After dinner, extended by congratulations to the newly-engaged couple, and the insistence of a delighted Agrippa Sorio on raising repeated toasts to Quintus and Julia, and even to Tiro, Quintus took Aradius Rufinus away to talk privately in his study. He quickly gave him an overview of matters in Rome.

'I'll get my written report to you as soon as I can, sir. But the news from Rome is not easy to hear. I am very sorry to have to report the death of your cousin. He was a fine and noble man, and it was my privilege to know him, however briefly.'

They drank to Ulpian. The governor sighed.

'He *was* a fine man, Quintus, and I fear the empire will be much the weaker for his loss.'

They sat in silence, watching the flames in the little fire Britta had insisted on having lit in the cooling room.

At length, the Governor said, 'Quintus, I know this trip was also a sad one for you personally, in so many ways. I am sorry for your losses too. I want you to know that I am nonetheless proud of what you have accomplished in very difficult circumstances. Please do not feel you have failed my cousin. Ulpian knew he was setting up enemies by his actions. He was proud as well as principled, and often that is a lethal combination.

'From now on, we need to take counsel for this part of the empire, for our island provinces. Especially in view of what the new chief minister has said to you. We need to strengthen relations with our northern province, and build new bridges across the seas to Hibernia, and into Caledonia. I rely on you more than ever to help me keep justice, prosperity and security the watchwords for Britannia. You and I, and your man Tiro, we have done our best to support the Emperor. We must take stock and look to our own people and our own borders.'

'I agree, sir. There will be precious little support from Rome, at least till the young Alexander Severus reaches manhood.'

THE CARNELIAN PHOENIX

Aradius Rufinus looked at Quintus keenly. 'And even then - who knows? Take some time to rest, Quintus, to celebrate your marriage and enjoy your home and family for a while. I will have important work for you soon. But it can wait till we have gathered more intelligence and taken counsel together. In the meantime, I expect an invitation to your wedding.'

Quintus smiled and stood to accompany the governor back to the salon where the ladies awaited them.

'And Quintus?'

' Sir?'

'I hear from my wife that you are to be a father again. Congratulations! Something good at least has come out of your journey. But tell me, is there anything I can do for you as reward and payment for your extraordinary loyalty?'

Quintus was surprised, and touched. As a soldier, he did not expect rewards above his pay for his work, except from the Emperor himself when occasional army-wide bonuses were issued.

But then he thought.

'Actually, sir there is something… there is a property in Iscalis which I believe has become available on the death of the previous owner, Claudia Claudius. Can it be released for sale? I know someone who just might be interested.'

The Governor laughed. 'Empire-building, Quintus? I'll look into it.' He rested his arm on the good shoulder of his Governor's Man, as they walked together along the corridor of the old house.

Quintus looked around in contentment as Aurelia bounced into view, hurrying to join them. He felt every stone and beam of this house calling to him. Beyond lay the marshes and silvered waters of the Summer Country, with enchanted Ynys Witrin just visible in the distance.

Part of him would always be a son of Rome, the greatest city on earth. But another part — the larger part — was now British. This was his home, and these were his people.

***

Five months later
To Tribune Justin Petrius near Populonium, Etruria

Dear brother, greetings.

I write to you rather than my beloved sister Lucilla, as I do not wish to alarm her unduly. Firstly, our congratulations on the birth of your daughter. My Julia asks me to tell you how delighted she is to be your little Julia's sponsor before the gods. Without boasting, I can say that Julia has a special relationship with the goddess Minerva, and we both hope that the mighty Capitoline goddess will bestow her blessings on your Julia as well.

Our own small Flavius has arrived in the world and prospers by the day, as does his mother. Aurelia would love to meet her cousins and sends her best wishes to you, Lucilla, baby Julia and the boys.

You may not be surprised to learn it came to my attention while I was in Rome last year that our family is unfortunately still under an imperial cloud. There are very powerful people — you may guess who — who continue to bear a grudge against the Valerii. I fear this grudge extends as far as Etruria and your own family. So I ask you: would you consider moving here to Britannia, at least for a while? This province is growing more and more prosperous, and I know of a property quite near us at Iscalis in the Summer Country, for sale or let at a reasonable price, that might well suit you. You could say it is in the family. In any event, once the babe is old enough to travel, please do come to visit us.

Lastly, I want you to know that whatever has happened in recent times to push us away from each other, and whoever was to blame, I bear no grudge. You are my only sister's husband, the father of my nephews and new niece, and my oldest friend. Let us both put the past and its sorrows behind us, and think instead of our families and our future together.

In hopes of seeing you soon, I remain your loving brother.
Senior Beneficiarius Consularis Quintus Valerius
Bo Gwelt, Summer Country, Britannia Superior

Epilogue

North of Lugdunum in Gaul, a tombstone is set high on a hilltop overlooking that glittering city. It is a narrow slab of golden stone, carefully dressed, with a smooth flat top. On it is carved the depiction of a Roman soldier in the prime of life. He is standing to attention, vine stick in his right hand, his helmet beplumed and his cloak thrown back over one shoulder. Underneath are carved these words:

TO THE SPIRITS OF THE DEPARTED. FELIX ANTONIUS, PRIMUS PILUS OF THE LONDINIUM COHORT. AGED 44, OF 26 YEARS' SERVICE, HE LIES HERE. HIS FRIEND AND SON TIRO SET THIS UP.

The End

Notes and Acknowledgements

In this second of the Quintus Valerius series I feature several real historical figures, including Ulpian and Epegathus (more are italicised in my Character List). The riots, fires and assassinations in Rome were real events recorded by senator and historian Cassius Dio, who also makes a brief appearance at Ulpian's party. I could not keep him out!

Ulpian himself, full name Gnaeus Domitius Annius Ulpianus, remains to this day an influential jurist and is regarded as the father of European law. He was the key adviser to Augusta Mamaea and Emperor Alexander Severus until his assassination at the hands of the Praetorians. This has been dated to between AD 223-228.

His associate, Julius Paulus Prudentissimus, was his eventual successor and may have come from Patavium. I have used fictional licence in portraying Paul's character. I hope he will forgive me.

Marcus Aurelius Epegathus is a more shadowy figure, who was implicated in the death of Ulpian. Soon after the events in my story, Cassius Dio records that Epegathus was promoted to prefect of Egypt, where he was arrested and taken to Crete for execution.

Pytheas the Greek geographer was real, although, alas, his great great-something granddaughter Fulvia Pompeia is my creation only.

JACQUIE ROGERS

The Latin quote in chapter 21: Arx Tarpeia Capitoli is an ancient saying, unattributed as far as I could find. It means *The Tarpeian Rock is close to the Capitol,* a warning that a fall from grace can come swiftly. In my story it is uttered by Epegathus, and I am pleased it so quickly applied to him as well.

The Carnelian Phoenix was largely researched during Covid lockdown, so I was unable to visit as many of the settings as I wanted to. For some of the historical detail I have relied on excellent archaeology and scholarship, including the enthusiastic advice of Professor Timothy Darvill of Bournemouth University, who answered my questions about ancient Poole Harbour. Any errors remain my own, of course.

My ongoing thanks also to Sue Willetts and her colleagues at the Hellenic and Roman Library at the Institute of Classical Studies, London, who helped with everything from the *pomerium* boundary, Roman commercial shipping, Mithraism, and Roman beliefs in ghosts. Everyone needs a good librarian, and I do more than most. Thanks, Sue, you've been a trooper!

In researching the Praetorian Guard at this period, I was keen to understand how cultures might develop in elite regiments, both good and bad. Major CF Lane, late Royal Artillery, and Lieutenant Colonel TG Kidwell OBE, late Royal Artillery, were both immensely helpful in this regard, and I thank them for their generous time. I should add that the particular Praetorian Guard behaviour as depicted in *The Carnelian Phoenix* reflects the opposite of the excellent qualities they described in their own British Army service.

THE CARNELIAN PHOENIX

My thanks to the scholars of Stanford University, creators of the wonderful ORBIS Geospatial Network Model of the Roman World. Without ORBIS I may never have got Quintus and Tiro to Rome on time, or Julia back to Poole.

My gratitude to readers who commented so helpfully on early drafts: Fiona Forsyth, Lynn Johnson, Stephen Finnemore, Ian Walker, David Orders and Louise Trafford.

Rhodri Orders was patient and meticulous with detailed feedback.

Thanks to my publisher, Sharpe Books.

And finally, but always first, my husband, first reader, critic and cook, Peter. Thank you.

[For a map, character list, and additional material and blogs, visit https://jacquierogers.substack.com. To follow me, go to https://linktr.ee/jacquierogers

Place Names

Annam: the ancients' name for Viet Nam.
Antipolis: Antibes.
Aquae Sulis: Bath.
Aquitania: modern Aquitaine, the west coast of France.
Augustodunum: Autun, in Burgundy. Capital of the Three Gauls.
Bawdrip: a villa and estate at the west end of the Polden Hills, Somerset. Home of the Sorio family.
Burdigala: Bordeaux.
Bo Gwelt: a villa and estate at Shapwick in the Polden Hills, home of the Aurelianus family.
Bol: modern Poole on the Dorset coast, a port of the Durotriges tribe.
Caledonia: northern Scotland.
Calleva Atrebatum: Silchester.
Castra Peregrina: the Roman headquarters of the imperial secret service on the Caelian Hill.
Cathay: the ancients' name for China.
Corinium Dubonnorum: Cirencester, capital of the Dobunni tribe.
Durnovaria: Dorchester.
Eboracum: York.
Etruria: region of Tuscany in Italy.
Flavian amphitheatre: the Colosseum in Rome.
Gades: Cadiz, in the southern Spanish province of Hispania Baetica.

THE CARNELIAN PHOENIX

Gallia Narbonensis: the most southerly province of Gaul, roughly modern Provence.

Garunna: river Garonne.

Gaul: loosely, France.

Gesiacorum: Boulogne.

Iscalis: Cheddar, home of Claudia, Julia's sister-in-law.

Kernow: British name for Cornwall.

Lindinis: Ilchester, the tribal capital of the northern Durotriges.

Londinium: London.

Lugdunum: Lyon.

Massilia: Marseilles.

Mare Cantabricum: Bay of Biscay.

Mare Nostrum: the Mediterranean Sea

Narbo: Narbonne.

Outer Sea: Atlantic Ocean.

Patavium: Padua, north Italy.

Portus: the huge artificial harbour near Ostia, on the banks of the river Tiberis (Tiber). It served Rome for both passengers and cargo.

Rhodanus: river Rhone.

Rutupiae: Richborough, Kent

Sabrina: river Severn.

Sagonna: river Saône.

The Summer Country: loosely, Somerset.

Tamesis: the river Thames.

Temple of Nodens: Lydney, on the west bank of the Severn river in Gloucestershire.

Ynys Witrin: Glastonbury and the Tor.

General note:

In naming places I have used contemporary Roman place-names, except where that name is not known. In that case I have tried to use ancient British names, or when that is not known either, the modern equivalent.

E.g., Bo Gwelt may be the British forerunner to Pouelt, used in Domesday Book to denote the whole Polden estate. The British name refers to the grazing of sheep. This estate no longer exists as such, but is thought to be the forerunner of the modern parish boundaries.

Glossary of Terms

Annona: the supply of food for Rome

Artemon: slanted foremast.

Beneficiarius Consularis: a Governor's Man, a senior centurion detached from his legion to serve as the Provincial Governor's high-level representative in diplomatic, investigative and policing matters.

Biturica: wine made by the Gaulish tribe native to Burdigala, ancestor of the Cabernet family of wines.

Birrus: hooded British woollen cloak

Caligae: Heavy hobnailed military sandal-boots.

Caracalla: ankle-length hooded cloak worn by a *beneficiarius*

Cardo (maximus): the main north-south street of a planned Roman city, often based on a preceding fort structure. Would be the commercial heart, lined with shops. The *decumanus,* or east-west main street, would often have the city's forum at the crossroads with the *cardo.*

Corbita: large cargo vessel, with a high hull designed for ocean-going.

Dolia: very large earthenware containers, used for storing and transporting wine, olive oil, grains.

Dominus/Domina: Master/Mistress

Frumentarius: an officer detached from his legion to take on an investigative/policing role, run from Rome and carrying out assignments across the Empire.

Garum: fermented fish sauce used in cooking.

Gladius: a short broad sword, once universal but being replaced with the longer *spatha* by the third century.

Harpastum: a game of teams played with a small hard ball, tossed or kicked, similar to rugby but with a central line between teams.

Hasta: a decorative spear, the badge of office carried by officers detached on Imperial or Governor's business.

Legio: a legion numbering around 5,000 men and officers.

Magister Navis: ship's captain

Mithraism: a highly secretive monotheistic cult, popular among soldiers, merchants and men of all classes across the Roman empire from the second century.

Mansio: inn for travelling officials

Matrona docta: an educated upper-class woman

Mulsum: wine mixed with honey immediately before drinking.

Palla: women's wool mantle

Paterfamilias: head of the household, father.

Peregrini: originating from "foreigner" and here meaning the secret service officers based at the Castra Peregrina.

Pomerium: border denoting the sacred bounds of the old city of Rome, within which it was forbidden to carry weapons.

Pugio: large leaf-bladed soldier's dagger

Optio: normally second in command of a century; sometimes detached to serve as assistant and *stator* to a Governor's Man, as in this story.

Stola: the long pleated woman's robe denoting respectable (and usually married) status. Worn over the tunica, usually made of wool.

Tunica: long-sleeved women's tunic

THE CARNELIAN PHOENIX

Vigiles: night watchmen and fire brigade in cities

Printed in Great Britain
by Amazon